THE SENTINEL MOTHER

AN FBI AGENT CHARLIE O'HARE NOVEL

THE SENTINEL MOTHER

AN FBI AGENT CHARLIE O'HARE NOVEL

anhappyappbook

HBG

PUBLISHED IN THE UNITED KINGDOM

The Sentinel Mother
ISBN: 978-1-7391331-0-8

Author's contact: scifi@giljacksonbooks.com

The Sentinel Mother is a work of fiction and the product of the author's imagination. All names (excepting two) are coincidental to any person either living or dead.

Published by Hiram B. Good, Plymouth UK

Cover design, Paper make-up and eBook formatting by:
hirambgood@giljacksonbooks.com

Cover images courtesy:
Katrin B., Stefan Keller, esudroff
from Pixabay

Dedicated to

GISELA AND VIOLET

The Author and His Work

Gil Jackson was born and raised in Wandsworth, south London. He is married to Rita, a Surrey girl. They have three children and two grandchildren. He writes sci-fi and time travel alternative histories.

His first book, **The Seventh Gift** in the, *An FBI Agent Charlie O'Hare Novel* genre series is a chilling story of the Order of the Most Divine Third Circle. An organization founded by scribes and scientific men of the day following paranormal activity seen and recorded by them after the crucifixion of Christ in Jerusalem. In particular, a mysterious man/angel, suggested by some to be God's guardian, the Holy Spirit. The Order's intention is to bring this creature to Earth for the knowledge it possesses. Not until Satan comes with the financial means in the name of one Marco Giuseppe in 1920s New York are the foundations for the possibility finally realized. In 1997 the man/angel was brought to Earth by the Order where its brain was subjected to a massive burst of energy from an electromagnetic field force and mind penetration machine with the name of AG-MX-960. The data on two hard drives was subsequently stolen from them by O'Hare.

The second book in the series, **The Sentinel Mother** continues with those two hard drives. One having what appears to be two document files of medieval appearance stolen back by the Order. Their experts failing to open them figure they need to work in unison. O'Hare wants them removed and stored in a safe place until such time as they can be destroyed or returned from whence they came. His fear is that if they are ever cracked open an apocalypse would fall on humanity that would make Pandora's box look decidedly tame. Hearing of the existence of data that can create worlds Aliens from another Time–Verse threatened with extinction in their own; with the technology to open those hard drives invade Earth to get them. O'Hare, a man continually trying to keep one step ahead of the game, now has another adversary to contend with along with the Order.

Third in the series concerns the Order's new CEO. ***Direktorin Elke Kriemhild*** after Marco Giuseppe. She is family connected to the old German Illuminati, who, along with the Order see one autocratic world of elitism. They will bring pariah states along with them to aid them in their endeavours that need that data for their new science. But is she all she seems? And who will the Alien's turn their attentions on to get the data they so desperately need for their survival; taking humanity out in their ambition. For they know human vulnerability.

The, *An FBI Agent Charlie O'Hare Novel*'s are based in New York, and as such are written in American-English.

His other book series, *A Barrister Phileas Cluff Novel* begins with **The Tinners Hut.** Part alternative history it features the young lawyer Phileas Cluff and his girlfriend. Cluff has to go back in time to 1716 to defend the life of a man already hanged for a murder he did not commit. The lives of 300 children in a 2008 hostage school siege against the English monarchy are the stakes. The man holding them hostage is from 1716. Without modern day forensics to aid him Cluff has his work cut out. Fortunately he has the founders of his Lincoln's Inn Fields legal firm to aid him. Ellick & Waite, Barristers in Law, 1716.

The second book in the series concerns the execution of Charles the First of England on January 30, 1649. Did it really happen? Or was it fake?

His, *A Barrister Phileas Cluff Novel*'s are written English-English and attempts to make the author's theories on paradoxes of time unique and believable.

He has two nonfiction books. **The London Apprentice** is a tongue-in-cheek autobiography of his time as an apprentice compositor. The other, **Hiram B. Good's, The Multi-Drop Drivers' Manual** is the definitive bible for courier drivers, an occupation he worked in for a time.

He attended what is now the London College of Communication where he studied hand composition, graphic design, and typography for the printing industry. Going on to study ancient writing at Aldersgate and Barbican College along the London Wall he quickly came to realize that learning to write in cuneiform was not going to be a way forward in his career. He has worked as an origination manager for several print companies. As well as writing he oversees an ebook, paperback formatting and print origination company with the name Hiram B. Good, Graphic Compositor + Allied. They can be found at his website https://giljacksonbooks.com

One

IT WAS 1996 WHEN TOM DORCAS a financial executive working for the US government's pension service came to realize his job of dolling out contributed benefits was to end. It was a phone call, personally to him, to say the government was closing them down and he was not to be concerned as he had come to the notice of those at the top. He was used to company staff wind-ups; guessing it was one of the guys working under him. He put the phone onto record mode telling him to fuck-off and get on with his work.

His career prospects came an hour after that call. All hell broke out at the civil service building the floor above his. A second call told him to hide up while the building was being cleared. He didn't tell the caller to fuck off this time. The caller had used his name, telling him he wasn't impressed with being sworn at. He didn't know why, but he did exactly as he was asked when FBI agents, office security and staff fire officers cleared the floor. The whole building was being assaulted. A third call asked him to copy, recover, and remove all documents from an upstairs desk after the FBI had gone. *You will not go unrewarded*, he had said.

On the floors above his were several offices. Although separate companies they were loosely connected to pensions (or so he had been told). Data security dictated pensions were to be held on three department floors. None of the staff knew what records the other departments' held or where. He had picked up stories from the staff working those floors they were not dealing with pensions at all.

Rumored a department of the CIA. He hadn't quite got the connection between the CIA operating from up there and the FBI raiding them.

Hell breaking out upstairs came by way of a team of heavily armed agents bursting into the building, cramming the lifts and stairwells on their way one floor up. Sounds of crashing, small-arm fire, explosions, shouting, and screaming filtered down to where his department floor was. He wondered if he was doing right hiding behind filing cabinets waiting for an assault to the building to die down before going to work. To cover his back he decided to photograph and record everything from this point forward.

It was two hours before the noise and shouting died down; before he tentatively made his way out from his office and ventured upstairs. Normally there were cameras and video screens on his departmental floor watching staff coming and going. They were off now, he couldn't be seen. Out in the hallway, he froze. Two of the video screens showing the ground floor foyer were still displaying. He double-checked the camera he was now under. Off. In fact, the cable carrying the signal had been severed. He waited for security to clear before he made his move. FBI agents in white coveralls were bundling a man out through the doors. He was wearing orange ones. The type the guards made the Islamic terrorists wear at Guantanamo Bay. This one also had a bag over his head. When they had got him out someone came running back in. He guessed he was heading the operation and had more business to attend to for he ran into the entrance leading to the stairwell. From here Dorcas lost his view of him, he heard the gunfire though.

He was going to have to stay where he was a while longer. If they discovered him then the game would be up, he would keep the door open watching the video screen.

An hour went by when the noise started up once more. This time it was paramedics coming into the foyer. They had four stretchers. Taking them into the stairwell he lost sight of them again. Twenty minutes went by when they started bringing bodies out. They were clearly dead. Their faces covered and the body blankets over them were blooded. When one slipped off one of the men he made out an FBI ID badge on his suit jacket lapel. *God!* This raid, whatever it had been about, had ended in a blood bath. *What had gone on here?*

It was another two hours before it had quietened down enough for him to assume everyone had left, and the building had been locked up. All the regular security people had been replaced by two FBI agents. He would have to be careful others could be checking out the building. Either way, he needed a coffee, and the vending machine was outside his department in the hallway where the lifts were located. The video screen was still showing the foyer. Whatever, he would risk getting a coffee first, make his way up the stairwell and go and do what he had been asked. If he was caught, he would make some excuse he had taken a fall during the melee becoming unconscious. Nevertheless, he was not going to go headlong into trouble without a coffee.

He found an office door signed, SPECIAL SURVEILLANCE OPERATIONS. He was under the impression they were a department of the CIA, or thought they were, for he was not so sure now for signed underneath was an exclusion zone to both the FBI and the CIA. He checked the corridors for any sound of movement. All was quiet. Across the way were two other doors. One had the title names OPERATIONS DIRECTORS. Dr. Nathaniel Johnson and Dr. Daniel Sullivan. Next door was PENSIONS ADMINISTRATOR. This was where he was told the documents he needed were kept. He went in.

The room had been ransacked tidily. There was a facsimile machine in the corner. A desk covered with reams of papers had been pulled over to it. He went across to it and saw the last call made was to the Pentagon. The number counter of the facsimile showed 40 sheets of records out of the pile remaining had been sent. *It was serious*, he murmured. He took his camera, without looking too closely at what he had in front of him, photographed the documents on the desk. The messenger recorded the recipient as CHARLIE O'HARE. Gathering up all the relevant documents needed for . . .

What did they need them for?

Would they be of more value to himself?

Dorcas plugged his camera into his 'special' computer and opened the folder. It showed files, asking him what he wanted to do with them. He was not to read them; only open them one at a time, print them off, then mail them to an address in Germany he had been given over the phone. The remainder he was to burn; not shred.

When he had finished printing he copied a set for himself, downloaded the folder to a flash drive then deleted it from his computer. He went into its hard drive and deleted the camera download from its own hard drive recycling bin folder. Having done this he ran a file shredder application. Gone. That will make life difficult for recovery by any geeks should it come to that. Lastly, he ran the file shredder through his camera removing the jpeg images from its memory and SD card.

He then cleared his desk and separated the originals out into some semblance of order. Dating them was difficult. He should have paid more attention to getting the top of the sheet where the dates were in the frame of his camera more carefully. Laying them out he pasted tags of paper for an easy reference. After giving them a cursory glance he then packaged up the flash drive and the copied printed documents of everything, put his name on it, and addressed them to where his mother lived with her sister in Connecticut.

All remainder original documents he had been asked to send to Germany he packaged up. Those connected with the Order of the Most Divine Third Circle, accordingly surplus to requirement, he burned. He then called the There-On-Time mail receiving agency in Washington DC, telling them he had an urgent international government collection for Germany with its reference number. An hour passed when a courier driver rang his doorbell to make the collection.

EXTRACTED NOTES DICTATED BY DR. SAX STONERCROP FROM THE ORDER OF THE MOST DIVINE THIRD CIRCLE

1920

. . . dating back to the time of the Christian Jesus of Nazareth when the spirits were first seen, recorded, then secreted away at the time of his crucifixion, that had carried on through various Christian religious factions; then there was The Order of the Most Divine Third Circle. Attempts to take it down had been thwarted by the first amendment of the American Constitution for religious freedoms. Although, they had been forced to take out their acts of child abuse and kidnapping had all been largely ignored by the security forces.

. . . the CEO for Oceans International, Frederik Spannocs. This was the holding company. Word was that he was in league with Satan himself. Whether he was or not, they couldn't say, only that he certainly fancied himself in that direction, for his name couldn't have been his real one. Prince of Darkness was an anagram.

. . . the entrapment of an Entity to reach out and pull in among us for the knowledge of creation it possesses would propel man to heights of unimaginable possibilities: The Seventh Gift is within reach. Stonecrop would be a hundred percent with them in . . .

. . . Johnson and Sullivan. Their involvement as undercover agents in the dockyard to keep an eye out for communists, radicals, saboteurs, and the like under the deputy head of the Bureau of Investigation, J. Edgar Hoover. There is a reference to a paranormal event, written by Commissioner Dore.

. . . keep officer O'Hare alive . . . Tammany connections . . . We are as yet not strong enough to take them on.

. . . The powers within the FBI should be allowed to think O'Hare had exaggerated what he had seen. In all events they should be encouraged not to take him seriously; also, it would not do for both of them to be removed, suspicions of conspiracy, etc. Lt. Weinberg, O'Hare boss, was not to be a player. A Jew. He should be discredited and taken out with blame falling on others for his death. Suggest a test of loyalty for Dr. Sax
Stonercrop . . .

. . . Stonercrop should be recruited to the FBI for his knowledge of cults and the paranormal. As an academic, he could be turned. It would be useful for

the Order to have an infiltrator in their midst with
such knowledge . . .

. . . recruited and given the status of CEO . . .
. . . imperative the name Teutonic Knights be
disassociated from the Order.

. . . as well as the Freemasons.

1950

. . . an immediate interest toward Marco Giuseppi was
to be shown. Marco Giuseppi, head of the Dockyard,
Ships & Rigging and Allied Workers' Union whilst at
the same time, two officers from New York's 7th
Precinct were to be prevented from investigating the
abduction of an immigrant family's daughter. Her
disappearance has to date remained a mystery.

. . . the authorities heading the organization into
this scientific investigation is Operations Directors
Dr. Nathaniel Johnson, Dr. Daniel Sullivan, formerly
of SSO . . . both immune from prosecution; any
attempts made to implicate other people are also
immune . . .

. . . the killer of Frank Weinberg was not Marco
Giuseppi, one of our FBI hitmen from the Seaburg
Inquiry; the same man had blown-up the restaurant
taking out David Weinberg, his wife Ruth, and
assistant director of the FBI Franklin Lomax.

. . . in the event, a full denial to the Vatican,

any other person(s) were in any way responsible for the death of one, and the near-death of another of their library staff. (We are not yet powerful enough to take on the might of the Roman Catholic Church should they act against us) . . .

1997

Daniel. Telephone conversation from Father Milligan to Sister Benedicta Marie. The angel has been taken into divine custody. Whatever possessed the form of Spannocs has departed. Go ahead with the replacement. The most despicable person Spannocs can think he would give up the ghost for would be a Jew. We have Hamilton Fitch (formerly Arnold Z. Weinberg) deputy editor of the New York Post with us. The Jewish curse will see an end of his line. See you in Alaska. Nath.

1997

. . . Frederik Spannocs, net worth $50 billion. Departed this world without a trace leaving the shell body of a tramp by the name of Marco Giuseppe, born 1890, died 1997.

1998

The program for the creation of the universe is now in the hands of Star Birth. The list of sympathizers to the cause however is not. Whoever takes over the mantle of the Order of the Most Divine Third Circle once more needs to be aware when the program for creation was downloaded a foreign file attached to the hard drive has not been able to be opened. The members list contains an aristocrat connection to the

```
English throne. IMPERATIVE: The list of members names
is destroyed.
```

Dorcas then sat down for a long read.

He took the scraps of paper he had copied and studied. Studied them with the intensity of the scholar he was. With an MBA from Harvard, it wasn't long before he realized he was sitting on a fortune if he handled this right. (His own father had lost theirs during the Black Monday global crash of 1987.)

He looked into the state of play with the Order of the Most Divine Third Circle. It seemed to be in limbo. Promising, he thought to himself.

Making discrete inquiries following documental notes he held as to the legal aspects of taking on the registered title he discovered no one was holding their hands up to its ownership. Hardly surprising given the historical funding of its operation. For the moment all was up for grabs including its trade name and logo.

Using his government pension program password from his own computer he searched for affiliates. Two names came up, Oceans International, and Oceans Galactica. Surprise! Should it be? Government contracts were all over them. Although to be fair to the government of the day, they were legitimate contracts. How were they to know they were dealing with companies associated with pedophiles and right-wing criminality? *Yeh, right!*

Aryan Farmers Association seemed to be the CEO Frederik Spannocs' favorite baby. Crimes credited to them ran to child abuse, child abduction, pedophilia, and slavery. Net wealth after.... *Oh look, they didn't pay any taxes on . . . $5 billion* he said. He paused to consider. If Internal Revenue were not keen to slice cash from the account sheets of illicit crimes, someone in government did and knew exactly what they were up to. More to the point, why did they ignore it? He asked himself, *Someone or many?* A tremble went through him. Was he getting in over his head with all of this?

Of course he wasn't.

Taking the name of the Order of the Most Divine Third Circle he registered it under new management as Tom Dorcas Inc. He appointed the largest advertising, publicity, and corporate legal firm in the world to act for him. Graf & Mayer were to begin opening up the organization into Asia and Western Europe, Central and Eastern Europe, Africa, and the Middle East, establishing his new order onto the world stage.

He would run the whole operation from his former offices. The lease was up for renewal and the US pension services hadn't made any applications to re-establish administrative (annex ii-38) section gov.pen here. Not a surprise, he thought. Not with all the bad press relating to them and pedophilia. Leverage all nicely documented in a list of members Poster Tacked to the wall over Johnson's desk.

A month later everything had been set up. Holding off the *Wall Street Journal* anxious to write an article for this new kid on the block, who he was? where he had got his money? who was backing him? until he was all set to go.

Having taken over the management of the building he began letting out office space to blue chips. Now companies were all moving in, the whole building was beginning to take on an air of respectability. Out on the junction road, he set a state-of-the-art illuminated board advertising the organization. Next he called in the *Wall Street Journal*.

Fundamentally a simple soul, Dorcas began to worry he had posted his death warrant inside that package to Connecticut.

TWO

Now walk the angels on the walls of heaven,
As sentinels to watch th' immortal souls,
To entertain divine Zenocrate.

TAMBURLAINE THE GREAT (1590)

SENTINEL MASTER– needed to be co-joined to ExtraVersialTerrestrialist if it was to fully function. In its constant state –EVT was invisible, neither absorbing, reflecting or emitting light. What were normal habitation circumstances of its universe where chaos and time did not exist – indeed were not needed, –EVT neither slept, breathed, nor consumed – until it crossed over to material Earth and Time. It had one sense and one alone, the ability to be aware and protect itself. Coming into this new world atmosphere of nitrogen, oxygen, argon, carbon dioxide and all other traces, –EVT had metaphysically adapted, its only sustenance needed was human body fluid. –EVT had a quantum engine core driver. This would deliver program instructions from the Sentinel Mother to its Time Traveller Servant. The manipulation by them of the Nature of Impossible Laws put –EVT one-third the size of a human before arrival on earth. Because of its biological base primarily wiped out by robotic engineering thousands of years before, the Sentinel Mother needed a re-creation program for furtherance of existence if there was to be any future. Extinction was imminent.

Sentinel Master was reprograming a malfunction. –EVT shut

down. −EVT came back on. Rectifying malfunction will cause understanding by Aliens for their reason for being here. −EVT felt deep underground Earth. A malfunction correction was causing overspill of data. −EVT cannot close itself down to prevent.

−EVT took information technology as a sponge takes water. Information images from the shadow of human activity through the doorway from their world into the other were noted. Their defenses insignificant. Not entering any equation for injury or shut down. The equality of the situation required no balance. −EVT had no means to assess the whole situation, as yet!

−EVT could not be sure −EVT had deliberately been shut down by Sentinel Master or program crash. −EVT remained reasoned. An unlikely event for quantum programming −EVT re-booted.

Re-boot came. Sentinel Master approved. Malfunction for time correction imminent. Function Time came and went. Program initiating up-date. −EVT was singular.

−EVT was isolated. −EVT ran a program to track. An instantaneous process. −EVT Time did not exist where −EVT emanated. For −EVT had errored. Program read-out showing Alien environment affected. Back up copy of first Alien seen. −EVT control seeing no change assumed no malfunction. Program failure dismissed. The −EVT ability to cloak had a malfunction. Reprograming needed. −EVT master program for others temporarily closed. −EVT would continue alone. −EVT picked up an Alien possessor for the data. Identity Earth computer showed a file picture program of a Harley Hare, an age and intellect showing source for a Creation Blueprint. Corrected malfunction: streamed social media platforms for identification of Alien. −EVT stored facial identities, names, voices, social security administration numbers, and any other data connected for it to locate its quarry.

 –EVT had arrived in a twin paradox multiple-connected space dimension. The running speed time analyzing charts from a two millisecond brane to Earth terrestrial Time frame co-ordinate starting point. No clear damage from source. –EVT would transgress Time and its semi components in tracing down and destruction of all. –EVT adapted and proceeded through its transparent field.

 Sentinel Master–EVT were locked. Now –EVT needed resources. Now –EVT was fully functional in this Verse.

There was another Master in this Verse. A virus to cause –EVT irreparable damage if it infected. Program up-date information continuing to stream was not accessing information details.

 Named White Bear Angel to those first seeing her when Earth came close to an apocalypse in the year of Their Lord One Thousand Nine Hundred and Ninety-Seven. The USAF base White Bear located on Earth's Arctic region being her last manifestation – was now her second. A creature with all the attributes of an – EVT – was unknowingly, to a select few – and Earth's only shield left to confront any Alien attempt to recover what White Bear Angel had been unable to return to its Maker: the Program of Creation to its library. Program now at large; and with its Creation Controller being in absentia; she faced a one-armed battle for its return.

 She locked onto the Sentinel Master and its –EVT extension. There was a channel of power emanating from the Cosmos's own. A power comparable to her own. She was aware of the Creation Controller. Unlike –EVT and any Sentinel Cohorts, she had a sense of what was right and what was wrong when it came to all aspects of the Universe's physical and philosophical direction. Unlike those eagerly sought by a maverick-God whose sole aim was the destruction of Earth's Time and place in a complex and orderly Cosmos for a throne of its own. She knew the destruction of Mankind was always on a knife edge; and even if she didn't know the importance for their survival, or why it mattered. She knew it did. She had confronted Alpha Omega only the once, and even though, So Be It, was not in her vocabulary, she would be destroyed if she had another confrontation with Him: His experimental doubts and loss of patience for success were not inexhaustible.

A Belgian Malinois. A guard dog leashed to US Army K-9 military policeman, Sergeant Bud Thomas-Kelly had a curious disposition. Even though the shoot first ask after career soldier with the close cropped bullet-headed the clean-cut, Lieutenant Descartes, had his way wanting to command, Shoot what fancies its chances had been given. In any event it was going to be unlikely anyone from security forces was about to open fire on a dog strolling away from a portal with total disdain for another world, cock its leg and piss up its sides.

Cheyne had other ideas. It smelt a rat. Against all its training and restraint it went for the intruder. Standing on its hind legs it pulled his handler off his feet, out from the ranks to the edge of the portal where dog met dog, dog melted dog to its rear paws, slinking off into the darkness, re-aligning itself as a military security soldier in a time not existing, leaving all including Lieutenant Descartes to wonder what the hell had happened to Bud's dog.

Looking back toward the portal, Thomas-Kelly, with the curiosity of one to touch wet paint, walked forward and stuck his hand through the object.

He drew back screaming. A limb was gone. Not in a bloody severed mess; but a sealed wound at the end of his arm showing no sign it had been there in the first instance. His mistake was to put his head into the portal. His thought, to collect his arm with the intent of taking it to a hospital for a stitch job.

Through the portal his arm met his head in relative position. What his eye saw was too much for his heart and the headless and one arm body in his real time collapsed, leaving his head and one arm a time fraction so small in advance to its own devices it no longer functioned.

If the command had been given to blast the Malinois back from whence it came, the order, now rejected in favor of the argument for exploration of new frontiers over annihilation being paramount in human understanding, ignored what fools' acted on. For, Shoot what fancies its chances in this world, was Descartes' best disobeyed order of the day, while his radio operator called to say they had found an Alien ship or portal on the ground giving a GPS location before the signal died in the air.

The United States President, Ryder 'Black Dick' Howe's first and only option for Earth's second chance for survival after hearing what had happened would go sailing down the Swanee river as a child's paper boat if he ignored the information and didn't follow it through.

–EVT stood by the side of an old scraped and rusted white trailer where one of their kind was answering a digestive system function command.

'Good dog,' Wulfhere the current dosser of this once classy camper said crouching to defecate, his bare arse exuding the waste products from a previous meal into the center of a small shrub while at the same time holding his hand out to stroke the Malinois. The slightly oily coat of the animal was the last sensation from the touch of a moving object he was to experience.

–EVT embedded itself inside the human to seek out its shut-down core. It was inside the brain. Life function enabling from brain disabled. Human extinct. In need of protein from the new form it had taken, it consumed the fluid it needed from inside out.

–EVT moved back towards the Transparent Portal Field leaving a patch of orange earth the only evidence –EVT had been here. The malfunction inadvertently marking presence needing attention. – EVT needed multiples to close verse down. Program error resolved. Installing. Program stalled. The Transparent Portal Field was going out of kilter. –EVT inadvertently bayed as a dog at its impending entrapment in this Alien verse.

'Someone shut that frickin' wolf up,' Descartes shouted.

The canine went silent. Padding up to him, looking up to him, for all the world wanting Descartes to pat its head, he softened.

'Merci beacoup,' Descartes said down to the creature.

–EVT transformed into a duplicate of the Alien and Descartes became two. Seeing his double-goer was too much for him. –EVT was his intrusive disease.

Descartes' eyes became bigger. He dropped to the ground.

A shout went out, MEDIC! Was too late. The Lieutenant was beyond repair.

–EVT proceeded to turn its attention to his men. Private First Class Andrews put his M249 to his head in an effort to take himself from the shock of what he saw as his inevitable grisly death. Capable of pushing 750 bullets up its barrel in 60 seconds he pulled the trigger rattling off four before his finger lost strength. The rest of the platoon held their nerve. Standing their ground, cocking their weapons in unison, before they too succumbed to the infiltration of an Alien mushing their insides out until none were left standing. They were being attacked by themself. One even tried to reason with his twin. It was all over in 9.001 seconds.

–EVT had malfunctioned into thinking what it had come for was among these people. If –EVT were to recover the information it needed breaking down human brain stems was not the answer. It would take too long. The ability to return from where it came within parameters of Time was critical here. The program link to the Sentinel Master was not finite. Transparent Portal Field came back. It was stable once again. The Alien –EVT had closed the door to this Verse once. The Sentinel Master –EVT needed to locate this creature and take it down before it did it again, permanently.

Three

PRESIDENT RYDER HOWE; Vice President, Joe McClusky; Assistant to the President for Homeland Security and Counterterrorism (CIA), Jean Ronstandt with his assistant, Madeleine Tubman; National Security Advisor to the Vice President, Abisai Campbell; White House Chief of Staff, Steven Kalo; Assistant Commanding General Joint Special Operations Command, Vice Admiral Carmella Rossi.

Charlie O'Hare walked purposely toward the White House Situation room. He was in the dark as to what he was doing here. Wonder what gives now? he thought. Everybody who's anybody is here. The President reached across and shook his hand. This was followed by Joe McClusky. He knew Joe better than the President, 'Howya doin', Joe?'

'I have called you together because of the situation occurring at Becland.' He turned to O'Hare. 'No need to remind you where that is, Mr. O'Hare.'

Indeed there wasn't.

O'Hare hadn't seen President Howe since then. They last met when Howe was Vice-President under the previous administration of Henry Clancy Montgomery III. He had been invited to Howe's inauguration when he had picked up the 43rd title. He was younger than Henry by ten years, although, the lines and the sag to his eyes didn't show. He did look tired though. It was O'Hare's opinion seventy was too old to become a world leader. Having thought that though, he supposed America was once again in safe hands.

'You are here because an Alien has turned up at Becland. This, by the nature of its strange happenings will concern you, Charlie. Not directly, you were involved in similar before. It's your advice I need now.'

There, just like that, an Alien! You'd have thought he was announcing a price increase of hamburgers. Howe was nothing if not down to earth in his appraisal of situations. Becland, the now uninhabited new Roswell, no longer on the map of America; once an end point, is now a start point. O'Hare never thought it was going to end just like that.

'The marines sent to investigate came under the orders of Lieutenant Descartes. The last signal received from Descartes was they had come across what appeared to be an upright mirror of glass positioned vertically over desert scrubland. We sent up a reconnaissance drone. It didn't look good down there. Eighteen marines lying dead on home soil is a fucking tragedy. And whatever was responsible I need it brought down in its tracks.' He handed out photographs of the area. It showed an out of focus glint of light with bodies surrounding it. 'Those are our soldiers down there, whatever took them out, and I've said it already. If it turns out it was an Alien, then it had better come from another planet and not this one,' Howe said.

O'Hare studied the picture he had in his hand. This was the Becland he recognized. Where a perverted excuse for a man by the name of Marco Giuseppi *alias* Frederik Spannocs met his end; not before bringing the world to the brink of another war though. The nuclear power station, stripped of its rods and as much of its contaminated material as was safely possible had been taken to a secret dumping facility in Maine before it had been made to look like a melt-down accident. Its roof all stove in after the marines had blown it apart back in '97 added to the lie, was to the side of Becland. The lie itself – subject to various conspiracy theories on social media platforms – was managed to be contained. Becland was derelict, its houses bulldozed by the military to give the impression the meltdown from its nuclear power house was its cause. Better to admit government and company money over negligence than a true Act of God no one is going to find credence no matter how faithful, religious and God-fearing America professes to be (I'll say no more on the matter).

He looked down on what had been the Becland Diamond Conference Center. Next to the last stand for Spannocs before White Bear. Where heaven engaged with hell in a confrontation still unresolved. As for his own, well, as long as the program remained here on Earth, there would be peace for no one. This was different though. He continued looking at the picture; and his own knowledge of happenings of the time.

The area was surrounded by double high wire fences. Signs in red lettering on white backgrounds placed at intervals of 75 yards read: RADIOACTIVE AREA: DANGER OF DEATH. NO ENTRY BY ORDER OF THE U.S. DEPARTMENT OF DEFENSE, all for a distance of five miles. Scrub and forest had grown over the area hiding it from casual visitors. Becland was how the government wished it to remain – testament to a truth never revealed.

Howe was right in what he said, assuming this photograph wasn't a fake, those were bodies down there, soldiers. A mirror of glass Descartes described before going off air as having a reflected rim of shimmering sunlight on its one edge circumference, which on an overcast day would have been lost to the lens from the drone's camera, prominent. As best he judged, it was in the same place the two world's collided in a white explosion of heat; when a quadrant portion of earth shook the shook with an intensity of two stars left all living souls between one second and infinite years incinerated where they stood.

'So what do you want from me?' O'Hare asked.

'I've organized a team of physicists to evaluate as to what they believe is down there.'

O'Hare gave him a look of caution.

'Whether I want to believe what has occurred or not, action has to be seen to have been taken. Anyway if an Alien had come through and attacked our men they're going to be the people to crack this. CNN will have a field day if we don't.'

'And you want me to go in?'

'No, Charlie. What I need are two reliable guys to fly them in and get them out in one piece. You know such people,' the President said opening his eyes wide.

He did.

Webb and Coleman came immediately to mind. A tinge of excitement went through him. A rescue mission of a religious order going badly wrong was when O'Hare and Webb's paths first crossed. The Bell helicopter Webb was piloting went down like a lead balloon after being hit by a Laws missile aimed at them by the Ku Klux Klan intent on bringing them out of the sky, and lynching them for their time.

Operation Daemon Crush, he said whenever he had cause to thank the Lord for small mercies saving all of their lives.

'The best two people I trust with my life, though where they are now is anyone's guess. Baxter Webb was the FBI's Critical Incident Response Group Operations controller back in the day. Zac Coleman, his co-pilot. If I can find them.'

'Trusted to keep the peace if it goes wrong, eh?'

'If what happened to those soldiers down there happens to your scientists peace won't be an issue. Will it, sir?'

* * *

Webb (he got the sobriquet Spider not from his surname as many supposed; but from his smoking the black Japanese cigarettes with the picture of an arachnid on its pack), flew F4 Phantom's in Vietnam where he achieved flying ace status. Retired out in his fifties, he still hankered for flying.

Both Webb and Coleman were part-time pilots for the FBI and CIA when unofficial missions' presented themselves; and with their moonlighting for banks, repossessing expensive aircraft and luxury boats for those who didn't meet their credit arrangements, they were doing very nicely thank you. Banks and credit agencies were going to be O'Hare's first line of inquiry to track them down.

He didn't have to wait long.

Both men had been arrested after breaking into a private airplane hangar facility when they tried to recover a Cessna Citation C525 from its criminal owner. O'Hare arranged for their release.

Four

THE SCIENTIFIC TEAM of specialists were made up of Wilfred Simpson, Stefanka Prishna, with their boss, Kurtz Konig. Konig was from the Helmholtz Centre for Heavy Ion, the rest worked for Conseil européen pour la recherche nucléaire. Anti-radiation suits were issued and loaded aboard the helicopter.

Marlyn Gibbs, a freelance photo journalist with National Geographic had to sign the Defense Secrets Act of 1911. She was armed as was the army medical officer, Lieutenant Doctor Wendy Mitchell. Webb and Coleman were never unarmed whatever job they took on.

Webb was to locate Descartes and his men, administer first aid to any of the living; body bag any in the other place. A transport plane was on Becland's perimeter to carry out the dead when it was required.

Webb brought the Sikorsky UH-60 Black Hawk over the disused power station out over the town for an informal recce. Happy he hadn't come under any Alien attack, he came close to the last signal coordinates Descartes had managed to pass over. Bringing the Black Hawk down with a bump in a cloud of dust, sand and tumbleweed, he knocked the rotors out of drive lowering the engine revs to a tick before cutting the engine altogether. It was midday, blisteringly hot, blinding sunlight, and an uncanny silence. The wind was blowing sand and soil east. He looked through the window.

So, this is Becland's infamous Ground Zero; out of bounds to all since, well, must be a couple of years now, he thought to himself.

'Okay ladies and gentlemen,' he said peeling the foil off a strip of Extra Mint gum with his teeth before popping it into his mouth, 'release your harnesses and get your suits on, you're summer vacation starts here. Kurtz, can you keep your people close?' Konig nodded. 'Zac, first off we need to find those marines. Wendy is it?' She nodded. 'You'd better come with us, there might be the chance some are still alive.'

Coleman jumped out first. He looked around him, his gun at the ready. Up on a ridge he spotted a body. 'Hey, Spider, someone up there. Someone I suspect shouldn't be. Enjoying the sun by the looks of it.'

'Better go check it out. Take it easy though, he may not be sleeping.'

Coleman called out to the man as he approached him. He might have been sunbathing … once … for sure he wasn't now. An old wagon he had been living in was close by. A plaque by the side of the door badly signed in duck egg blue announced it as, WULFHERES HOME. The man himself laying by the side of it looked chewed, mushed, then eaten. He instinctively touched his body for any sign of life.

A once white Winnebago, the camper languished off-level with three of its six wheels inflated was dirt spattered half-mast in a sea of bright orange muddy ground surrounded by a sea of natural brown. The natural brown, the color of the surrounding terrain, was not amiss, the orange was. He pushed open the door of the camper and squeezed his suited body through the entrance. His fit for duty Colt M4 carbine at the ready.

For sure it had been lived in. The bed was unmade. One of an old pair of boots was on the pillow, the other further down the bed.

The gas stove, fortunately running low on fuel had one of its burners still alight. A frying pan with a lump of bacon dried and crisped to a frazzle had welded itself to the base. That was going to take some cleaning, he thought. He turned the gas off. Satisfied the man was living alone (he assumed he didn't have a wife, or if he did, she had left him years since), he turned to leave. He stepped outside into the sunlight with one thought in mind. The man's culinary skills having recently been interrupted, suggested his dinner date seeking preference to the chef over the bacon, could well be searching for a second course.

He pressed his intercom switch with his chin, 'Spider.'

'Reading you, Zac.'

'Civilian. Dead.'

'You sure?'

'Not in uniform. Not in much at all. Jesus! He's one mess of a man though. I reckon whatever done this to him is still in the area. Likely watching us, the body's still warm.'

'Thanks, Zac. Stay where you are, I'm sending Wendy up. She'll need to decide cause of death.'

Webb double checked the GPS figures of Descartes' last position. They were where they were supposed to be. So where were all these marines? *And tick the empty box for Alien space craft*, he muttered.

Gibbs came through coms asking Baxter whether their helmets were still important as they were when they first landed. She was having trouble taking pictures.

'Konig's your boss, ask him. The FBI's ours. We're under orders to keep them on.'

Kurtz came back telling his team it was up to them. He had had no directive, it had been a recommendation.

33

Simpson checked his Geiger reading. It read slightly above normal. He double checked it. For an area supposedly having had a nuclear melt-down he found curiously strange. He was satisfied. 'Geiger says good to go, Kurtz.'

'Fair enough. Your decision people.'

Prishna unfastened her helmet.

'Sorry, Baxter, radiation levels are low enough for us to survive here for a day or two. Levels are less than a dentist's x-ray machine. The others' took their helmets off, leaving Baxter and Coleman to sweat their balls off – and Mitchell to, perspire hers.

'Kurtz, I'm sending Wendy to look at the body up on the ridge. It might be a good idea if Marlyn goes with her, the President will find close-ups useful,' Webb suggested.

'Roger that, Baxter,' Kurtz came back.

She nodded.

'Got your weapon, Wendy? Just in case. Zac suffers premonitions, knowing when to get a last drink in before closing time is called. I'd hate for you to get caught out.'

'Heard that, Spider.'

Mitchell and Gibbs approached the sunbathing man with trepidation, for what remained of the tourist that had strayed into the worst caravan park imaginable was not good. When she thought tourist the term came loosely, for there was to be no more sightseeing for this one. She put the Geiger counter up to his remains. It read 3Gy. As Mitchell was here to take samples, as well as tendering to any sick and injured, assuming they found any, it would be as well if he stayed.

Gibbs held her camera at arm's length. 'Nice!' she said staring at the mutilated remains and fired off half a dozen shots. 'How did he come to look like this I wonder?'

'The man has been eaten alive, that's how,' Mitchell answered.

'And recently. In summertime with this heat, I would have expected to find maggots. Not yet though. Give it a couple of weeks. Bluebottles . . . start a fly-paper production plant there's so many.'

What was left was half-eaten flesh and droppings of defecated soil and shrub mixed together. She smeared together the undigested human remains between her two rubber-gloved hands and put them into a sampler bag. Whatever had done this was fussy about its diet. For the creature (and it must have been animal, possibly mammal) having dined here was not keen on the unfortunate's eyes as well as one of his testicles, for along with the mangled and bloody mass, matted out with pubic hair, it looked as though an attempt to chew the meal had disagreed with it and it had retched them up. Holding the translucent bag up to the sunlight, the Scotch broth soup remains squeezed hard against the inside of the bag gave a bizarre image of a Cycloptic-eyed creature from, Monsters, Inc.

'Open it up, Marlyn,' she said indicating the sampler box. She placed the meal in and hasped the lid closed. 'Enough,' she said. 'I'll do the rest when I get back to the lab.' She looked over Marlyn's shoulder and pointed, 'What is that?'

'Our team,' Gibbs answered.

'Not them, out there, further on. Her eyes were sticky from the heat. She blinked to clear them. 'Oh, this damned vizor.'

Gibbs looked at where Mitchell was pointing. The sand was funneling across the landscape. A wind phenomenon, perhaps. She watched mesmerized waiting for it to settle itself back down. It didn't. She expected a rocky outcrop or a hill to be causing it.

'KURTZ!'

Konig looked up. Mitchell was waving. The Winnebago was 200 yards away from him. 'Got you, Wendy. Go ahead.'

'Can you see? Some distance further on from where you're

standing. The weather pattern is all over the place.'

He stared into the distance while his eyes adjusted. 'Y-e-s! I think so, what about it?'

'There is a shift in the wind debris,' Simpson chipped in. 'It's blowing off course. Something's causing it to do that, and it's not natural. A sandstorm?'

'Yes, I can see what you're on about now. Thought I was imagining it for a minute. We're coming back, we're finished here,' Konig replied.

'Best take a look then,' Webb said. 'All of you, Zac and me will take the lead.' Coleman nodded agreement.

Coleman walked alongside Webb. Both men had their weapons in readiness. Both men anxious not so much for themselves, for they were used to war zones and death, but for the civilians they were responsible for. The object appeared out of sand storm as an illusion. A circle of glass standing vertical that both would have sworn wasn't there before took the men's breath away. In this wind Coleman would have expected it to have blow over. Coming within ten yards of it they saw the explanation for Descartes' going off air. Mutilated bodies of soldiers and equipment were strewn out and away from the object in all directions. All they could do was stare.

'Everyone, stay where you are,' Webb said over the com. 'God, this is one awful mess? What do you think, Zac?'

'I'm thinking, where's the fucking creature that did this? Why didn't we see them after we landed?' Coleman asked.

'Because they weren't there. If they were, they were fucking invisible,' Webb said. 'One for you, Kurtz. A David Copperfield illusion. Bring your people in, we've found what you've come for; and what we have.'

Konig said, 'Jesus! What happened?'

'Good question,' Coleman answered. 'We won't need the services of any medics, that's for sure.'

Mitchell looked through her helmet at the dead marines. The remains of bodies told her all she needed to know. Coleman unwrapped the body bags in readiness while she went among them collecting up ID tags. The search for life would be as elusive as that on mars. Those not with any particular body she placed as close as she thought was appropriate to the marine it belonged. DNA may or may not make identification possible. She had never seen anything like this before. All the bodies showed signs that attempts had been made to eat them. If that was so, then it was clear to her no animal of the mammal species had carried this out. Where she expected teeth marks or saliva, there was none. Something had just sucked the life out of them.

Webb called up the marine lieutenant in charge of the ambulances waiting beyond the perimeter fence to enter; after what he had witnessed, he suggested they organize a battalion from the Marine Corps before they collect the dead.

'No survivors!' Lieutenant Braque queried.

'No anything actually, Lieutenant,' Webb answered. He turned to Konig, 'If that's what you've come to investigate,' he said pointing at the object, 'don't be too long about it, Kurt. I'm fearing for our lives the longer we remain here.'

Dr. Wilf Simpson – scientist and part-time science fiction writer – excited about coming across an Alien portal; who had more salient facts at his disposal than Google, expected to stumble straight into a purple blob of pulsating jelly with condensing air coming from its center. So far he was disappointed. No purple blobs here. What there was though, appeared to be a force field of energy coming from the ground below the portal (for want of a more scientific explanation of what it was); and to all intents and purposes headed up into the atmosphere.

Prishna and Gibbs came closer. Prishna made the comment it looked like a lens from Mauna Kea's Observatory. Gibbs began snapping away with her camera, moving around towards the edge of the lens as she went. 'The diameter of this lens is only . . . what? Kurtz!' She took off her glove and pointed her finger at its edge.

Konig nodded. She took a laser measure from her overall. 'Twenty eight feet? It doesn't seem possible a glass object of this size and thickness is capable of supporting itself without falling and breaking into a thousand shards on those rocks,' Konig said pre-empting her measurement.

'And a millimeter thick,' Gibbs answered.

'If it's an inch, yup.'

'Is it glass though? It's performing as is. It seems to have the same properties for reflection,' Gibbs said adjusting the focus of her Nikon. She clicked. 'Wonder when I can get these to National Geographic?'

'Don't even think about it,' Zac said. 'You'll get ten years.'

Simpson came up. 'Let me have a look.' He studied it sideways on. Getting down on his knees, he got himself as close as he dared without touching it. He looked upwards along its plane. 'It's not glass, Kurtz. Look at the surface of it. Have you ever seen glass vibrate like that?'

Konig couldn't see at first, not until he also got down on his knees.

'That's the weirdest thing I've ever seen. It puts me in mind of a child's soap dip ring. You know, when the kiddie blows on the liquified soap and it expands until it reaches an optimum point when it no longer holds itself together and breaks away into a bubble.'

Gibbs continued taking pictures moving along and over its surface before going to the back of it. She saw Coleman through it, his automatic in his hands. She took a shot of him. And another. Only later did she find the digital pixels had distorted to the point where the image couldn't be identified properly. And only then did she wish she'd brought her film camera with her instead of the latest tech she did bring.

Simpson got up from his knees. A window, he thought. A time traveler's fucking portal no less. To worlds beyond ours. He was experiencing what he and other sci-fi writers dreamed. His fantasies into worlds of myths and legends. His world of physics working for CERN was a whole lot more tangible. There he had seen mysteries of the universe up close. Where time travel allowed other worlds to be explored was an approaching possibility. For even though youth was close enough to the child in him, to imagine a man on a time travel mission would one day be a reality. As a boy he read superhero and Martian comics. Now he was a valuable member of Konig's team, along with Prishna and others who were amongst the top physicists in the world looking into the existence of hypothetical particles. Of particular interest to him, tachyonic fields (particles traveling faster than the speed of light of Higgs boson fame. One of the Standard Model).

'Watch where you're standing,' Konig said. 'Get any closer and Higgs' theory will have you in a flash.'

Simpson turned and smiled. With the words hardly out of Konig's mouth he went off balance forward putting his hand up against the surface of the object. Before it had gone an inch in he withdrew it.

Gibbs cried out, *Whoah!*

He looked at her and at what she was pointing to. His finger from the top knuckle was missing. Seeing it, and this time without purpose, he fell face first in the sand.

Gibbs grabbed him. He was off balance causing the pair of them to go down together. She turned him over onto his back and lifted his legs. He came around in seconds asking what happened. She reminded him, at the same administering water from her bottle, while he, looking at the end of his finger was trying to figure out why it was not bleeding, showing signs of being crushed or having a cracked distal phalanx even, exhibiting instead a perfectly shaped stump. He didn't complain of any pain, for there was none. In truth, he had a trophy. A lecturer's visual aid to beat all. A science fiction writer's, *I've seen the truth.*

Webb suggested they take their samples and photographic evidence and get out of here as soon as possible. 'Whatever it is, is to be treated as dangerous.' He turned to Konig. 'If you've everything you need, Professor, we'll move out.'

'You do know we're going to have to face down whatever occurred here some time or another, don't you?'

'I'm no scientist, Prof; my feelings are we're going to have to destroy it. Because if facing it down later means someone has to enter it well good luck with that one, because as sure as hell, it won't be me holding any of your people's hands.'

–EVT program responsible for its Time–Shift cloak had gone down, exposing both the Transparent Portal Field and the dead inhabitants of Earth in this Time–Verse. When the program containing the location of its quarry –EVT was to locate was uploaded there came another hitch. The security of the program was not attached. Another had locked onto it. –EVT had been located once more. The data stream had been hacked. Sentinel Master had no choice. Unable to operate it would have to close down until a new program was streamed in. Losing control of the Transparent Portal Field –EVT was now isolated and trapped.

–EVT bayed as a dog. The howl deep and ghostly, resounded out and across the desert floor of Becland to echo back from the hills at the edge of the valley. The entrance back to its own world was closed off to it.

The team on the ground gathered themselves into a group fearing an attack to their party similar to the one the marines faced.

'Back in the helicopter, ladies and gentlemen, the holiday's over,' Webb said.

Alien Predator 1, Sentinel Master–EVT 0.

On the ground lay a soldier's helmet. The headgear, along with the micro video camera attached (partially smashed) was still running. At the US Base of Fort Sam Houston, army signal officer, Sgt. Tamsin Tass picked up an image on her screen. It was of a man wearing a bowler hat, with a white . . . *Is that a clay pipe poking out of his chest pocket?* she said.

The man turned and walked away from the remains of what Webb had reported back to them as a potential danger zone for the military before flying out. *That's our Black Hawk going over the horizon*, she said to CIA officer for Homeland Security, Jean Ronstandt standing over her watching.

'So, who in hell is the clown they've left behind?' Ronstandt said asking the hypothetical question.

Five

DIREKTORIN ELKE KRIEMHILD waited for Johnson to pick up the telephone in America. In front of her were the historical and removed documents connected with the old Order of the Most Divine Third Circle over the years. Or would be, for the small matter, they had all been copied. Twice. For sure, by that upstart shit Johnson had employed for the task.

When he answered he knew what she was going to say. Sitting at his old desk he was looking at a screwed into a ball sheet of A4 in the waste bin. It was tinted red. *Dorcas!*

The paper they use for documents is special in it retains its color for one pass in a copier. A single green light pass of the document doesn't affect the color of the paper. Another pass and it will turn red tint. Knowing who was responsible, Johnson had to ask if there was likely to be any ramifications with him having them?

'If you ignore the fact he's re-named the organization, the Church of the New Order under Tom Dorcas Inc., registered it as a religion under the First Amendment of the United States constitution, walked off with $5 billion of our money. Not at all. Happily, we own Graf & Mayer, the company making all the arrangements for him. Schmerzen im arsch, and all a matter of unpicking it and returning. You will find him filing for bankruptcy after having his balls removed with a blunt rusty knife very soon, Nathaniel.

He smiled. He always liked her pain in the arse comments. So much more refined when spoken in German. As for Dorcas, he had organized him to steal the documents a month back. He wondered why it had taken him so long to organize such a simple task. Now he knew. He was not the fool he had taken him for.

'The documents Dorcas sent me are red. He's sitting on another set. We're not prepared to allow him to use them as leverage when we take the Order back. Of more immediacy, the list of members is not among them. I hope you destroyed those before you let him loose on your desk?'

Bollocks he hadn't. Another age memory encounter. The list's still on the wall, along with the sticky note reminding him to destroy it. Hope to God Charlie has been in there and taken it.

'If it falls into the wrong hands at least two crown heads of Europe will fall. Shortly before yours. Old age is taking them out quick enough as it is. I notice the cheeky bastard has got his company address in the same building we used to lease. Except, unlike you, he's not in the basement. We're not pissing around here. Though, on reflection, Dorcas might be useful with or without any balls. Have a quiet word with him, Nathaniel. And find that list. Tschüss.'

The peculiar arrangement Johnson had with O'Hare in keeping with both their agencies and histories he never did trust. Not completely. He supposed it went both ways. For diplomacy's sake, neither man was who they purported to be when it came to acting out their roles for the prevention of an autocratic world order.

Johnson sent an electronic message on his private mail server to O'Hare. He was hoping against hope to be able to recover the list before Dorcas, seeing it stuck on the wall, recognizing its value, would create diplomatic mischievous for Europe and Direktorin Elke

Kriemhild.

'If you were wondering, Mr. Wharfmaster, I have it.'

O'Hare's reply snapped straight back.

Six

THE SENDING OF THE DOWNLOADED hard drive, with those immovable and stubborn folder files to two of the world's leading black hatters in the penetration business was a resort (not necessarily a last) for Direktorin Kriemhild. Not out of any lack of computer expertise on her organization's part (for didn't they build the program to hack governments of the world) . . . more . . . the Seagate Medalist 3132 hard drive containing those two medieval folder files required an unlawful expertise. People that advertised their illegal arts on the dark web; and importantly, could easily be disposed of for the knowledge those folders contained when they finally revealed themselves, without the law, or companies that had been held to ransom for mega bucks shedding a tear for their demise.

COra8 & AsC (Corate and Ask) met at university where they began their hacking careers to make ends meet. Those 'ends meet' soon became surpassed with an embarrassment that brought the university's dean and the Internal Revenue down around their heads looking into their business activities. The dean, reluctant to let two obvious high flyers be sent down, allowed them to carry on their degrees. The IR were not so charitable, forcing them to auction their cars they tried to hide in the university car park: Corate, a Mercedes SL 60 AMG; and Ask, a BMW Z8, for unpaid taxes.

Now older and legit they were cracking open software company program files searching out unpatched holes companies were vulnerable. With an office staff of twenty graduates they were coming close to respectability – with a certain caution still – in Silicon Valley.

If they had been told who was sending it to them they may have been given a clue. Clearly it wasn't any breakfast cereal company despite arriving at their offices as a, 35 x Kellogg's Cereal 5 Variety Packs carton. The address label, CORASK Tech found their Morgan Hill, Northern California offices with little trouble, where it was duly signed for by one of the early rising turner-ins. She regretted her decision to make an early start, for she was lumbered with having to explain to everyone as they came in through the door, seeing a green and red cockerel printed package on the goods-in counter, they were not being treated to a company bonus breakfast as it was far too heavy for corn flakes.

Intrigued, Corate, who had tech gear secured in plain boxes with their contents bubble wrapped looked at what they had. This had none. The order note asking to open the file, mark it up as the key used, then call this number and await its return care of person, Direktorin Elke Kriemhild to collect.

Ask was looking over his shoulder as he took it out.

'Kriemhild. With a name like that it's gotta be from a government agency. CIA. FBI. You think?' he suggested to Corate.

Corate took the Seagate from him. He studied it closely as if it were an explosive device about to take his hands off. He put it down and began rifling through a box of of miscellaneous wires and plugs he had at the back of his bench. Finding what he thought looked promising he plugged it in. He connected it to a monitor and switched it on. Two icon files of medieval appearance came up. Looking as if it had been copied from an historic hand tooled leather book jacket, carved from an ancient stone even, came up on the screen.

'What are they? Jewish, Islamic,' Corate asked by way of suggestion.

'Resembles more Jewish Shin than Moslem,' Ask said. 'Which, considering computers are modern in comparable time does seem a tad strange.'

There was no file extension giving clues to its opening. Some kind of key matching the physics for computers seemed reasonable to both men. They systematically went through archiving, compression, data recovery, containers and compressions, database and document files. Thinking of the Islamic or Jewish symbolism, seeing as God the Architect and Engineer would have opted for similar they downloaded specialist software such as CAD. Neither folder was having any of it. They came to conclusion that the software needed to open it didn't exist. Not on this planet, at least. If it did, then they would have it. More intriguing for the two black hatters and their world of penetration, was that the folder would contain binary code that a human wouldn't understand if did spring into life. Whatever had created it was a divine programmer leaving them a hacker wall to hit them face on for the first time in their careers.

This left COra8 and AsC with the only alternative for its opening. There must be an outside source required, or, the folder designation was fake. There were however three peculiarities about it since starting to crack it. After working on it for half an hour they began to suspect it was giving off levels of radiation (Ask was complaining of head aches). For peace of mind they got a Geiger counter and checked it out. It read three hundred millirems. A level that wouldn't toast bread. Second, was the sound coming from it. In computer-speak what was known as the 'click of death'. Such a click would have been from an actuator resetting itself after hitting a damaged sector on a disk. Which was all well and good if the clicking was coming from inside the device. It wasn't. This clicking was coming from somewhere else. Looking closer at its casing Corate noticed some screw heads holding it together showed signs of wear. He took a fine screwdriver and undid them, lifted off the shield exposing the disk.

'There's your problem. It's jammed,' Ask said satisfied he alone had cracked it. He reassembled it, reconnected it to a power source, and ran it once more. Then the third peculiarity came into play. A multimedia music track began to play. Somehow, some comedian had laid down a Barry Manilow track inside. On a loop it began playing, ♪ *At the Copa – Copacabana – The hottest spot north of Havana* ♪ which every time it came around had their staff looking up from their work stations to sing along in an accompaniment.

They called Kriemhild to tell her that they had failed to open the two folder files. Diagnostic assessment: an electronic key from a sister hard drive to be run in tandem was missing. They asked if she had the secondary device?

'What kind of an organization do you think I work for. Everything you needed was in that one hard drive. There is no other. If you cannot open a couple of simple folders, then you had better send it back and I'll find another company that can,' Kriemhild said. 'I'll arrange collection.'

Corate and Ask looked at each other.

'No! Fuck her. We'll keep Barry Manilow to ourselves. We nothing about it, yes?' Corate said to his partner.

'Don't know what you're talking about,' Ask replied grinning.

They repackaged up the 35 x Kellogg's Cereal 5 Variety Packs carton along with their findings and an invoice. An hour later a There-On-Time courier arrived taking it from them.

Direktorin Elke Kriemhild was at her office deep in the mountains of Weinberghöhe below Drogstadt Castle. Hewn from the mountain in 1542 on the orders of Pope Paul III for the torture and imprisonment of heretics during the Roman Catholic Inquisition it had been bought by Johann Adam Weishaupt, a law professor in 1776 who intended it for his worldwide Illuminati. Now in the hands of a new elite, they had skewed away from Weishaupt's and Bronisław Trentowski's unpopularity of title names such as, Freemasonry, Intelligentsia, even the old name, Illuminati. For this was now Star Birth, instilling into its followers beliefs in new found sciences such as particle physics, as opposed to God and His Divine associates now out of favor by the masses. Religious dictates requiring obedience without question were always doomed to failure, unless a religious fanatic pointed a gun to ones head. From Star Birth's aspect they had the guns.

Religion was no longer the opium of the masses.

From the Star Birth point of view questions of a God over science depended not on faith; on the demonstration of hard physics over 2000 years of myth they were intent on burying. Problem was, those true members of the Order of the Most Divine Third Circle proving the myth to be true was going to take time.

On the roof of the castle, under a dome purported to be a planetarium from an outside world, was a sophisticated network for communication. Locked by a metal door from the rest of the castle massive cabinets contained search engine servers. Alongside were air conditioning units to keep them from overheating. There was a crew of twelve computer engineers servicing them, on three shifts around the clock. The floor below held the organizations World Operations Center. Programed to eavesdrop on the USA as well as Europe, this was run by five high-tech people with experiences of working for Microsoft and Google. From here they had access to one of the first face recognition systems in the world. Their undetectable scammers were hacking into the United States drivers' license offices of state, territory as well as the District of Columbia.

From this vast network they were at the forefront for controlling the politics of the new and emerging social platforms. For this was where people, that could be instilled with propaganda and false information, were to be found. Though based in Europe totalitarian states were offered access to technologies of the West to manage their own agendas in other countries.

The computers and ancillary facilities had access to all telephone companies in America. The list ran to facility-based wireless service providers as well as AT&T, Sprint, and US Cellular. From an array of keywords the computer running the system locked into all providers and callers. From there, the caller could be isolated down to within ten feet anywhere on Earth. Such was the intensity of operating these systems all staff were replaced at six week intervals to keep them free from burn-out. The whole operation was controlled from Munich (Bavaria being its preferred nation state name), in Germany. For the Order of the Most Divine Third Circle was Direktorin Elke Kriemhild's first love; who in turn represented those seeing democratic republicanism for a world order the only way its population approaching 10 billion would survive.

Inquiries of her people involved at White Bear on the AG-MX-960 project when the top blew off the Arctic region were equally divided between them that died, those doing time for child abuse, abduction, and under age sex with minors, and those enlisted into the US government's own scientific programs at at the place known as Area 51, Becland. Whatever dirty project that happened to be. It would be the latter of that divide that would know how to open what they had downloaded, otherwise, what would have been the point if that had not been given consideration?

There was no doubt they had come close with their experiments to proving the existence of God. In fact, she was sure, were it not for those crimes orchestrated by Frederik Spannocs, the divine would not have intervened by falling into the trap of coming to Earth. It was said that abuse against children was the ultimate sin that heaven would not stand for. If you believed that to be true (a myth she was partially coming around to as she got older) then God's intervention by a divine spirit stepping up to the plate was a clear response. Why had it all gone so wrong for them? A secret mission, a section of the US government being aware, must have had its share of detractors and moles.

Not for the first time had she given that any thought. She had a potted history of the Order's intent and what went wrong. The two masterminds for directing operations of the Order of the Most Divine Third Circle in America were Daniel Sullivan (head separated from his neck by an instrument of his own design), and Nathaniel Johnson. Those two men, not forgetting O'Hare, and Spannocs (presumed dead welcomed into hell), would be well over a 100 years old now. Mortals coming into contact with a divine spirit – she had been told – can be killed, murdered; but not by any natural cause pass away. How many others were there like that in the world, she wondered?

Which left one working for the organization from that time capable of undermining Birth Star. Johnson! Although, his involvement in murder directly or indirectly for Spannocs and the organization, would go a long way to dispel any questions of disloyalty there. Nevertheless, if he was a mole within the organization, he would be in the same league as a British police officer working under cover within the Irish Republican Army. A double agent, overseeing kneecapping – using countersunk drill bits attached to a power unit popular with the IRA – and execution. The organization's hierarchy carried out an investigation prior to reforming the direction of the Order; and even though suspicions' fell on Johnson, he was cleared with a recommendation that a close eye be kept on him. She would return to him after the folder files from that hard drive had shed their light.

She communicated through their secure telephone network to the CIA man responsible for arresting O'Hare when he returned to United States from Ireland, relieving him of the hard drive.

'I want to be sure about this. And I want you to think carefully about your answers. The hard drive you sent to CORASK Tech, is it the same one you took from O'Hare when he arrived back at Kennedy Airport? Could it have been confused with any other? And being refused entry into Ireland, would O'Hare have found a way to doctor it? Put simple, did Irish customs send him straight back to the United States without his feet touching Ireland's soil?' Kriemhild queried.

'Our people swear he never left Dublin Airport. Customs had him back on his plane within twenty minutes of trying to enter.'

'Was there anyone with him having access to the hard drive on the plane? It was his own charter flight wasn't it?'

'A Lear, yes. Apart from the pilot, just him. He gave it up into our hands as soon as he stepped out of the plane.'

'Well, doesn't sound like the O'Hare we've all come to know and love over the years.'

'Oh, wait a minute. There was somebody else on the plane with him apart from the pilot. He had an Irish landing lips to pour drinks.'

'Well I think you can discount her.'

'Perhaps, he doctored it himself. I assume that's what you're implying?'

'What! An old man! . . . well, I suppose it's feasible. Being the slippery bastard he is, you never can tell,' Kriemhild added.

'So, where's that leave us now?'

'I'm going to have to get my people to have a look at it. There-

On-Time are collecting it from CORATE Tech. When it arrives at your office take it straight to the German Consulate.'

'Anyone in particular?'

'Just say this is for Prince Artur of Prussia, they'll know,' Kriemhild answered.

'Prince Artur of Prussia!'

'*Yes!* Bist du taub? Did I not tell you? I am that middle aged aristocratic Bavarian lesbian, transed as a man everyone in your CIA speaks of, darling?'

Seven

IN ATTENDANCE: Charlie O'Hare, Annie Carter, Hamilton Fitch, and Jean Ronstandt.

' "But I've a bloody good idea what it's come for!" ' Ryder waited. 'Those were your words, weren't they?'

'Aliens. They've come for it,' O'Hare answered.

'Why?'

'Because of the data it contains.'

'You're still insisting the data for the creation of the universe, assuming such data exists, is on that hard drive, are you? Listen!' Ryder looked at Ronstandt before turning back to O'Hare. 'I've got one of those new fangled laptops at home. The First Lady and I share it. Do you know what we put on it?' O'Hare looked at him and shook his head. 'I'll tell you. Family pictures and music. Do you know how much room we have left on it?' O'Hare was still looking him in the face. 'Well I'll tell you. We've got so much room left, it keeps asking us to download the files to a separate hard drive to save space.' He looked at Ronstandt before looking back at O'Hare. 'Now you're telling me you have a hard drive capable of storing all the data needed for the creation of the universe . . .'

'Two. It needs two . . .' O'Hare interrupted.

'Oh! That's where I'm going wrong.' He looked back at Ronstandt. 'It needs two hard drives. That's all right. It takes two. DO YOU TAKE ME FOR A BLOODY FOOL, CHARLIE?'

O'Hare kept his resolve. What Howe was sounding off about

made perfect sense to the average person in the street owning a computer. It made sense to Ronstandt. And if truth be told – a man with little knowledge of computers with their capacity for storing information – to him.

'Mr. President. With respect. When a man feeds five thousand people with five loaves and two fishes, managing to fill twelve baskets full crumbs at the end, who are we to say, He can't get the data for the creation of the universe onto two computer hard drives.'

O'Hare had him. And Howe knew it. For any argument concerning the Lord and His miracles, in this case, the same one recorded by the famous four of Matthew, Mark, Luke and John in separate passages from the Bible, was difficult to argue against. Even more so for Howe who not only had a doctorate in religion from Cambridge university in England, but had been a lay preacher for the Christ Episcopal Church in Bethel, Vermont. A position giving him approval from his side of the political divide when standing for election.

Howe allowed him to continue.

'One of two Seagate hard drives I was forced to give up to the CIA when I was refused entry into Ireland,' O'Hare said. 'The Order have been trying to break into it using a company of hackers well versed in such methods. I . . . I say I . . . what I mean to say is my own expert managed to doctor it between Dublin and Kennedy. She was the air hostess with the mostest when it came to computer technologies,' O'Hare said smiling.

'And she weren't bad at dispensing whiskey neither, Mr. President,' Carter came in.

'Sounds about right. I've heard about his drinking sessions with Henry. So, if these people can't open it, what about this Alien in our backyard. Will he?'

'An Alien! I wouldn't have thought it would have too much trouble, providing it has the key,' O'Hare said

'Wouldn't be the other hard drive would it?' Howe came back.

'Yes.'

'The one you have hidden.'

'Yes.'

'Out of curiosity, Charlie,' Ronstandt came in. 'What would happen if it was opened?'

'Yes, I was curious about that too,' Howe said.

'Seriously.... Ohhh ... it'll blow us all to Kingdom Come.'

'You serious?'

'I don't know, it's possible. Although, such fears were expressed when it came to science smashing up particles in the Hadron Collider. Nothing happened then, so I suppose nothing will happen when those hard drives are eventually cracked open.'

Howe and Ronstandt both nodded with relief. O'Hare's likelihood of an apocalypse always came with the hint of reservation.

'But if it happens, it could all come with God sans hope. His Seven Seals and what follows. A not for human consumption hard drive containing God's data may not have come with His stock health warning: that no man can look upon Me and live; nevertheless, it could extend to the modern age of computers with an appendix to His data: nor open My files, look upon them ... etc,' O'Hare said.

'So these people, this German order, is prepared to bring widespread havoc for some cranky new world to get their hands on this thing and open it?' Ronstandt asked.

'Or the Alien, yes. Because they never did reason what they were doing. Oh, it was all some innocent scientific experiment at the start, and one the government backed for a brief time ...'

'And we're still looking into who they were,' Ronstandt said.

'Good luck with that one. They should have been reined in years ago. Back in the day when I was with the NYPD I was warning about a secret government department that was operating. Sure it was under the management of a criminal who happened to be keeping the dockyard running for the government during both world wars at the time, nevertheless, a criminal organization along with this inner government, encouraged the development of a computer delving into human brains, decided it would be a good idea to bring—' He hesitated.

'Say it, Charlie. Or if you won't I will,' Carter came in.

O'Hare looked at her. Of course it was still all too embarrassing to admit to what they were doing, even if the Order, its beliefs and people going back to the time of the Crucifixion of Christ, when they in all innocence was first established. He waved his hand out to her to continue.

She smiled.

'Okay. It was a two-pronged Christian belief at the time to bring the Divine Spirit to Earth. First to save souls, and second kick out the Romans. Of course, with divine intervention being as rare as a Pope named Cohen, didn't happen. No offence, Hamilton,' Carter said.

'Well there were rumors of a 5th century one name of Pope Zosimus, my educated Sister of Mercy,' Fitch came back.

She acknowledged him.

'Assuming such was achievable, how were they to go about bringing a divinity down from heaven? Even if you believed such existed there was no technology,' Ronstandt asked.

She continued.

'Only faith. Bible's full of the belief that a God will come to Earth. Those believing consolidated that faith in prayer. In all faiths, God is great, God is merciful, God is forgiving. All those believing in God will know He will one day come tor Earth to right wrongs of man. Fast forward 2000 years, when the Order had the wherewithal to force the issue with heaven they took a pragmatic approach. Ultimate sin was where the binding of His book came away at the spine done it for Him. The Great, the Merciful and the Forgiving bollocksed Him, if He'll excuse me for saying it. He, with some infinite wisdom, so the story goes, created man in His image. Image doesn't mean a copy. Call it behavior: the need to procreate. A fundamental need for all creatures on Earth; all in the universe; even our Alien friend. You can't get away from its power. Everything has an entitlement to life, it runs through the universe as blood through veins, and it all begins with the child.'

'Ultimate sin IS the killing of children then?' Ronstandt asked.

'Can you think of another? An unforgivable! It wasn't God's way to dispense justice, He was more interested in forgiveness. His Divine Spirit had other ideas though. Holy Ghost, Spirit, call it what you will. That ghost has been His dirty rag wipe since He first created the universe. And now He's gone, leaving this servant to run the universe as he sees fit. As well as dispensing justice against ultimate sin where he can he was gifted the program for creation. Inside his brain. Now all you have to do is encourage sin against children as bait, bring him to this mortal coil; and while he's as weak as Superman after a dose of Kryptonite you can empty his head for the knowledge it contains using the technology that is AG-MX-960. Which is exactly what happened.'

'Jesus!' Ronstandt said. 'And I understood all sin was forgivable in the eyes of the Lord.'

'God's plan for peace and harmony in the world is a joke,' Carter said. 'One of the reasons I could not continue as a nun with the Carmelite order, instead choosing a more proactive approach to Christianity by working as an archivist for the Church of Rome among others. The legislative body of Vatican City are hoping for my recantation.'

Her words gave no grounds for hope. Fitch put his hand on her shoulder.

The President sought to change the subject. 'The problem administrations have is being able to find criminality, Miss Carter. Difficult when it comes to religion, you get accused of all sorts. New religions are coming on-line daily. You can no more prevent them setting up than bring about gun control,' Howe said.

O'Hare came in, 'Well, the keyword there, Mr. President, is criminalize. If they commit crimes in this country they should be held to account. The problem we have here is this lot are now based in Germany. We had a hard enough job getting to them when the Order did operate here, what chance with them in a European country. The FBI won't be able to move for lawyers breathing down their necks. If you produce evidence against people in high places, someone somewhere is seeking an election and it's put on the back boiler. We know it is an organization having powerful alliances with an aim for world domination using authoritarian countries for models. In particular the Democratic People's Republic of Korea under Kim Jong-Il. Politically half the world's countries are democracies. For how much longer that figure will remain low will depend on people's apathy. Treachery by intellectuals against the people, and with the new social media outlets, they will have no trouble in enhancing apathy.'

'Enough talk, can they be stopped?' Howe asked.

O'Hare looked around at everybody before continuing.

'Excuse me, for I'm having a déjà vu moment, and not for the first time. I have been trying to warn about the criminal activities of this organization for sixty years or more. There have been government departments involved in all of this over the years, FBI, CIA, Special Surveillance, none I particularly trust to do the right thing. But, having said that, there is one individual that can help here. His code name is Wharfmaster. He was a beat cop, one of two, with exceptional talent for undercover work. When the head of what was the Bureau of Investigation at that time, Alex Bielaski – himself an undercover prohibition agent who operated a decoy speakeasy in New York City – came upon the name Marco Giuseppi and his operation. He sought to get inside. You must remember Giuseppi established a child slavery and pedophile ring, not for criminals, oh no, for they were not politically powerful enough, it was for America's rich that had political punch; when the Order of the Most Divine Third Circle came to his notice. For Giuseppi's operation was organized from New York's dockyard management to encompass the Order by bigger fish.

'Bielaski approached the NYPD in the name of Commissioner Dore asking if he knew anyone capable of pulling off an undercover operation that would be politically dynamite if it ever came to light. One demanding total allegiance; right up to the very end if necessary. So begins the story of the Wharfmaster. Dore suspected of being the agent was murdered shortly after. Bielaski distanced himself from the operation, not out of fear, but to protect the Wharfmaster.'

O'Hare asked Carter to pass him a bottle of water from a trolley set to one side in the Oval office. He unscrewed the top and took a sip. He was breathing heavy as if he was living out the incident.

'You okay to continue,' Howe asked him. He nodded he was.

'Where was I though?'

'The Wharfmaster,' Ronstandt said.

'Right. Of course I knew none of this at the time. Why would I? I was just a humble sergeant at that time; but good as his word the man did infiltrate the Order, and had to witness and watch appalling acts of violence taking place while at the same time keeping me up to speed with the necessary intelligence to bring the first of these people to book. I am the only person knowing of his existence, and when this is all over, I shall be seeking a Presidential pardon for him.'

'And you say he's still operating?' Ronstandt asked.

'You have to go all the way back to President Roosevelt and the National Bureau of Criminal Identification for any sense of the operational skills of this man. He has had to deal with corrupt persons in government organizations, the likes of the Bureau of Investigation, which is where I came in with my old boss, Lieutenant Frank Weinberg,' he pointed to Fitch, 'his grandfather, and where we lost control of who was in charge. And that was often a toss up. You had J. Edgar Hoover on one hand and the United States Supreme Court on the other. What I do know is someone high up in public office using the legal framework of malfeasance set them on their way. You are fighting kings, princes, dynasties and bloodlines with these people that see themselves the Elite of the Earth.'

'Two you said?' the President said recollecting his words.

'He had an assistant. He's dead now. Weren't sure I trusted him much. Having said that, not sure I trust the Wharfmaster much, although I am slowly coming around, but it's taken me sixty years. He's as old as me, has mortality as me. And as the Japanese soldier found in the jungle who never did surrender, the Wharfmaster remains entrenched body and soul in order to pass information to his country. And up until now this has been a successful arrangement for the organizations being kept in check. Never beaten. Never going to be.'

'So who is his go-between, and what happens to the intelligence he passes out?' Ronstandt asked.

'You're looking at him. Some I've kept in my head. Some I've stored. What got back to the government . . . well . . . I guess archived not always acted upon. Don't look at me in that way, it happens. For sure, for much of the crimes of child abuse against the Order are still awaiting justice. And don't forget the murders, and attempted murders against me and my team.'

Howe looked at Ronstandt.

'God! What a fucking mess. I never realized. Makes me wonder if my being in office is not the same as being in power,' Howe remarked.

'You wouldn't be the first President to arrive at that conclusion,' O'Hare said. He knew this to be a simple fact of life. 'Put in and take out as many agents, double agents, shadows, ghosts, cloak-and-dagger merchants as you can into an enemy, all the while keeping them at a distance from the American administration, and you will always have an advantage.' The President looked shell shocked. 'It's as much for your protection as head of state as it is for anything else.'

'Suppose there's no point in me asking if any of you in this room are working for them? Just thought I'd ask.'

Ronstandt shrugged. Despite their misgivings none of them felt trustworthy after what O'Hare had said, he knew enough of the world he operated in when it came close to the point of impasse.

'You have your pardon for this man. Are you happy with what's been said here, Jean?' the President asked.

'Up to a point. Happy for the history lesson. These people are, as Mr. O'Hare would have it, kings and princes . . . dynasties and bloodlines. At worse, we will be fighting fire with blankets dampened with kerosene. All we can hope to achieve is to make life as difficult and embarrassing for them as possible by the sound of things.'

'Answer me one question, Charlie. What became of this computer AG-MX . . . what was it again . . . this Order used to bring this data to Earth?'

'Ronstandt looked furtive. 'Ah, perhaps I can help with that one. Sorry, Mr. President I should have mentioned it sooner, I didn't get around to it. We are in the process of bringing it back into service from dry dock using some of their engineers. We are also constructing a building over the portal in Area 51 for Konig's team to make closer scientific study.'

'That'll be one of those "keeping them at a distance from the American administration" you spoke of Mr. O'Hare,' the President said.

The President was coming to realize what his predecessor, Henry, had on his plate with all O'Hare had told him. Trying to keep a lid on all going before, persuading the public, as well as the two party politicians all was under control as the world around him descended into an abyss, had been a nightmare of politics. The man had had to make some astonishing choices. Getting them wrong would have tipped the human race into oblivion, and it was clear the organization, with or without any Frederic Spannocs, was never going to be in retreat. With evidence brought to him by O'Hare through his intermediary that Bavaria were planning to kickstart where Spannocs had left off. What was going to be difficult for him as President was that this new Order was managing to lock into the major communication networks of the free world already.

When it had been put to him, mindful intelligence sources of their own, vague and without purpose, when analyzed and loaded with O'Hare's own were starting to make sense. America and the free world was under a deadly assault from people that seemed to have the whip hand. He needed to take them seriously or the world would take one more step towards mind bending autocracy. And they one time thought communism was evil. Inch by inch is the name of their game. Civilization was already half way there, it wouldn't take much for the rest to be swallowed up as lambs to slaughter.

O'Hare had asked him for assistance for a plan that may or may not work. He would have to play it by ear as it progressed. If it came out the President had assisted O'Hare it would not look good; for that reason no one else was to be in on it. A new kid was on the block vying for the American section. With O'Hare's assistance, Tom Dorcas Inc would be the unwitting undercover operation. If O'Hare could control events giving Dorcas a kick arse chance, then the Order could be controlled and managed by more than one mole in America.

'Sounds like you have a plan. A good one, Charlie.'

He put his hands together in prayer and lowered his head towards the President.

'You've already set it in motion, haven't you, Charlie?'

O'Hare caught up with Fitch and Carter as they were leaving the building. He was smiling.

'I need you to meet some friends of mine.'

'Oh no. Not this time, Charlie. For all her years, our Sarah will kill the both of us. NO! Whatever it is . . . NO!' Fitch said.

'Well, I'll keep you half on board, deal?'

'Yeh! Like that's going to happen.'

'Annie. Will you take my confession?'

Eight

O'HARE MADE HIS WAY down the steps into the basement of the vault. Wells Fargo, a high-security bank for people with loose change in their pockets close to being taxed, was how he saw this place.

Thinking to himself about the locks down here, and the advantage the set of keys the jailer had over them was a mystery. The man handing them over to anyone off the street would still take them fifty years to get to where they were now. There were hundreds of them hanging from large key hoops about his person, each contributing to the man's limp.

Eldred Crook was not interested in what this client of Wells Fargo was going to collect or store. He had had all sorts down here over the years. For this was one of a number of hub quarters for the company. Ever since a boy of fifteen Crook had been employed by the company and had risen. Now working out of its secretive and secure Apache Junction Arizona office, he was their head clerk. He was their only clerk. His demeanor resembled a latter-day gun fight auditor from Dodge City, his clothes would have made Doc Holiday stand aghast with envy. In consideration of property having been down here since the Civil War, he might well have been the same man first securing them at that time.

Black lace tie, tasseled high-heeled boots – all a-jingling – along with an old Colt six-shooter holstered to a belt lower than his waistband gave O'Hare a taste for three fingers of whiskey. He had an imaginative mind. He saw it come a-sliding from the other end of the counter in a three-ale bar by a nervous tender. He licked his lips, his taste for the malt would have to wait.

'H, Mr. O'Hare, we had to relocate property from certain box initials since, I've left the key for O in case there's property in there still yours. You would have been informed,' he said checking the small cheroot he had stashed behind his ear was still there. 'In your case we dropped the O in favor of H on 'count of the number of Irish immigrants comin' threw Ellis. Beggin' yer pardon, no offence—'

'It was the only way in.'

'Yup! Bring the O key back when yer done. Phone on the wall. Press the blue button and speak into it when yer ready to come out and I'll be right down fur yer . . . oh yeh, nearly forgot.' He rummaged inside the deep pocket of his too long cream jacket, pulled out a contract, opened it out on the wooden table hinged to the wall, a pot of ink glued to it. He unscrewed the top and sticking his nose to it sniffed. He disappeared his hand into another pocket pulling out a nib pen. 'Scratch yer signature there. Sign or cross, I ain't bothered which. Stick the time you've finished, there's the number of yer box.'

O'Hare stuck the pen in the bottle of ink, took it out, shook it, sniffed it (damn catching this sniffing), then scratched his name. Crook took the contract off him, rolled it up and stuck it back into his jacket pocket. He then stuck the cheroot in his mouth, took a red match out of his pocket. Striking it into life from a patch of sandpaper stapled to the back pocket of his jeans he lighted it. Satisfied with his work done he walked back up the same stairs he had come down. The smoke from the cheroot drifted with him and over his eighty-year-old grey hair. Hair flecked with orange from the years of tobacco juice he wiped from his mouth, before running his hand through it. Ten minutes later O'Hare heard the last of the cell doors being slammed shut and locked. He was alone. His eyes went along the lines of safety deposit boxes until he saw the M-O. Then the initial letter O. He put the key in the lock and opened the safe putting the stapled sheets of paper he had with him in. He locked it, moved over to F-H.

He inserted his key into the lock and opened the door. Oh, God! he thought to himself. Frank Weinberg's sworn affidavit of paranormal activities, were it ever needed from all those years ago was lying there. A folder with a red ribbon, its seal of wax broken, right where he had put it. He pulled it out weighing it in his hands. Thinking back to those distant times in 1920s New York when he had carried none of the responsibilities he had now become entrusted by default; when as Sergeant to Frank Weinberg's Lieutenant, a man forever taking the can for his Sergeant's corner-cutting activities to secure convictions. He wiped the corner of his eye and replaced the document. *Some respects, they were good days*, he said. Going into the leather case alongside he withdrew the hard drive. He then closed the door of the safe and locked it. He was not here for sentimentality. He went to the phone on the wall and picked it up. 'All done, when you're ready, Mr. Crook.'

No answer. The phone clicked off. He listened as the cell doors started to be unlocked, slammed shut, locked again, repeated. Repeated all the way down three flights. *Should have got someone younger*, he muttered. Sitting down, he pulled a flask of whiskey from his case, undid the top and took a swig, replaced the lid and settled down for a ten minute or so wait.

He had his back to the door when the man unlocked the last one. The man had been quicker than he thought by five full minutes. He turned. The man in subject wasn't Crook. His six-shooter was a Colt peacemaker. What this was, was an M9 Beretta being held at arm's length pointing to his heart. The suppressor attached to the business end was still smoking.

That's the end of Crook, he thought to himself.

'I'll take that, Irish. The hard drive. And, any lists you may have.'

The smell from the Beretta's latest action inclined him to pass over the hard drive. He then put his hand and took out a list. He sniffed before answering, 'What this? It's of no use to anybody except me. Just a laundry list of arseholes that have pissed me off over the years. Can I, perhaps, add your name, you'd be in good company?' he said handing it over before closing the safety deposit door then locking it.

The man looked at the list of names, then began to smile. He was right, there were names he recognized. And had pissed him off. 'Well we do appear to have friends in common, Mr. O'Hare,' he said handing it back.

O'Hare wasn't sure if he recognized him or not. He had short cut gray hair putting him in his late forties. Neither clean cut, or shaven, he did have the faint whiff of a whore's handbag about him though. Someone must love him. A pair of round vintage reading glasses gave the appearance of him being a librarian. Which was unlikely given the circumstances, although, he was wearing a cheap looking brown suit with leather elbow protectors. Who wears those these days? For sure a librarian. Or a sniper. Apart from that he was all round inconspicuous in appearance. A man you wouldn't look at twice. He did have a nasty demeanour about him. An aura of bad feelings and reputation exuded. O'Hare sniffed once more. 'Nice aftershave, mister. Sorry didn't catch your name. What is it, sort of . . . animalic, what – beaver – monkey glands – wet dog? Has it a name?'

'Fun-nie! Hold your hands out.' He beckoned with his left hand. 'Open the box back up. What else have you in there? And none of your Irish shenanigans.'

O'Hare shrugged and put the key into the lock, turned it, and pulled the door open once more. His revolver, old, pulled through clean and loaded was to one side. He hoped, being wrapped in brown paper, the man wouldn't notice it.

'You'll have to tell your people they've sent you all this way for a Barry Manilow recording. You can pick one of them up for a dime at any Value Village store.' He watched his face for any reaction. For his Manilow reference only Howe knew. And it wasn't showing in this man's eyes. He was one from the wrong side of the CIA, that much he was sure of. One of the same that had relieved him of the hard drive when he landed at Kennedy.

'Empty the locker.'

He shrugged. 'If you insist, but you'll be wasting your time.' He reached in with the intention of going for his revolver, then fumbled the move. The man seeing the barrel of the gun sticking out of its brown paper wrapping panicked. He brought his gun straight up to O'Hare in a move with the intention of shooting him. 'No! No!' he said sensing an imminent reaction that was already too late. All he could do was ask who he was?

When the thud came he heard him say, 'Lieutenant Coxly Hess, sir.' His legs went from under him and he went down on the cold red-painted concrete floor face down.

Hess was not sure if O'Hare was feigning death or not. In life he had been a tricky son-of-a-bitch. And now a second bullet was going to settle it once and for all. Putting the barrel to O'Hare's head he wrapped his finger around the trigger, then hesitated. Thinking better he removed it. The thought of blowing a man's already dead head wide open was not palatable. On a one-to-one it would be different. Not like this. Under an old worn-out and yellowed fluorescent light wasn't right. Too barbaric. Too uncivilized. For none of this was personal. Kriemhild wasn't fussed whether he killed him or not, and from her point of view it was job done. Finished with.

He hooked his foot under O'Hare's chest rolling him over onto his back, then startled when his lower body followed a fraction of a second later causing him to bring his gun back to O'Hare's head. He breathed a sigh of relief when he realized the body was taking up the slack. His index finger relaxed. O'Hare's jacket and front of his shirt showed where the bullet had entered his chest. The buttoned tweed jacket he was wearing displayed a single burn hole. He was gone. He stooped down and looked into his face saying, *Lot of people will be glad to see the back of you, old son. Heard you were 108 last birthday! Can't complain at that. You don't look a day over fifty. You've had a good run, Irish . . . so you have! Nothing personal, eh!*

He bent closer over him.

'God! However much whiskey you had to drink. Not good for you, you know. No, siree . . . not good at all.'

Hess stepped over the body of Eldred Crook on his way to leaving the bank when a light caught in the corner of his eye. Coming from the alcove corner of the ceiling. A red busy light on a cctv camera was blinking. The video cassette for the camera was going to have to be found and disappeared. He needed the location of the office the bank kept their computers. Easier said than done for the door leading to the upstairs office was locked. Well, it was a safe deposit box establishment belonging to Wells Fargo, he thought. And that had to be where the computers were located. There ought to be a key this side of the door.

The better part of half an hour and the KEY SAFE LOCKER was located. Putting his hand inside his jacket pocket he took out a pair of eye protection goggles. Taking his gun at arms length he shot the door lock off. Removing his goggles he returned them to his pocket. A key with an orange plastic tag hanging up was written, COMPUTER ROOM. He went back out into the reception area, unlocked the door and ran up the stairs. Time may no longer be on his side. There was another room. Opening the door he saw a bank of computers with clear plastic fronts. He looked through and found one with a cassette recorder. Putting his goggles back on he opened the front and shot into the device twice. He then fired his pistol several times more until the electrics did the rest of the destruction work. He half put his goggles into his pocket, getting them hooked onto the door handle as he left. He got into his car and drove away. A hundred yards up the road he scarcely noticed the black private ambulance parked up in a lay by.

Tommy Scripps pulled up outside the bank expecting O'Hare to be waiting. With no sign of him outside, he went inside. What met him was a scene of devastation. All the security doors were unlocked. Was that a good sign when it came to omens he wondered? Probably not. Fearing the worst he went down the stairs looking for O'Hare. At lower level there was one door open, on the floor, the bad omen presented itself. O'Hare was laid out face up. Dead as Aristophanes. He had come to deposit a list of names. Now, whoever shot him had them. Unless. H was still open. He shoved his hand in and went through it taking out a revolver wrapped in brown paper, an ancient looking red folder, and an empty leather case. There was nothing else. Was there another? he thought. This was H for Hare. Was there an O for the remainder of that particular name?

'If events go awry,' O'Hare had told him. 'Don't worry about any hard drive. In fact leave it. Bring the list out. Get it to Fitch. He'll know what to do with it.'

Well, Scripps old boy, there's no list here. But what he told you suggests otherwise.

He took the keys from F-H then casually picking through he noticed half a dozen marked M-O, and one marked O. The tag underneath attached to the key was written in red ink, Obsolete. Bollocks! O for fucking bollocks! he thought to himself. When he thought he heard someone stirring behind him he startled. Was it Charlie? He looked down at the body. Nope, still dead. He went back to the lockers for another look. O was still locked. Nothing to lose, he thought, putting the key in and turning it the door unlocked. Bingo! Bollicking bingo! And it has sheets of papers in it. He put his hand in and took them out. No more than half a dozen pages stapled together, it was a list of names of European leaders, ex-kings, south east Asian military rulers, dictators, military juntas and general arseholes around the world ruling by terror. Ye God's, he thought, I wouldn't want to be caught by the wrong people with these. He rolled them up and put them into his back pocket. He startled once more, What's the matter with you, Scripps? You're a bag of nerves. What the—

O'Hare was stirring on the floor. Well, stirring was not the right word, for the man appeared closer to death than life.

'Chris'sake, Charlie, what you trying to do to me?'

His first priority had been to get the list away. Now he regretted not checking if O'Hare was alive or dead. Now he was still alive and he had to get him out of here. Easier said than done, for there was no way he could get him out by himself with all those steps.

He got down on his knees and leaned over O'Hare's face.

'Charlie, it's Tommy Scripps. I've got the list. If there's life in the old dog, I'm going to have to coax it from you. And it's going to be violent and not pleasant. I've got to get you out of here. His eyes had no sooner opened than they had closed. There was an imperceptible movement of his lips which he took to be an acknowledgement of sorts. Whether they were or not, he was going to have to move him out one way or another. He got his arms under his and pulled him to a sitting position. His chin was on his chest. 'Come on old son,' Tommy said to him. 'Let's have some sort of effort from you.' He got him upright and tested his ability to take some of his weight onto his legs. It wasn't good. They were folding, straightening, and folding again. He was going to have to go for this, he needed to get him out of here, alarms were already starting to go off. On top of which O'Hare was beginning to yell blue murder.

By a miracle, ten minutes' of struggling had him out by the side of the ambulance. Holding him with one arm under his arms he slid the side door open to the ambulance and half and half dropped him onto the floor. With one final effort, he had him on the mortuary bed inside. With a sigh of exhausted breath he strapped him down.

He was shouting, *You bastard! You bastard!* from the back of the vehicle as he drove them away. He needed to get him to a doctor.

Wells Fargo's security services rang the number. Instead of the coded response coming through a voice activated recording in another part of the building came into play.

This is the offices of Wells Fargo; all our phone lines are busy right now – your call is important to us – might we suggest you call back later – or leave a message after the tone – or – alternatively – hold after the tone – when we will get an operative to you as soon as one becomes available – thank you for calling – have a nice ... EMERGENCY! BUILDING COMPROMISED! EMERGENCY! BUILDING COMPROMISED! EMERGENCY! BUILDING COMPROMISED!

With the break-in warning giving it stick on an annoying loop to anyone listening for any period of time longer than a couple of seconds, the all-girl singing group the Dixie Chicks cut in with the musical phrase, ♫ Give-It-Up-Or-Let-Me-Go ♫ in musical time while all hell was breaking out at the San Francisco headquarters of its bank.

Nine

SENTINEL MASTER–EVT despatched der türöffner standing outside the German consulate at the United Nations Plaza building in New York as someone might squash a fly. The contact between an advanced race of Aliens on the edge of extinction and a human will always be 'no competition'.

The doorman went down, the revolving doors behind him with its architectural glass portico followed in a heap of rubble and crushed body parts. The Alien didn't walk or fly, it ascended and drifted (was how one witness would have it), into the foyer area where two girl receptionists ran for their lives leaving the CIA officer holding the hard drive to stand and gape. He dropped the 35 x Kellogg's Cereal 5 Variety Packs carton containing the hard drive and attempted to run for cover into the building. He didn't make one step. His back was opened up by a vicious metal claw aimed at him from the Alien. He was in two pieces. The hard drive was in two pieces.

White Bear Angel's data transfer to the brain of O'Hare took less than a second, leaving the Seagate by the side of the reception desk vibrating with one folder file remaining out of two inside being the cause.

Sentinel Master–EVT took up what remained. Needing to source the location of this Predator Guardian responsible for stripping the data out, Sentinel Master–EVT sought a program to match the powers of Predator Guardian now in possession of the data. When it did it would be as doomed as der Türöffner, along with the

CIA man wearing a bowler hat, opened to his spine in a pool of blood on the sidewalk of 871 United Nations Plaza.

The *New York Post*'s office went wild when Johnny Bingham caught A-C7 news link on the screen. He watched the German consulate at its United Nations building in New York come under a terrorist attack.

'Hey! Everyone! Get a load of this.'

Fitch looked up from his desk to look through the glass separator of his office from the open plan subeditor's area.

'Boss, you looking at this?' Bingham shouted to the man now on his way out. Reports of an Alien!—'

'How much as he had to drink?' Mike Crawford asked. 'Always the way, innit. Any decent pics going begging and where am I, sitting here scratching me arse doing a menial's job. This is your fault, Ham.'

'Get out there then. Take Heinz with you,' Fitch said approaching his desk. 'And I've told you before about calling me Ham. Your nothing but a Philistine. If the food can't be koshered, then say my name. Hamilton!'

'Is anyone watching what's going on here?'

'Sorry, Julia.'

They turned back to watch the A-C7 news feed coming in from a bank of tv screens they had in the *Post*'s office. A reporter was interviewing a girl. Holding a mic to her face, his cameraman in front of him, he asked the question of what she saw.

'I was strolling down East 49th street coming into the Plaza when I saw a spiral of energy land right on the sidewalk outside the embassy. The doorman didn't stand a chance. It all happened so quick. The man was split in two right there. A second later, the creature had the broken remains from a computer wrapped in a cereal box caught in its arms. Thought to meself that's never going to play any more music. The police have covered him up, he's under that red blanket.'

The channel went to live cover. It showed a Special Weapon and Tactical team of specialist FBI officers from its Albany field office, who along with the police and marines were sealing off the area. The reporter moved across to another witness.

'Thought it was a stunt for some Iron Man movie. Unbelievable,' he said.

A guy next to him said, 'The doorman was standing there one minute, the next he was crushed under a pile of glass from the front of the building's roof. Well, I'm saying he was dead. It wouldn't have taken a doctor to pronounce death from the butchered remains of what I saw.'

A-C7's reporter queried, 'And was it an Alien you saw?'

He answered, 'Well, I'll tell you now.' He looked from side to side as if what he was about to say would create a stampede of buffalo down East 49th. 'My brother's an army medic, see. He was sent to that place that's off limits, Becland. You know? The nuclear power station. The place that went into melt down about eighteen months back . . .'

'Go on . . .' A-C7's reporter encouraged.

'There was a military exercise, see. A group of marines died. Word was they died after an Alien ship landed.'

'Anymore?'

'I watched the news to see if what my brother said at the time was going to be shown again. There was no more mention of it.'

'Thank you, Mister. What did you say your name was?'

'If it's all the same, I'd rather not say.'

The news feed cut to politics. It didn't return. Too late, the cat was out of the bag. A-C7 had not helped by broadcasting live, but, Fitch supposed they were a news channel – it's what they do. Although, apparently; and according to Crawford A-C7's reporter told him his bosses had received a request from the White House to kill the story until more information was available. Fitch tried to contact A-C7's editor for confirmation but he wasn't available. His boss – no friend of Howe's legislation – was giving him a grilling for pulling the feed before the station had had the chance to slice it up for the Eastern Seaboard.

'FITCH! What is it?'

'It's Annie. Hamilton, Charlie has been shot and killed.'

'Ben-zonna! Was that part of your arrangement?' He laughed. Over the years, O'Hare had been up to all sorts of exploits. Getting himself killed in the course of his investigations was one of many. There was a pause from Carter, one that went longer than he would have expected. 'Annie!' She didn't answer. 'ANNIE! Tell me you're not serious?'

And now there were others joining the illustrious group after witnessing the German consulate attack by an Alien. Although, to be fair, it had all happened so quickly it would be easy enough to convince the public they were mistaken in what they saw. Assuming they hadn't taken photographs. And those assumptions cannot always be relied upon since the advent of camera phones last year.

'We've got real problems of national security here,' Howe said turning to Ronstandt. 'Late evening news pulled in a witness saying how his brother, a medic was ordered into Becland to pick up the bodies of dead marines. That's not good, Jean. Denial has to be your number one priority here now,' Howe said.

'When we find who it was, I will. I've already been in touch with the base at Sam Houston,' Ronstandt said.

'That's all very well, you've still to find a way around the story. For starters I suggest you get somebody on it immediately. Something on the lines Disney is making a movie, remake of Fantasia, anything,' Howe said.

'Call for you, Ryder. Hamilton Fitch,' the Vice President said.

'Thanks, Joe. Sorry Hamilton, but I had no choice, we had to pull. . . . What! When?' He clamped his hand over the mouthpiece. 'Charlie O'Hare has been found dead, Joe.'

Ten

For we wrestle not against flesh and blood,
but against principalities, against powers,
against the rulers of the darkness of this world,
against spiritual wickedness in high places.

Wherefore take unto you the whole armour of God,
that ye may be able to withstand in the evil day,
and having done all, to stand.

Stand therefore, having your loins girt about with truth,
and having on the breastplate of righteousness.

EPHESIANS Chapter 6, v12.

CARTER WAS AT HER DEVOTION. A veneration for a man lately died. She did not need reminding her church not only confined itself to this world, but extended into the next. On her knees. Head bowed. The altar of Our Lady of Mount Carmel the object of her adulation; her sorrow for her brother was clear. She was wearing the religious clothes of the Carmelite order, not because it was demanded of her in this place (for she had already levelled to the Vatican status of special envoy to Pope John-Paul II, as well as UN advisor to the Ecumenical Society of World Religions), but because of her affiliation to Carmelites when she had first met O'Hare. Even though no longer a

Carmelite, her spirit was with them still.

She opened her eyes to face the statue of the Virgin Mother closing them as soon as she had looked on her face. Her fingers autonomously working through her rosary, she murmured to herself:

St. Michael the Archangel, defend us in battle; be our defense against the wickedness and snares of the devil. May God rebuke him, we humbly pray. And do thou, O prince of the heavenly host, by the power of God thrust into hell Satan and all the evil spirits who prowl about the world for the ruin of souls.

In nomine Patris, et Filii, et Spiritus Sancti. Amen.

She got to her feet. Crossed herself, and turned to leave. With thoughts of recent conversations in Rome, in which she had once again been mandated, she felt secure and strong to continue with the job she was to do.

Cardinal Francis Evgeni, a progressive within the Church – therefore out of favor with the majority of the College of Cardinals – made a full and agreeable reference to Sister Benedicta Marie by Fr. Michael Joseph after his brutal killing stated:

For although following the monastic vows and devotion of mundanity of her community, Fr. Joseph considered this Sister had over the years far superseded the title that encompassed thought of care, selflessness (cloistress extraordinaire he had been heard to say of her on occasion) and all other attributes of Godliness sufficient unto themselves, he was sure. And to Fr. Joseph, with her consideration as mentor, the man saw no reason either theologically or theoretically why it shouldn't be possible for a woman to become a Cardinal (the laughter ringing still in the cloisters from the Vatican fraternity the Pope was naming her in the next consistory gave them mileage).

Nevertheless, Fr. Joseph being enshrined as he was with authority for final proof by Pope Benedict XVI, finding no reason from texts that a woman should be excluded, nevertheless considered her a princess of the church in waiting . . . in consideration of which a review of this anachronistic job title of Sister bestowed on women of the Catholic order was ready for a make-over.

She had faced down demons to bring evidence of tangible existence of a spirit world (how he hated the phrase). A throwaway remark for a body without material substance bordering on faeries, ghosts even, despite evidential written descriptions and sworn statements in the archive to the contrary. An archive Fr. Joseph shared with his Jewish brothers. *Oh yes, we are all brothers*, he had told Pope Benedict after the Holy Father had asked him how he saw and reconciled their differences of faith?

Fr. Joseph's statement that 'we are all brothers', did not especially apply to his co-conspirator, Rabi Spiro Jackson, but inclusive of all other religions, faiths and peoples of the world. Their papers and collected evidence recorded and passed down through 2000 years one to another was, as far as Cardinal Evgeni knew, the same question put by St. Peter of his predecessor up to Pope Benedict XVI.

'Son of God, or not the Son of God, is the human point at issue between them. We neither of us recognize the relevance of such argument as superior or inferior over the other. How else do we carry forward our both philosophies for our understanding of God to our people?' Fr. Joseph stated.

A point of view accorded with the Holy Father. One that would have enhanced his position to higher status within the College of Cardinals were it not for his premature death.

* * *

Two of them remained now Charlie was gone, she thought to herself. The last of his disciples. Now they were back where they were, having to pick up the pieces of another being, and why it had come to this side of the veil. There would be no reason for his guardian angel to hang around any longer. The last recorded spirit on Earth. Without whose help in facing down Satan's progeny, the late great (*sic*), Frederik Spannocs, man would have been wiped from the Earth in a cataclysmic world war. A single tear came from her right eye and rolled down her cheek. She left the cool darkness of Our Lady of Mount Carmel and made her way to the presbytery of Fr. Edwin Shaughnessy. Raising the large knocker on the door she banged it down. A hollow echo rang from inside. For an old large oak door it uttered not a squeak or a creak from either its hinges or its hangings as it opened.

'Hello, Sister, come through. Tea, coffee?' He paused in the corridor and turned to correct himself. 'Sorry, force of habit. Miss Marie . . . Carter.'

'Annie.'

'Right. The NYPD said he'd been to an out of the way branch of Wells Fargo when he was shot and injured. I heard a friend of his happened . . . or not, to be in the vicinity at the time. Scripps. He died later from his injuries. Scripps! I know the name. Can't place from where,' Fr. Shaughnessy said.

'His undertaker.'

'Right. Well, I've heard of ambulance chasers – but coffin! Tell me, Sister . . . Annie. If he was murdered why weren't the police involved?'

That was Charlie all over, she thought to herself. Straight forward thinking is not in his tool kit. How did the murderer know he would be at a Wells Fargo bank in some backwater was the question?

'As far as police involvement was concerned they didn't seem interested. They left everything in Scripps' hands. I suppose, with his reputation they were happy to leave everything to him. If he turned up anything untoward, they trusted him to contact them, I don't know.

'What was he doing there, robbing the place?'

'Now there's a question, Father.'

'So how can I help, Annie? By the way, I received your letter asking if I would officiate at Charlie's funeral, of course I will. It would be an honor.'

'Thank you, Father. But I do need to impose on you further.'

'Anything.'

'I'm making arrangements for his funeral . . . quite frankly . . . Father, I'm struggling.'

'Of course you are. Who wouldn't be after all your years of knowing him. Look, he was a beat cop on the Lower East Side back in the day, Mount Carmel being on the patch kind of puts me in the frame, what with him having no family and all, I'll do what I can.'

'Well, Father, it would be a weight off my mind. As I said, Scripps are the undertakers.'

'Of course, Scripps. Undertaker to the stars. I've seen his funeral ads on television. Not sure if I agree with undertakers advertising. Still, it's a different world these days. What a face though. Have you ever met him. If you ever needed an undertaker with the look of the crape hangar about him, he has it in spades. Excuse the pun. Calls himself Tommy of the Tammany on the ads. Now I think of it wasn't Charlie's father a Tammany? A ward boss?'

'Tammany! Heard the name, don't know anything about them though. Charlie never mentioned them, not to me anyway,' Carter said.

'You haven't. There's a surprise. Political party. Of sorts. Connected with the Democrats. They looked after the interests of Irish immigrants in New York back in the day. If I'm right, Charlie's father will be buried in Green-Wood, Brooklyn, that's where a lot of the influential and not so go. William Tweed was a Tammany boss, he's one of the no so's buried there. A man that did Tammany no favors.'

'In what way?'

'On the corrupt side. In fact, he was a lot on the corrupt side. He took New York for a couple of hundred million dollars in the mid-1800s!'

So, our Charlie has history, she thought. 'Well he won't be going to Green-Wood, Father, for he's to be interred in Ireland.'

'Is he now. Has he family there?'

She smiled. 'County Wexford. He has relatives living there. In a castle, if you don't mind. Whether he was spinning a yarn, I don't know. But, we shall find out now won't we. He's to be shipped out after the service. Scripps will be dealing with all of that. Which leaves the service to be arranged. You know cars, flowers . . . the usual trappings. I suspect it'll be a bit of a grand affair, he had a lot of friends you know.'

'Not a problem. I shall need to know his lawyer, address, friends, dignitaries, phone number etc., etc,' Fr. Shaughnessy said.

'Here's a list of the details,' she said passing them to him. 'Everything's there apart from lawyers. Charlie had no time for them.' She was looking concerned. 'You have something on your mind.'

'I made a second visit to the mortuary after Daniella Scripps, the undertaker's daughter, rang to say there were some bits and bobs of Charlie's that needed collecting. When I got there a car belonging to the New York's Chief Medical Examiner was parked outside. Scripps asked me to stay in the outer office while he went away to fetch Daniella. When his daughter came out from the mortuary with them I saw a man through the open door I took to be the Chief Medical Examiner standing over Charlie's coffin. Which was strange. He had been dead a week, and the doctor had already signed his death certificate with cause.'

'I must admit it does seem all a bit on the strange side. Who was the doctor that signed the death certificate off, do you know?'

'His own doctor, I assume. I don't know his name. I could have all of this entirely wrong, it's just that the procedural order seems to be all over the place, Father. I was asked to verify that it was Charlie, which I was more than happy to do, although perhaps happy is not the right word. Normally the job of a family member. In this case there are no living relatives here, so it fell to either me, or his other close friend, Hamilton Fitch to make a positive identity. Then his doctor signs the death certificate; and then a week later the city's Chief Medical Examiner pops his head round the door of the undertakers. Suspicious, or what?'

'Another medical? Doesn't sound right that another medical examination is carried out after death certificates have been signed off. Wasn't a police forensic examination?' Fr. Shaughnessy asked.

'Well funny you mention police, that's another thing. There has been no police inquiry into his death anywhere. Open and shut.'

'There hasn't.'

'When I queried Scripps as to what the Chief Medical Examiner was doing there, he said it was to confirm he was dead. When I reminded him the doctor had already signed the death certificate to that effect; and what was going on here? He shrugged.'

'Or wasn't going to let on. Suspicious you say . . . I'd say.'

Eleven

CURTAINS DRAWN, CLOCKS STOPPED. Any mirrors on the wall overlooking where the dead were laid out should be covered with crape to prevent the deceased's spirit from becoming trapped in its infinity.

Tommy Scripps had taken none of these precautions.

To say Scripps and Daughter Inc were undertakers was likening to saying Leonardo da Vinci was a stonemason. They were THE undertakers to the discerning of New York. From presidents to celebrities, they've all been buried or cremated by the Scripps's.

Tommy Scripps and Charlie O'Hare were the sons of immigrants who arrived in New York in 1850 after Ireland's Great Famine. With families to support, and with hostilities against the Irish from employers as well as City Hall they needed protection. Coming by way of the American Irish Society of Friends; and what would become known as Tammany they were an organization to be reckoned. Even New York's mafia kept to their side of the street where they were concerned. There was safety and security among its members.

With children dying of disease among New York's immigrant poor population; and with funeral costs out of reach to most, Percival Scripps, with loans from Seamus O'Hare (Charlie's father), along with the Tammany, they set up business. Seamus and Percival became lifetime friends. Tommy was the great grandson bearing the name

Scripps forward. Daniella, his daughter (if she ever got around to getting married and having children) likewise.

'Isn't it Sin O'Hare that's supposed to be older than both Methuselah and Charlie?' Daniella asked her father as she removed the brown rubber sheet from his body.

'Don't ask me, Ella. For the first time, despite your mortician's training, you're going to have to use make-up for age rather than youth.'

For even Daniella Scripps, a licensed cosmetologists, had to admit to herself, cosmeticizing the look of a man of 108 to make him appear more and not less was going to be a challenge for her. To make the dead appear as they did in life was not always easy. To make them older – much older – she had not been asked before. For this man, if he was to rise from the dead and walk out of here right now, it would have been no great surprise to her. She would have preferred doing a make-over as any other, which wasn't going to happen in this case. He was Irish! All bringing its own problems. Most funerals allowed close relatives a passing view of the body to say their goodbyes before the lid was screwed down. A wake! Well, that would be friends, relatives and half the village standing close over him; getting closer and more personal as the evening turned to night, standing over him with a pipe-full of tobacco in one hand, a whiskey in the other, all wanting to drink his health; a give away if she got the ageing process wrong.

She opened her make-up case ignoring the fingernail clippers. His fingers were to remain untrimmed. Next tweezers. Not for plucking. She began putting false hairs in his ears and up his nose. She ignored going for any clean look normally associated with her job, instead she added blemishes using a heavy conditioning marker pen. Now the face proper. She went over this with an airbrush gray foundation lightening making sure she covered the neckline. Now lips. She took a purple lipstick from her make-up case and began dabbing it on. Satisfied with the look of cyanosis, she applied some blot powder for lasting color. She stood back and looked at him. He didn't look over a hundred, sixty, maybe closer? Going to have to do. He would resemble a wax work if she did anymore to him. She went to cover him in preparation for her father to put him in the coffin and hesitated. There was a red mark on his chest. A color she used to beautify? Not on this occasion it wasn't.

A smidgen, of what looked to her to be blood, the size of a pinhead appeared on his shirt which wasn't there before she began. If the body's circulation had not ceased, for whatever reason (occurring after death), it would not show scarlet colored as blood but bluish-red. She had not received the body before it had gone through the stages of rigor mortis (there had been a delay of two days getting the body here), interval secondary flaccidity had loosened muscles with the internal body temperature rising ambiently. Which was occurring now.

She didn't know the doctor that examined O'Hare after her father had rescued him from a shoot-out at the bank. He had taken him there instead of a hospital. *It was a complicated story*, her father had said to her. Do what you can.

She hoped whoever he was he had diagnosed death correctly; and not systemic or suspended animation as death had been declared wrongly on more than one occasion in the past. Oh yes, there had been occasions when bodies awoke, raising themselves from mortician's slabs. Even knocking on the coffin lid trying to attract someone's attention after it had been screwed down. If it turned out to be fresh blood she could be in serious trouble.

She retrieved her stethoscope from the medical cabinet.

Plugging in the ear tips she placed the diaphragm to his chest and listened for signs of a heart beat or mutterings from his lungs. She came away and looked at him. She shook her head, drew a deep breathe, pulled a pair of clinical gloves on and placed her finger in the blood. Rubbing it between her fingers, bringing them close to her nose she sniffed. Iron. She removed a tray of glass slides from a drawer, slid one out from its sterile bag, touched the sample of blood onto the glass, labeled it, put it into a drawer in the clinical cupboard. She covered the body, went to the phone on the wall, saying, *I need a decision here, I'm not qualified to make this one.*

'All done, Ella?' her father said as he came into the mortuary. She was on the phone. 'I've brought you a tea. Problem?'

'Fresh blood. I'm calling the doctor.'

'No need for that, Ella. Let sleeping dogs lie, eh!'

A strange phrase for her father to use. She wondered what he meant by it. 'It won't hurt to have a blood sample analyzed. It's my decision to make.'

'It is. Overrule me . . . on this occasion, please trust your father and put the phone down. You are Scripps and Daughter, Ella there's nothing to be gained analyzing blood on this occasion. You've cut yourself without realizing. Let it go.'

She studied her father. She wasn't convinced she was doing the right thing, but put the phone down anyway.

'For the best.' He changed the subject. 'You taking the lead hearse tomorrow? If you are I'll take the doors. Morrie and Able will handle the second.'

'That pair of bouncers. Look, I said before, I wouldn't be using them as chauffeurs again. They're an embarrassment and bloody useless.'

'I know . . . I know. In case of trouble. Where Charlie's

concerned rioting in the wings.' He laughed. 'You'll be glad of them if fighting breaks out.'

* * *

It was a white coffin affair. How Charlie liked it to have been, Carter imagined. Imagine. Now there's a thought. For you cannot say for sure what arrangements people would prefer if they hadn't expressed them when alive. Even so, he would have enjoyed what she and Fr. Shaughnessy had arranged for his final send off. Half-draped with the American stars and stripes on the front end, the Irish tricolor of green white and orange at the other. Tones of color bringing a pleasing contrast to an otherwise morbid occasion were all around. The carriage, a white Cadillac, to match the coffin with glass all round view. Of course, all unappreciated by the man in the box. Alongside the coffin there were three enormous wreaths of flower heads and leaves from government and federal departments, O'Hare at one time or another was involved with. Inscriptions on cards and plaques inside along the inside window read: *To That To Which We Aspire*: New York Police Department; to *A Man's Personification of Achievement*: Federal Bureau of Investigation. The hearse's roof rack was decked with more flowers and wreaths, their names and organizations written on small cards indecipherable to readers as the hearse moved off at a snails pace.

The first of the following vehicles carried friends of the deceased, Annie Carter being one. Hamilton Fitch; former president, Henry Clancy Montgomery III; Sarah Weinberg (Fitch's grandmother, now 98); and Sergei Bezukladnikov (Russia's former premier and Charlie's one-time backgammon opponent and drinking partner).

A second vehicle (a presidential bullet-proof affair) driving a yard off the rear fender of the first. Ryder Black Dick Howe was seated in the back. A nuisance of security walking alongside the vehicle, keeping the president in the shade. Their heads moving side to side searching for any would be assassin, their hats held close under crooked elbows. They were all dressed in dark suits. In one hand some held sun glasses, all, if not inside their jackets, were close enough for an assumption by those watching they were ready to pull unseen weapons from unseen shoulder holsters. Watchmen. Two police outriders astride Harley Davidson's were balancing at a slow two miles an hour ready to accelerate into the first sign of trouble.

The procession continued its way between crowds of curious people, not out of any particular acquaintanceship with the deceased, from his reputation and what they had picked up from the media. A community, stopping, walking, turning, stepping out from their daily business, all to wonder who this man was. If they did not already know who he was by now – for it had been shouted long and hard from the rooftops by the newspapers and television since his passing – they must have been residing on another planet. A former Irishman with the New York Police Department, whom, working rough and tough street beats of 1920s downtown Brooklyn, had risen through the ranks to become the first honorary member of the Federal Bureau of Intelligence (common sense more than intelligence, he often reiterated to those suffering attitudes of self importance for their positions within the organization). Was saving the world stretching going too far for some New York barbers, cab drivers, burger flippers, flower sellers, and news vendors? A secret truth known to a select few some said.

Saved the world, eh! Brother, no bum accolade, a woman walking a dog said to a man shouting from the sidewalk, *Savior of the World?*

That's the word on the avenues and bars, ma'am.

Only I heard it was New York, she said.

Forget New York! The World! The World!

Apart from the doppler affect from the siren of a Fire Department New York Engine 10 as it hurried through, a handful of dogs woke; before seeing nothing out of the ordinary went back to sleep. Quietness descended at the arrival of the cortege to the Church of the Blessed Virgin.

Daniella brought the Cadillac she was driving to a stop. Her father got out and opened the door for the mourners inside. He spoke to Morrie and Able to give a hand with the coffin when their passengers had alighted. The three mourners walked the procession of followers into the church.

Fitch straightened his suit. Wearing a yarmulka, and though O'Hare was not Jewish, he had followed his tradition out of respect for him by having his suit pocket torn according to its faith ritual. His head bowed, he had the arm of Sarah Weinberg. Her face draped in black lace weeds, to some, believing it was her own husband they had come to bury this day were a long way off. Walking slowly, she wore a modern cut black tailored suit with matching grey buttoned blouse. A large gold Star of David and chain hanging on the outside blazed wealth where none existed. For the briefest of moments she turned to look at her grandson then bit her lip.

Worn 1890 to impoverished Russo-Jewish immigrants, Sarah Weinberg was wife to Lieutenant Frank Weinberg – she never got over him being murdered by an unknown assassin after his part in Judge Seaburg's team looking into corruption of New York's mayor, the Honorable James Walker back in 1925. Weinberg and O'Hare were with the NYPD, only later were they enrolled into the FBI. The occasion they first mixed it with Marco Giuseppi was the beginning of the end for her family.

By God, how she rued that day.

Frail and small now with a curvature of the spine; even though wearing weeds about her lined face all could see her true age. Fitch saw neither age, frailty, or her large rheumy eyes standing proud from her diminishing facial bone structure. It was enough that she was his last living relative.

She had forced him into changing his birth name of Weinberg for his protection. An evil man, a name she could never bring herself to repeat, had besieged all of them, and their lives. Out of necessity to put his great grandmother at ease, he covered his face by shadowing it under his large homburg. Steadying her through the church portal as they entered its cold dark gloom he sensed her shudder on his arm, not from any cold or dark.

He gripped her tight as they took their seats.

Shouldering the coffin the bearers' followed. Placing the casket on the bier they straightened up from the weight. They lowered their heads towards the altar, standing to one side allowing others to take their places. The organ ending its recital of Handel's Messiah was the invitation for Fr. Shaughnessy to step forward. Bowing his head he asked all to stand.

Fitch put his hand on his grandmother's shoulder saying, *No need, Bubbeh.*

'Let us pray.'

Speaking slowly and coherently, avoiding differing faiths present by refraining from using the name of Jesus, opting instead to keeping to God the Father, he gave a brief homily for Charlie ending saying the man wished to be known as Sergeant Charlie O'Hare of the New York Police Department, before continuing with a prayer:

All we can expect in this life, how it is cut short, how we are all sinners, how He will accept our frailties, and what better we can expect in the next world if we seek redemption in this life. He paused before whispering the last of his homily, and safe deliverance from evil into the next.

For Sarah Weinberg, the deliverance from life's evils couldn't come soon enough. The sooner the better.

Fr. Shaughnessy looked up from the lectern at this gathering of mourners. Some he knew, many he didn't. So quiet now, apart from the traffic passing outside. If he tilted his head to one side, he sensed the sound of a mouse sighing. There it was again. Although he knew it couldn't be. Close to the limits of human hearing, a screech, unoiled metal on wood. A brass screw – as an example – being turned by hand out of seasoned oak as somebody removing the hinges from an old door perhaps.

He listened and watched for any reaction from the mourners. It appeared not. He needed to continue and draw the service to a close, the time between the end of the prayer, an allowed pause for reflection, was common enough for an experienced priest; for he had taken longer than he normally did the result of listening to . . . a mouse sighing.

Sentinel Master–EVT functioned as intended. The program location files had returned its state of mimicking its quarry as well as locating it. Although erratic, the data had located Hartley Hare, although the Time–Verse differential model was continuing to malfunction. The Transparent Portal Field data, hacked into by the Predator Guardian, was continuing to prevent correct function. Sentinel Master–EVT had no way to return.

Entry into the container had turned all eight thumbscrews. Before they had even began to unscrew, an outside source created a Time–Verse malfunction screwed them back tightened.

Twelve

WHAT IS MORE HUMILIATING than a group of security men and women being ejected from a building by another group of security people in what could only be described as a coup? They attempted to stand their ground; take them on, but, they were outgunned, out numbered, outmanned and all round outed, three to one.

To Nathaniel Johnson there was actually.

It was seeing them having their shoes removed, their Ray Ban glasses trodden underfoot, a single sleeve scissor-cut removed from their immaculate dark suits while they stood to attention in line. They were then made to walk off out of the car park into the rural Malaka's Corner shrubland to catch a Vamoose bus from the Washington DC junction main road. All avoided if they had listened and followed the directions to leave by the German security firm of Graf & Mayer, and not stand and make a fight of it. Indeed they were lucky – considering – to have lost only two men dead, and another forced to give a blow-job to the German he had kneed in the bollocks after they had first removed his teeth with a rifle butt.

Johnson drew a rapid breath between pursed lips.

That's O'Hare's work undone, Johnson thought further watching the action unfold through a periscope from his underground offices. All those financial maneuverings for what?

And my word, what are they doing with him now? Strapped face down across the bonnet of a Humvee with his strides around his ankles. Phew! No front teeth, mouth full of cum, now they're raping him? Lucky day for someone, or what?

Direktorin Elke Kriemhild laid down her guidelines. They were not negotiable. Dorcas was to sign everything he had transferred to his Church of the New Order over to the newly established, Star Birth (Bavaria Section). All bank accounts were to be closed down with all monies transferred to Star Birth (Bavaria Section). All Asia, Western Europe, Central and Eastern Europe, Africa, and the Middle East branches registered in the name of Tom Dorcas Inc. were to be re-directed to Star Birth (Bavaria Section), and his name deregistered from incorporated businesses in America.

'I don't know who you think you are, Direk-torin Elk-ee, or whatever you call yourself. This is the United States of America, ma'am. We don't take orders from companies in other countries losing everything over here. In your case, two world wars. As for transferring power and assets over to you, well, it's not going to be that easy. You're going to need more than my signature. Do I make myself clear. Now tell your people to get the fuck out of my offices.'

'Very well, Mr. Dorcas. I need to speak with Kerstin. Is she there?'

'She wants you,' he said passing her the phone.

Hartmann listened for a second or two before directing her attention to one of Kriemhild's heavies with a click of her fingers, while at the same time carrying on her conversation. Dorcas was grabbed and punched in the kidneys before being dragged to the window. While gasping for breath, with a deal of pain, he was forced to watch his front desk reception security man, strapped across one of the jeeps being raped. Finished with that, he watched as another pushed a bottle up his arse, before dropping him into a sitting position on the ground. Inserted neck first, Dorcas was sure the bottle still had its crown metal cap in place. The man was screaming, his mouth bloodied beyond any reason he could make out, sent a chill through him. The remainder of his security forced to stand and watch, now released, dragged themselves barefoot through the dust and heat off the site as quickly as their legs carried them. His face drained from the punch to his kidneys; and with his body shaking uncontrollably he screamed out at whoever was listening to stop, adding, 'WHAT DO YOU WANT ME TO DO?'

Hartmann relayed the conversation from Direktorin Kriemhild who was no longer interested in speaking with him.

He shouldn't have mentioned the wars!

'First off, Mr. Dorcas,' Hartmann began. 'There's a rather large payment waiting to be settled with Internal Revenue, in the region of ... how much did you say, Direktorin? Right. I'm to tell him there's a federal criminal order pending for the responsible person when they catch up with him. He's nodding he understands, direktorin. The Order of the Most Divine Third Circle had those assets. In the region of $5 billion. There's a considerable amount of tax owing. Does he have it? ... Do you, Mr. Dorcas? ... He's nodding he doesn't think so, direktorin. He'll get five years for tax evasion. I'll tell him, say again direktorin. Did you ask, does he have any personal assets? He's nodding he has, *I've a house in Connecticut. My mother lives there with her sister*. Hartmann paused ... Yes direktorin, it is very touching ... Can I tell Direktorin Kriemhild you are now under our direct orders and you will comply with all our requests, Mr. Dorcas?' Hartmann asked.

Dorcas, who thought he had everything watertight, wondered how his world and bank accounts had disappeared into oblivion. He didn't know what hurt the most, the pain in his kidneys needing medical attention, or the thought of a metal capped bottle being removed from up his caboose. All thoughts were now academic.

It was a different work force confronting under cover agent, Madeleine Tubman (aka Corinne Diaz), when she returned after the weekend. Kerstin Hartmann was now manager in residence, Nathaniel Johnson was back in his office doing what he always did for the Order of the Most Divine Third Circle (his sign, sans the 'S', being now only the one of them, OPERATION'S DIRECTOR. Dr. Nathaniel Johnson, over the door), while Tom Dorcas was in charge of accounts (what trustier person did they have now).

Addressed to Corinne Diaz, there was letter on her desk. When she opened it she saw it was a form from the contracts and management founder, Heinrich Stein, of Graf & Mayer Recruitment Consultants. They were offering her the position of deputy director of operations for Star Birth (USA).

Thirteen

LIEUTENANT COXLY HESS (RTD BUT NOT OUT): A sharpshooter trained at US Army Sniper School, Camp Perry, Ohio where his professionalism and bull hitmanship cut him out for special assignments. The taking out of Fidel Castro being one of them. The killing of Castro was not considered by the President of the day as being useful for American–Russian relations, and as such the man and his cigar in Hess's cross-hairs, a late and direct order to 'have your rifle jam' from his top sawyer within the network put him down as an insubordinate.

Now Germany was seeking his services once again.

Direktorin Kriemhild was turning over in her hands the repaired hard drive recently put back together by one of her people in communications (inscrutable these Chinese). Its condition when it arrived from the German Consulate was, to put it bluntly, a half-eaten dog's breakfast. Then it was only a platter, the plastic disk out of a hard drive, had been posted to her in a jiffy bag. Bambang Xie had installed it into another holder. She held her breath and plugged it in to her computer. Then going to This PC she went down to Seagate (G) and clicked on it. When it opened the first thing she noticed was that there was only one file folder. She was sure CORASK Tech said there had been two. She clicked on it. Then again. Then a third time. She sighed. Nothing.

She would have liked to have thought that the damage done was the reason it could not be opened, but she would be deluding herself. The explanation given to her over the phone from the Consulate for its condition was, to say the least, bizarre in its extreme. Bizarre it may have been but ... *An Alien! Come on*, she said. That was all bullenscheiße to cover someone's tracks ... *from another planet. They must take the American public for fools. Well not me!* It had to have been a film publicity stunt gone wrong; that had caused the death of a commissioner and the CIA courier that had first relieved O'Hare of it at Kennedy. O'Hare! She spit his name. Now, he would have been the person having any sister hard drive if there was one. Now Hess had killed him! A double-edged blessing? Perhaps. Dead or not, he would have kept control. Passing the hard drive to one of his people would certainly have been his thinking.

Intelligence from Malaka's Corner was that O'Hare was to be interred in Ireland after a short funeral service in New York. With arrangements to take the body to Ireland, if there was another hard drive the chances were it would be in his coffin – along with that list. If not, a euro to a dollar, someone connected with the deceased possessed it. She made an AT&T video call to the CIA offices asking for Hess.

Over-confident, hypersensitive, hostile towards people, money driven, possessing a psychopathic personality disorder; a man ideal for the job. Embedded in that section of the CIA that was beyond government. A department for extraordinary dirty tricks, subterfuge, and the working for other countries' interests, all at the same time unsure who they were answerable to. For sure it wasn't Uncle Sam. That much they knew.

'So you shot dead Liberty Valance, nicht wahr! You'll go down in the annals of history when you're credited for it, Lieutenant Hess. Pity you came away with a useless piece of kit with no more on it than

Barry Manilow. I take it you didn't find that list. No, you would have said, wouldn't you? On the same, my sources tell me when Wells Fargo's security team turned up there was no evidence of O'Hare's body to be found anywhere. O'Hare either walked out of there or was assisted. Which was it to be?'

'There was no way he walked out. Stood up, or went for a piss. When I kill a man he remains in that condition,' Hess said.

'His funeral confirmed you right there. Then he had an accomplice,' Kriemhild said.

'There was no paperwork, list or otherwise in his safety deposit box,' Hess said. 'I stake my life on it.'

'Careful what you bet with, Hess,' she said with menace adding, 'well, it's got to be found along with the other hard drive. Now, I've organized a flight to Dublin, England for a game of follow the coffin. If its anywhere a compartment in that coffin has to be a safe bet. Or one of his close associates has it with them, and I'm thinking Hamilton Fitch or Annie Carter. It's too dangerous to be left in America now. They may well be going with him to secure it somewhere over there. Either way, you need to get yourself there and do some research.'

'When?'

'Out of Kennedy, tomorrow morning. Nine-thirty. Tickets will be with you by our good friends, There-On-Time. You've been booked into a hotel in Wexford. The Jigging Leprechaun is close to where O'Hare's body will be laid to rest. I have it on good authority he's being buried in his family home. Castle Rose. Ja?'

'And how am I supposed to get my tools on board a commercial flight?'

'You won't have to. Everything you need will be in place when you get there. We have friends in Ireland. And they have more weaponry at their disposale than you can shake a Wurst sausage at.

'What, paramilitaries, likely as bad-arsed as me, yeh right?'

He was no fool. He knew the troubles Ireland and Northern Ireland were having. Shooting the kneecaps off people seemed to be punishment of choice and fun in the two countries, and a dollar to a dime O'Hare would have friends a-plenty, willing and capable of taking his off, if he was to get caught interfering with coffins. Over there – whichever side of the border you happen to find yourself – was a dangerous place. Had been since the 1960s, if not before. Caught as a police informer, or a plain and simple spy for the British army, being shot in the kneecaps would be the least of his troubles. And trying to persuade anyone he wasn't a double agent would only make a bad situation worse.

Direktorin Kriemhild laughed, 'Not a problem for you to worry about. We Germans have had friendly connections with the Irish Republican Army since both world wars. We have sleepers in place. There are still those sympathetic to Germany and the Abwehr intelligence agency; also on friendly terms with Star Birth. You can rest assured, Lieutenant Hess . . . everything will be as tight as a, how you say, ente in den arsch – a duck's arse.'

'Not if you send me to Dublin, England it won't be, Direktorin Kriemhild—'

Direktorin Kriemhild would have one last look. She plugged the one battered Seagate into one of her computer's ports, then plugged the one Hess took from O'Hare's safety deposit box into the other. She opened them. Nothing. She heaved a sigh of frustration and clicked the remaining medieval folder once again. Was there something those tech boys at CORASK had overlooked. To her surprise, there was. Without the aid of speakers or earphones she could hear the faint wisp of sound coming through. Getting louder and louder, without realizing she began singing and toe tapping to its beat.

. . . ♩ At the Copa – Copacabana – The hottest spot north of Havana – At the Copa – Copacabana – Music and passion were always in fashion – At the Copa don't fall in love – Don't fall in love – Copacabana – Copacabana . . . ♩

She turned off both hard drives, ceased her singing and toe tapping and listened The music was continuing to play. Barry Manilow was coming from the original hard drive they had removed from O'Hare at Kennedy. She considered. *Donner und Blitzen, you can't move for Manilow round here.* Somewhere out there; and Hess has to find it this time, she thought. There's another hard drive that is the key. *Eier!*

She had not had to go too far to find out who O'Hare's associates were. They had been involved with him for years. The newspaperman, Hamilton Fitch and Sister Anna Marie from the religious Carmelite order. Both, along with O'Hare himself, instrumental in bringing the original Order down. Two unlikely candidates to go shifting bodies up steps from a vault though. That would leave, one of her own. She was thinking, the man close to the Order, was he a mole in those years? Was it he that was responsible for removing O'Hare's body from the bank vault

Nathaniel Johnson!

Now there was a need to look closer into the activities of the man, she thought. There had been too many leaks of information about them to be coincidental. He knew the scientists and engineers responsible for constructing AG-MX-960. The electromagnetic field force mind penetration analyzer (the fourth of its line) having the capacity to trap and hold a supernatural creature. Not a ghost, but

Christianity's Divine Spirit, the one the Order of the Most Divine Third Circle had sought the last 2000 years.

A creature that carried all the power and the glory within. Every physical law of the universe. To just reach out to him was to have monumental enlightenment bestowed. Ageing stopped in its tracks. All that power channeled to Jesus while He was a mortal on Earth, not because He was the Son of God necessarily; but because he was chosen. The classic tale from the Bible of the woman being ill for years reaching out to Him in a crowd and touching his clothes without his knowledge was only to be found out after He noticed some of that power leaving Him went out to her:

Daughter, your faith has made you well. Go in peace.

That power – one such example of many that had done the rounds, Direktorin Kriemhild thought, was quite possibly to Johnson and O'Hare the woman's story for the modern age.

She was a Calvinist with ambition. Her faith in the supernatural was a reality. For she had the evidence on photographic film. Film from a time before digital image cameras. Film, not computer-generated imagery capable of being manipulated, but celluloid. Celluloid put under the microscope and examined by experts demonstrated that reality. Whether it had any alliance to God, well, the jury was out as far as she was concerned. For the moment the organization – their new Order – had elected her direktorin and she would take them forward without the sexual trafficking of children they had engaged in the past under Frederik Spannocs. There was no need. She would keep crime within international law to drive Star Birth forward. Corruption and money laundering were the new buzz words. That alone would be enough to drive populations to their knees to create a unified autocratic world state; and all without a weapon of war being fired.

The enigma that was the Seventh Gift of God as a scientific project following its 2000 year history was her number one priority. The opening of those hard drives was imperative to cracking the enigma. For who wouldn't want the physics for the creation of life and the universe in front of them? What would they pay? What's the going rate to sit and converse with God? The world's wealth! Four hundred trillion-odd dollars worth! His knowledge would far and away surpass that meagre amount as a return. Anyone standing in her way to achieving that . . . well, there were more than enough betrayers, thugs, and assassins willing to murder others for less than any biblical 30 pieces of silver.

How much is that in the scheme of things?

Fourteen

THE BAROMETER NEEDLE swinged south.

Late afternoon, Friday the 23rd of June and the sky over John F. Kennedy International Airport was black tulip. The fall of the barometer came out of the blue threatening any further take-offs. Two minutes before there wasn't a cloud in the sky. Now there were dirty black ones everywhere. Standing beside the privately chartered Saab 340 plane overseeing O'Hare's repatriation to Ireland were Carter and Fitch. Fitch was to accompany the coffin to Castle Rose, Carter was to remain. An arrangement based on experience. As she said to Fitch, *Should events take a turn for the worse.*

When didn't they where O'Hare was concerned, Fitch thought to himself.

Tommy and Daniella parked the hearse as close to the plane as was possible and opened the back door. Tommy directed the fork lift driver as to where he was to position the forks. Straps were placed around the coffin. The forks were hooked under the straps, the coffin lifted out, then lowered onto the tarmac for the next stage.

The banksman overseeing the unloading looked up at the darkening sky and gave the forklift driver the hurry up before the weather took a turn for the worse. Fitch looked on. He had a laptop in one hand, an envelope in the other.

'Got the paperwork ready,' the banksman called across to him. He nodded in the direction of the airport's transit lounges. 'Your official send off is on its way.'

The Customs and Border Protection officer arrived in an electric trolley. 'Good afternoon, who's in charge here? We need the burial transit certificate.' Fitch passed it to him. The man studied it. 'Someone's got friends in the Medical Examiner's office, official paperwork takes 72 hours to process. Yes they seem to be in order. Have a good flight now.'

DOWNLOAD | SENTINEL MOTHER TRANSFERRING DATA PROGRAM. SENTINEL MASTER–EVT PROGRAM RUNNING. – EVT SINGULARITY ISOLATED. SENTINEL MASTER–EVT PROGRAM ACCESSIBLE. SENTINEL MASTER–EVT PROGRAM FUNCTIONING. PREDATOR GUARDIAN ISOLATED. ALL SYSTEMS NORMAL. PROTEIN FUEL OBSOLETE | DOWNLOAD COMPLETE | UPLOAD INITIATED

'Thanks, Border. Right you boys let's get this show on the road,' the banksman said.

The forklift driver secured the coffin in an air tray, pushed his truck as close to the plane's ramp as possible without knocking into it. He inched the truck forward until a plane crew member gave him a thumbs-up to stop. The two crew members were readying themselves to slide the air frame and coffin into the hold when without warning the hydraulics for lifting and lowering of the forks came to an unscheduled halt. One of the lashing straps had slipped off the coffin threatening to drop the whole caboodle onto the airstrip damaging the coffin and the ramp leading onto the plane. The coffin was hanging part on the loading ramp with its remainder on the forks. It teetered. The driver's heart went into his mouth. 'Bollocks!'

'Fucks sake, Mart. You still got a safety certificate in date. Can't you tie off a simple box without losing it,' the banksman called after him. 'The fucking thing will be on the deck in a minute.' He then remembered there was a lady present. 'Sorry, ma'am.'

'Don't worry about it,' Carter said smiling. She'd heard and given the same since leaving the Carmelites.

Martin jumped down from the truck and checked the dolly lines for any leakage. Clean. A corpse tumbling from a coffin onto an airport's runway (not any old airport – JFK!) would be more than an embarrassment. What he couldn't understand was why when the loading of the hearse onto the forks had been straightforward the operating controls decided to play up now. He was an experienced operator, everything had been checked over before he had taken the truck out of the depot. The load was the problem. For some reason the coffin was moving on its own. As if the body inside was moving around (perish the thought). He was going to have to take an unsafe measure to secure the load away from the plane. He would take a flyer. He climbed back into the truck and reversed it away from the plane's ramp with the coffin still teetering. He held his breath and pushed the lever to bring the coffin back to ground level. This time it worked. It came to rest on the tarmac.

'What are you doing now, Mart? Come on we've got to get this plane away before the weather grounds us in. We could have handballed it ourselves by now.'

Martin was not to be hurried.

''Stead of giving me grief, give me a hand to straighten it.'

Between the two of them they repositioned the coffin.

'Okay, let's have another go. Get out of the way,' Martin said.

The banksmen stepped aside and Martin got back onto the truck. He started it up, engaged the lift to take the load up, but all he got was a whirr from the motor . . . nothing. He put both fists up and clenching them cried out, 'Ughhh!' In his frustration he went through the fork's movements. Fork movement: forward, nothing; fork movement reverse, nothing; fork drive, nothing. 'This truck is going nowhere.' He got down once more, this time to check the battery power indicator. Although displaying less than a full charge, there was more than enough energy for the truck to operate. The forks with the coffin and air frame were three feet from the airstrip and they were going to have to handball it onto the plane as the banksman suggested by way of a joke after all. And a coffin the weight of this one was would be a riot.

Both men set to undoing the strapping in readiness. Tommy Scripps suggested he lend a hand, assuming it wasn't going to break any union rules. The fork lift driver said probably, but, *Who cares?*

Fitch was checking over the paperwork for the transfer of a coffin and body from one country into another. It was a lawyer's charter, consisting of export clearance requirements for where death occurred, death certificate and autopsy report, consular mortuary certificates, affidavit of foreign funeral director and transit permit, CDC import permit in the case of a quarantinable communicable disease, such as an urn containing cremation ashes, casket, body transfer case (oh, I've signed one without knowing). He was delighted to see there was no certificate requirement for the importation of clean, dry bones or bone fragments, human hair, teeth, fingernails or toenails or a deceased human body and portions thereof already cremated before importation. He looked up from all this depressive paperwork to see Carter staring in horror at him. *What?*

If Charlie was dead, she thought. What in God's name was causing all of this to happen?

The fork lift driver had both hands out to everyone around in a gesture suggesting he was no longer in control. His hands were off all controls and still the coffin was moving violently up and down, side to side threatening to remove itself onto the tarmac. There came an interval of time when it ceased all movement. They all breathed a sigh of relief. A short lived sigh. For it started up once more.

'Can we get him out, Mr. Scripps?' Carter asked.

'For God's sake!' Fitch shouted to the guys handling the loading, 'Get it down and open it.' He went to put his hands under the bottom of the coffin to support it, but it was too heavy for one man alone. 'Somebody give me a hand here, quick. I won't be able to hold it if it comes off,' he shouted in panic now. The tips of his fingers were bending under the strain.

The two crew members inside the plane seeing his dilemma dropped down onto the runway to give a hand. Everyone had a hold of it now.

'You sure you got no power,' the banksman said to the fork lift driver stood next to him. 'Go try it again.'

'Never mind let's get it on the ground,' Tommy said. 'Ella, stand back. If this lot goes with the weight and all, lead—'

'Man! were you about to say lead? You telling us this thing is lead lined. I thought it was heavy when we slid it out of the hearse and onto the forks. I've already got an hernia, me balls will be in me throat next,' the fork lift driver said.

The words were no sooner out of his mouth when everything happened at once. Everyone jumped back not caring whether the coffin fell off the forks and smashed or not. The lid of the air tray came away, followed by a screaming and splintering of timber joints as if someone were going at the coffin with a crowbar. The thumb screws holding the coffin lid tightened down were unscrewing. Eerily turning from the woodwork, at the depth of human hearing they gave a juddered and quiet squeak as a — mouse sighing. Tommy Scripps was not a man who succumbed to fear, but he was terrified of what might happen to O'Hare.

Daniella's understanding was that once burial had taken place the deceased was in God's final charge; while natural law dictated that the corpse of the deceased while on Earth fell to a designated responsible person. She was that person. Her responsibility was to accompany the body to its final resting place, on into the ground for the final hand over to God and any decision as to whether it remain with Him or went to some other place His. Now her charge was being desecrated by unseen forces threatening to overtake her responsibility. Seeing her father frozen in fear, unable to intervene, it would fall to her to take action. Whatever manifestation this was (for manifestation she was in no doubt), daring to interfere with her charge, was going to have to take it up with her.

Tommy had not expected the simple act of transferring Charlie to Ireland would be so fraught with danger. Seeing his daughter approaching the coffin he broke from his torpor. Running to her side he grabbed her arm in time to see the lid from the coffin coming away in a caterwauling sound of splintering wood, lead and lining, crape, and copper tacks. Father and daughter stood side by side watching as the creature came from nothing becoming a living entity before their eyes. In words, the best Daniella could bring to voice to exorcise demons she knew, she screamed to the highest octave she had, *In God's name, get the fuck out of there . . . you . . . daughter-of-a-bitch!*

Sentinel Master–EVT reached out. A crew member stepped forward and was evaporated. He resembled an un-embalmed 2000 year old Egyptian mummy look-alike to those close to the remains. Sentinel Master–EVT no longer resembled its previous version of Hartley

Hare becoming a cross between a Malinois dog and an upright machine. Tearing at the inside of the coffin it searched between the body of the man inside and the edge of the box containing him, pulling the lead lining away as if it were tissue paper.

Without panic, for what had happened to his workmate, the other crew member pushed an alarm button inside the aircraft. A terrorist threat alarm activated the airport's security putting an armed response team of officers and police into an immediate heads-up. Organized and ready they responded and were out towards the plane in less than three minutes to begin sealing off the area. In the next three minutes a second followed, then by a third wave of armed police.

Arriving in cars and heavy four-wheelers, blue lights flashing, they surrounded the plane. Gathering into an armed surround for protection they watched as the coffin was rolled across the runway. It was being dismantled with no apparent cause. When the cause was unmasked to the Response Commander she froze in horror. An eight-foot high part human part machine, with metal clawed hands on outstretched arms was hovering a foot off the ground. The remains of a coffin, with the body of a man hanging by his legs half in and half out, was being dragged along as the creature tried to escape its predicament. It was struggling as if caught in a net it was unable to escape from.

The head of the creature was turning from side to side trying to establish where it was to go from here, as having come into this Time–Verse, not finding what it was looking for, was seeking further options from its controllers.

What the . . . fuck *is that?* Jane Schwartz, Response Commander shouted turning from a static living statue into one that was now mobile. She fired off five rounds from her 5.56 mm caliber automatic at the creature. Whether she thought such a response would make it go away or not she didn't care. Her irresponsible shoot first, ask questions after went the way of a bounty hunter seeing dollar signs on a dead or alive poster.

Sentinel Master disengaged from −EVT leaving it vulnerable to annihilation. Predator Guardian was in the field; its first duty was to the Sentinel Mother.

If Fitch was about to say, What now? to Carter it was not so much for his observations of an Alien (with Charlie and Annie as companions, neither were strangers to visitors from Satan's front door), more, the upset of seeing O'Hare's temporary place of rest being desecrated, said instead, *What is that?*

After all they had gone through, witnessing and bringing to a close the years of suffering of innocent children, hadn't they done enough to satisfy God yet? And now the body of O'Hare, the man that had brought peace and order to the world, was being dragged from his coffin − and by what? Half a dog and half stripped down mechanical clock; unable to be stopped by an armed response unit with enough fire power to take on, Alien Machines from the Great Martian War.

Fitch, uttered one word. *Ahriman!*

DOWNLOAD | SENTINEL MOTHER DATA PROGRAM MALFUNCTION. −EVT INACCESSIBLE FROM SENTINEL MASTER PROGRAM. PREDATOR GUARDIAN CLOSING IN. ALL SYSTEMS LOCKDOWN | UPLOAD COMPLETE

She came—

Carter watched her pull the sword from the scabbard strapped across her back. A sword as long as herself. She threatened to strike the Alien if it didn't back away.

—EVT, now isolated, abandoned this theatre of conflict to fight another day.

Carter shouted to Fitch, *No! . . . White Bear Angel!*

Tommy and Daniella lifted O'Hare from what remained of the coffin and placed him onto a trolley. His body had not been touched. The lead lining pulled away from the inside of the woodwork of the coffin as if it were the crape now needed replacing. Torn and buckled, Tommy was having the devil's own job believing a creature from the supernatural had got inside Charlie's coffin to carry out this degree of damage just to get at a hard drive. Whatever did it contain that would bring a hound of hell to Earth to do that, he wondered.

Carter was comforted by Fitch. She had gone into a post trauma state with the sudden realization one of the plane's crew had been . . . she said vaporized . . . Fitch had to agree.

'Oh, that poor guy,' she struggled to hold back tears. 'He couldn't have been any older than thirty, having life taken from him.'

Daniella, in keeping with her designated responsibility checked the body of O'Hare over. To her surprise, apart from his shirt having been torn, he was in as good condition as the day they put him in. The oak coffin itself did not fare as well. The tattered lead combined with the remains of the coffin resembled a pile of firewood taken from a roof after a storm. They were going nowhere today.

The four of them were escorted to the airport lounge by the security force. Tommy had to organize another coffin, but he was having a difficulty. An official one. He told Daniella New York's Chief Medical Examiner had to be called in. They needed to inspect his body for possible contagions.

She hit the roof. As if it wasn't bad enough that her charge should have been subjected to a vicious assault by a creature from the black lagoon, now this.

'What kind of contagions?' she asked.

'Something about bacterial, or viruses.'

'Which would have died twenty-four hours after he had. Which leaves gastrointestinal infections and bloodborne viruses such as Hepatitis B before that time. Neither of which I have; and I handled the body. And if that creature, wherever it came from, had any of those it would have died. Didn't anyone notice it was part human. Dead bodies constitute no more a public health risk than do the living. Less in fact. So what kind of Chief Medical Examiner doesn't know any of this?'

All of which Tommy knew.

'I collect him! He's my responsibility, do you hear me, father?'

'Of course. He'll be ready in an hour.'

They were given a clean room environment allocated for such an event (how many allocated occasions do they have like this one round here, Daniella thought). A new coffin was delivered by one of Scripps' usual suppliers. The body was eventually released and brought over in a medical ambulance. *And I hope you inspect it for contagious diseases before you carry any injured in it!* she called out to the Medical Examiner as he passed Tommy their clearance to papers to proceed.

Daniella gave O'Hare another chance to look his best. She removed the blood dotted shirt replacing it with another clean one. Her father smiled at her mouthing, *Thank you.* Fitch called President Howe to tell him what had occurred. He had already been informed by airport security chiefs. He organized another plane for them with the directive, if there was any chance the Alien had made its way onto the plane with them they were to remove themselves from the airplane leaving everything behind (including the coffin) where he would make arrangements to hit it with a missile from an F-15 Strike Eagle coming there way now.

In twenty four hours, they were good to go. The coffin was loaded without incident, dressed with a new and replacement Irish Tricolor and a Stars and Stripes. The Scripps, Fitch and the coffin left JFK without further incident. Carter was to remain. She had been called back to the White House for an emergency briefing of the situation. President Howe was convinced the video image of O'Hare taken from a marines head cam at Becland was an impersonation of him by the Alien; that was clear was seeking him out, and he alone.

Asked if she had any ideas as to the reason why?

She had opined all reasonable answers; but declined what she knew to be true. That he was a vessel for the return of His Seventh Gift, she considered was a hallowed message no man on Earth was worthy for the telling. As to how that was to be achieved now he was dead would be for his maker to work out.

Banksman Stott, along with his colleague, Martin were called into the security office for what was to be a de-brief as to what had happened out on the runway by two officers from a response team. An emphasis was put on them not so much as to what they had seen, more, what they were to forget.

'Yup! It's not every day you get a grand shoved in yer bin for keeping your mouth shut,' Martin said.

'Yeh! Makes you wonder what the other's got,' Stott added.

Martin queried him asking, why he would say that?

'Well, we were not the only people to see . . . more to the point, what did we see, Mart?'

Fifteen

CARTER NO SOONER arrived at the White House than a call came in for her on a secure line set up by Jean Ronstandt. She knew who it was, having been briefed by Ronstandt that Tubman was now undercover with Star Birth.

Tubman was sitting in her car outside the former government offices. She didn't normally pass on information so soon after hearing it, but urgent responses demanded the dangerous passing of intelligence. She would risk her cover being blown in the case of this. She was not sure if the recipient's phone was being bugged, over listened to, or on loudspeaker. For this recipient was not one of her official CIA contacts. This one had been given over to her by Homeland Security when Ronstandt was out of the building. Despite this, she was still worried if they were to be trusted or not. She was at the point of ringing off when the call was answered.

Annie Carter . . .

She breathed a sigh of relief. She knew this woman. A nun. They had both been witnesses to events at White Bear, when she was an army officer under Colonel Lennox, and Carter was part of O'Hare's team.

Tubman used no keywords to trigger the Star Birth's AI robotics. Developed by Ronstandt himself, it involved notations of numbers once used, would send robotics off in another direction. At least the theory, as it was still in the development stage. AI robotics worked on a list of 30 million keywords triggering any unauthorized security breaches into Star Birth's telephone system. These were added on a daily basis making it next to impossible to find keywords having no meaning. Binary numbers were ignored by AI robotics. Tubman had triggered Ronstandt's secure line number from the car park outside the building.

'We met at a snow sports venue. I'll keep it brief. If a certain journalist is covering the St. Patrick's Day parade in Dublin, expect company from another newspaper looking for reports of the match and a hard drive to record them on. He will be staying in a hotel the band use for gigs, the Jigging Leprechaun, County Wexford.

'And does this journalist have a name?'

'Coxly Hess. Not necessarily the name he will be using. It would be as well your journalist friend doesn't take gifts from strangers.'

She was gone.

'Tubman?' Abisai Campbell, National Security Advisor standing in for Ronstandt asked Carter. She nodded it was. 'That'll test Jean's theory.'

'The point is, Ryder, I cannot get to the bottom of who has what, where, and how. I assumed being Commander-in-Chief you would have been filled in with such mundane details. The reason my department is now having to keep a close eye on Star Birth now is that O'Hare's arrangements for Tom Dorcas taking it over have fallen foul. It is back in the hands of Germany. They are powerful and dangerous. Madeleine may have blown her cover getting information out to Annie Carter. Hamilton Fitch is on his way to Ireland for the interment of Mr. O'Hare. He's carrying paperwork belonging to the Order passed to him by Scripps the undertaker for safekeeping.'

'And now we can't recover it without going there,' the President said.

'No, sir.'

'You've earned a trip to Charlie's interment to bring it back, Annie.' President Howe said. He turned to Campbell. 'In the meantime, get Tubman out of there before her cover's blown?'

'No need, sir.' Campbell replied.

Nathaniel Johnson has been watching Diaz since she first arrived for the interview for a position with Dorcas. As she had been the only applicant alarm bells rang in his head. Until he spoke with O'Hare he couldn't be sure if she was working for him or not. He'd heard he was dead. If that was the case he was forced to work on his own initiative. Fortunately the government's security operations were sloppy; the number Miss Diaz had called had been used before in another life. He recognized it, if Star Birth's system didn't. Which didn't solve the problem for it had come from their building, and, as such all the system recognized was another number coming from somewhere needing an explanation. As far as explanations were concerned, Star Birth, as the old Order, operated an ask questions first, shoot later policy. If it had been recognized, someone was going to come for Diaz and he needed to prevent that – somehow.

Fortunately computers and high tech gear allocated to himself and Dan Sullivan from their earlier days with the Order, after the FBI, O'Hare and his team came for Spannocs was still intact and working. From his basement bolt hole below the building's basement, he put two and two together. Seeing Diaz sitting in her car on her phone with the number flashing up at the same time on the screen he was watching he went into action. From the strength of the signal it was clear to him it was her. He went to the screen where the number was displayed and hit the delete key.

* * *

A security Humvee came out from the garages below the office building. It was heading to where Tubman was sitting in her vehicle. When it stopped two men got out and approached her car. They were wearing earpieces and video cameras on their chests. She saw they had weapons drawn. Her heart skipped a beat. One of them put his hand up. It was clear he was listening to a message coming into his earpiece.

'As you were, Mattie. We've been called off.' He signaled to Diaz as she was opening the door of her car. 'Sorry for the scare, ma'am. Wrong call.'

Sixteen

TO THE IRISH AVIATION AUTHORITY Vic Hall was writ large, except when it came to his peers. Often pointing out to his controlling masters the stupidity of some of their management decisions. *You lot shouldn't be let loose with a bus route let alone an airport*, his oft times worn mantra to them.

Following a directive, no one outside of his department was to know of the arrival of this plane, he had asked, *And how am I supposed to do that? Throw a camouflage net over it as it lands.*

A cocky no-it-all from management answered him by saying, 'No need for the dramatics, Mr. Hall, we asked Kennedy to cover the Presidential decal by the side door, also not use Executive One over the radio, instead Executive One Foxtrot on its approach to Runway 28L.'

'That's all right, I'll put the net back into store.'

Hall knew everything there was to know about airports and passenger planes up to the point of flying one. Often asked why he hadn't his reply was always the same, *Too bloody sanitized!* A former Royal Air Force pilot during the Cold War he had been forced to land a Vulcan bomber during a blizzard after an operation of hand-waving salutations to Russian pilots doing the same job for their side. It hit the runway, braked, and losing its footing on the ice went sideways at a rate of knots that left those watching to hold their breaths at the inevitability of a fire ball that would put runways and hangars out of service for weeks. Hall, not to be over excited, mumbling a stream of expletives to his co-pilot, kept the leviathan as close as he could to airport fire engines approaching him. With judicious use of the brakes he brought the fully-armed Avro Vulcan high-level nuclear bomber short of a hangar with not a scratch on either. The sobriquet, Skidmarks, had stuck ever since. Although the emergency team present at the time had all agreed he exhibited more judgement over luck, it was more than the recognition he got from his superiors who instigated a Courts-martial for pilot negligence against him, duly losing

The radio crackled into sound. 'Good morning. Executive One Foxtrot to Dublin tower we are nine miles out of Dublin request landing procedure and Radar number.'

Passengers without a flight to catch, watching from Dublin's Terminal One were exhilarated to watch an unusual plane arriving.

'Begorrah, will you look now,' a woman standing next to her husband said. 'The President of the United States is landing, so he is.'

Looking from the tower of Dublin's air traffic control as the plane came closer flight Hall's mouth dropped open. Executive One Foxtrot was still displaying the Seal of the President of the United States of America emblazoned on its fuselage. He called ground control.

'Get that plane downwind to hangar W14 quick, Henry. Another first. They couldn't organize a . . . never mind, I despair. There's a coffin to come out of her isn't there? We don't want anyone seeing one of them being unloaded out of a plane, they'll be getting wrong ideas.'

MacLeish got up from his computer, took up his binoculars and looked across the airfield. A man of sometimes infuriating habits, to Hall, when it came to airport safety, although sometimes driving him to distraction, was a good man trusted and true.

'Today, Henry! Today! We haven't time for twitching. The President of America smuggling himself into Ireland in a coffin will not make good copy in *The Irish Record* by morning true or not. And by midday it will have escalated to Gerry Adams seeking funds for the Republican cause doing a deal with him in the snug of Shaughnessy's. Never mind the London press. And kill the tractor driver when he's done, we don't want any witnesses,' he called after MacLeish as he was going out the door.

Fitch took his case down from the overhead compartment and began to make his way down the aisle of the plane to the exit. Going down the steps he was relieved the plane had been diverted away from the usual parking spaces in front of the airport. He was in no mood to answer questions from the press asking what the the editor-in-chief of the *New York Post* was doing in Dublin coming in on a Special Air Mission 26000.

A steward was waiting for him at the bottom of the steps alongside a golf-type shuttle vehicle. The driver was wearing a high visibility jacket. Around his neck, a pair of ear mufflers.

'Afternoon, sir. Put this on please?' He passed Fitch a yellow jacket. 'Good flight?' he asked. 'I'll take you to Customs. You and your party have clearance to go straight through.'

The coffin was loaded into a private ambulance parked alongside the plane. Tommy Scripps got in turned the ignition key then drove away leaving the golf trolley driver behind to hold out his hands in a gesture that he was supposed to follow him, not the other way round.

Hall was watching through his binoculars from the control tower. He had been alerted by a ground controller. A black ambulance was being driven the wrong way toward the crosswind runway. He called into his two-way radio, MacLeish! MacLeish! Where the hell are you? Where is he, anyone? MacLeish! For Chris'sake, come in. He was shaking his head in disbelief. He was watching a bowler-hatted man in morning dress heading his ambulance toward a Ryanair flight reversing out from its parking bay.

'Did you call me, Skids?' MacLeish's voice came back through his communicator.

'I'll give you Skids! You're supposed to be ground safety officer here. There's an ambulance about to collide into the safest air carrier in the world, and it's not even in the air.'

'O-h-h-h, bolloes!' the voice came back.

Fitch put his keys and loose change into the tray. His carry bag and the package went along the conveyor into the scanner coming out the other side. He was then waved through as McLeish said. He headed for an executive suite between a money exchange bank and a Costa coffee house, grabbing an Americano as he went. He would wait for Scripps and his daughter in there. He opened his briefcase to replace his passport to find a brown envelope he didn't recognize. It had an address. Opening it up he took out the contents. There were three sheets of red tinted paper stapled together. Badly reproduced photocopies. On them typed tight and small, a list of names. Foreign and English: kings and presidents. He held his breath. At the bottom was the company name with an address of the organization it was to be priority sent. Star Birth (Bavarian Section), Direktorin Elke Kriemhild, Drogstadt Castle, Germany. He skimmed it taking it in as much of the document as he could in case it needed to be recalled at a later date. It did. He put both hands to his brow and muttered, *Oy vey! My life!*

The list was a Who's Who, of world leaders. Most, if not all, among some of the nastiest bastards on the planet. Criminals beyond all laws, natural and real. It had always been a mystery to him why honest (he assumed there were still some left) democratic leaders of the Western world were reluctant to call them out. But then that's politics, he thought. For the moment though, with this document in his hands – and as to how he came to be in possession of it – the wrong people finding it on him; with him being editor-in-chief of the *New York Post*, would put him on a list. A death list. Did he need another excuse to be murdered? He put it back in his briefcase.

Standing in line waiting to go through Irish customs, he became aware a woman was standing close to him. So close he smelled her perfume. Samsara. So close one of them was going to have to move away. He decided it would be him. As he did he saw she was wearing an American insignia in her red jacket lapel. A Customs officer was close by. The woman spoke first.

'This is the man who stole my envelope officer,' she said.

She moved back into his space while the customs officer called for assistance. She whispered to him, 'It's me, Ham.' Her voice took on a higher pitch. 'You picked an envelope up from the conveyor belt and put it in your briefcase as you went through, it doesn't belong to you.'

Annie! He spoke her name in a surprised voice. She was the last person he expected to see. 'What are you doing here?' He looked over her shoulder. A private jet was parked in a holding bay close by the terminal. A Stars and Stripes decal on its tail fin; being fueled by an aviation tanker told him all he needed to know. That was no unobtrusive flight of the President. He didn't need to ask what was going on, for he trusted in her integrity. Glad to be shot of the envelope he handed it to her. He shrugged at the customs officer and smiled, 'An honest mistake, sir. Sorry ma'am.'

Daniella Scripps gave over the U.S. Transportation Security Administration manifest and burial transit certificate to the customs officer. The man looked her up and down, gave a cursory glance at the documentation, stamped it, tore off his section and handed over the other half.

'Lá Fhéile Pádraig sona duit!'

Daniella looked at the date on her watch. Isn't St. Patrick's Day, is it? she wondered.

Seventeen

DANIELLA DROVE INTO THE GROUNDS of Castle Rose with her father. She stopped the ambulance as a man hurried across to them. Not so much to greet them, for he seemed too officious for such formalities.

'Ned McCoy. That'll be, as in Sin O'Hare's estate manager if you're interested,' he said.

With all her years looking into the faces of the dead from all ages it was difficult to tell which end of the fifties this man belonged, for although he had a healthy tanned face with a hint of collagen loss and elastin in his skin, he looked in his mid-forties. He was wearing a dark blue suit over a high neck blue tee-shirt. Whether he was aware his gun holster was showing inside the left shoulder of his suit jacket she couldn't be sure. Either way, from not being bothered, or design, he buttoned his jacket closed covering the evidence. He stepped onto the running board of the ambulance, took hold of the mirror mount to steady himself and pointed a direction she assumed he wanted her to head in.

'Chapel's over there, Scripps. Behind those trees.'

She looked at her father with an expression, rather than what she would have liked to have said which was, Who the fuck's this clown! She drove to the side of the chapel and stopped. McCoy stepped off the running board and onto the gravel. In front of them, obscured by trees and bushes from the main house, was the chapel. A stone building with a steep angled slated roof covered in lichen and moss. There was a slit window high above the door on its front elevation. Or rather, the remains of one (it had been sealed up years since). Over the front portal was the date 1545 engraved into a white key stone, now gray and spattered with yellow lichen. Signs of birds picking away at it by nest builders was evident.

McCoy was at the door now. A stubborn construction of oak and black rusted iron stanchions and supports. He put his shoulder to it and worked away at the gap he had made by the insertion of his left foot. One of two sported hand-made brown brogues. Daniella reckoned to herself 1545 was about the last time the door had been opened judging by the effort needed. McCoy had a well-rehearsed system for opening it. A kick to the bottom left corner, a lift of the handle – still not quite bingo! So on reflection, closer to January 1998.

'Will the coffin fit through there?' he said after finishing off opening it with his shoulder.

Daniella looked at her father. They had had a long drive from the airport, not to mention the flight and its attended excitement. All she wanted was a cup of tea and a sit down before starting work like – tomorrow. Her father, already far from impressed with their welcome in words loud enough for McCoy said, 'Stay there, Ella. I'll deal with the man seeing as he's all fired up to get Charlie and his coffin into the ground.' He then directed himself at McCoy. 'Come on, you. I'll open the back door, you take the trolley out and put it together. I'll slide the coffin onto it when you're finished. Take care of your hands with the trolley when you open though, they have a habit of snatching trigger fingers from unwary strangers.'

'Put it back in the van, father. I can't be doing with all of this now,' Daniella said.

McCoy's attitude had changed. He was smiling as he showed them into the castle. 'You'll take whiskey, Mr. Scripps?'

'And I'll take a cup of tea if you wouldn't mind,' Daniella said far from happy with their first meeting. 'My father and I have had one hell of a day . . .'

'Your father!'

'And I trust our rooms are better prepared than your funeral arrangements, Mr. McCoy,' Daniella said.

'They are, Miss Scripps. Rest assured they are,' he said as they walked into the castle's foyer. They were no sooner across the threshold than a voice called out to them from one of three doors at the far end. 'Ah! The castle's housekeeper, Janice Caffrey,' McCoy said.

'Housekeeper, be boll--! Ned McCoy,' she said as she approached them. 'Gerty told me to make you and your daughter welcome,' she said giving Daniella a hug, then shaking Tommy's hand. 'We're heartily pleased to meet you, aren't we Ned? Ned!' McCoy had taken umbridge. 'Don't take any notice of him. Sin took himself off fishing earlier and didn't take Ned with him. Never mind about whiskey, did someone mention tea?'

Daniella smiled.

Despite advice from Tubman that Fitch should not book into the Jigging Leprechaun as Hess would be staying there he chose to ignore. Tubman had got the information out to them through Carter. It would be doubtful if he used his real name, but then, you can never be sure. If he was cocksure of himself he would. If he had been sent to find another hard drive then he was going to be disappointed. Far as he knew, with O'Hare's aptitude for deception (he was not privy to on this occasion), a maverick group of CIA operatives had it now. Although his vagueness as to there being another, well, he never did spell out. Leastways not to him he didn't. Not the hard drive, then he was here to find that list. Disappointment on both counts for him.

There were two other tables in the dining area. He figured as they were both strangers in Wexford, Hess would need to eat as he himself. If he was here then this would be the place to find and keep an eye on him. There were two guests sitting at table as he came in. A priest. He guessed of the Catholic Father persuasion, sitting with a woman. Both politely nodded at him as he came in. He acknowledged them before sitting down. Clerical celibacy being the discipline within the Catholic church by which only unmarried men are ordained to the episcopate, he guessed, it was either his mother, sister, or mistress. A man in his fifties, she fortyish. Both were dining on steak and kidney pudding. A carafe of red house their accompaniment. He had noticed a Chef's Recommendation of the Day was chalked on a tripod blackboard as he came in. So much easier than having to make a decision, he thought.

He had no sooner sat down than the landlady approached him. A woman in her fifties wearing a black skirt with a white blouse. A red silk scarf tied in a reef was round her neck. Short black hair had been styled as a man. He nodded at her and smiled.

'Hello again, Mr. Fitch. How's the room? Sorry about the storm window, its inclined to stick. I'll send my husband up later to take a look at it.'

'No, all fine, thank you. Don't trouble yourself.'

'What can we get you then, sir?' she asked. 'Chef has shredded poached Loch Duart salmon served on a niçoise style salad, or perhaps . . .'

Fitch looked down at the menu. 'The gammon steak with the fried egg, please.'

'Práta or fries?'

She smiled. He asked. She answered.

'That's Irish for plain boiled potatoes.'

'Fries, I think. If I'm not being disrespectful to the chef. And a Martini, lemon, no ice.' She nodded. He changed the subject. 'Tell me, the Father over there. He sounded American.'

If it was Hess he was playing the being in plain sight card. Who was going to take notice of a priest in Ireland? But the woman . . .

'He is. Do you know him? He said he was here for a funeral.'

'No I don't. Did he say whose, only I'm here for a funeral as well?' Fitch asked.

'I took it to be Castle Rose. Sin O'Hare's place.'

'No, I've never seen him before, as for his companion—'

'For sure you wouldn't have seen her before, not unless . . . I'll get your meal, Mr. Fitch. You must be hungry after your trip.'

'Why?' he asked. She had gone without answering.

He finished his dinner, took his Martini over to an empty table and sat down to Gmail Carter. The Father and the woman had already left in a taxi. A young man – a student if appearances were any judge – coming from behind the bar sat himself down at his table. He brought a drink with him. Fitch looked up from his Gmailing.

'Sorry to disturb you, I work here and couldn't help overhearing your conversation with Amanda.'

'Yes,' Fitch said. 'And what else do you do, apart from listening in to people's conversations behind bars?'

'University. Dublin. Politics and journalism.'

'Very good,' Fitch said.

'Her grandfather was hanged by the British for passing intelligence to the enemy during the second world war you know.'

He shrugged. He didn't expect a statement like that to come out of the blue. As a journalist himself, it was more a question of having to drag information from people rather than them giving it away. In this case, old news as opposed to new (the second world war was done with a long time since) given by people wanting to show how much they know of world events. For sure, this boy knew something he wanted off his chest.

'He was an Irish Republican involved with Abwehr, the German intelligence service operating here then.'

'Sorry, you are?'

'Finbar Nolan.' He put out his hand to shake his. 'Pleased to meet you. Yes, her grandfather was hanged by the British not for treachery – although, treachery by another country against a host I don't consider as being treacherous – but because he was a double agent for British intelligence. He was part of a network sacrificed to convince the IRA there were no informers in their ranks connected with him or German intelligence.'

Fitch didn't interrupt him for he had more to say. He took a sip of his drink and continued.

'But there were. And still is.'

'And how do you know all of this?' Fitch asked.

'Call it my thesis. You're a journalist, aren't you? I saw your name after you registered. Hamilton Fitch, editor-in-chief! Of the *New York Post*, no less. I'm impressed. I'm looking to work in America when I finish my degree, I could do with a leg up when that day comes. Call it networking.'

For sure, he was one cheeky bastard. Whether the news had any relevance to him being here was doubtful.

'Don't happen to know the priest with her?' Fitch asked.

'Booked in as Fr. Montgomery. A punt to a dollar, he's no priest.'

'You don't think so?'

He shook his head no. 'She's making up good terms for her

grandfather against the English government. Word is she's an active arms dealer for the IRA, and he's a buyer seeking friends.'

'Well, Mr. Nolan, pop your CV in my in tray behind reception and we'll see what we can do – after you've qualified. In the meantime some advice. Don't get involved with either of those two persons if you wish to finish your degree.'

He got up to leave. 'Did you ever take your own advice, Mr. Fitch.'

'No. I didn't. But then, I had threats against me for being who I am before I ever thought of a career in journalism. You just might live a little longer to get yourself established if you do take it. What did you say her name was again?'

He had not been able to get out of his mind the attack on Charlie's coffin at JFK. Most people seeing someone's coffin being vandalized would look on it as sacrilege. When the attacker turns out to be Alien from another planet or time is that sacrilege or something else? Horrific and frightening to most, to him, as it was to Carter, one of many similar experiences they had been through before. What was weird about this one though was they had both seen incantations of previous Aliens. In his case it was Ahriman, while Carter, Irinushka. Ahriman was the alter ego of Satan. Irinushka, was not so defined. His Jewish faith wouldn't convince him Irinushka was an abducted daughter that had taken on the form of an angel as Charlie had always imagined. But despite their initial reactions they had seen neither, for this was half machine half human of average height that bore no similarity to either Irinushka or Ahriman.

For Ahriman was an incarnation of Satan, while Irinushka (according to Charlie), was a mortal woman taken into God's keeping. (*Huh!*) All thinking on those lines depended on whether a belief in bible interpretations of good and evil rationally stacked up. He was Jewish. Carter and O'Hare, Catholic. He aside, two people educated and logical of mind. None of which made any sense for what had taken place. But here they were (albeit without Charlie) locked into myth and legend once more; where the physics of other verses would test our own. Not of heaven and hell (at least according to Professor Kurt Konig), but of this world from a different time. In his example, half machine half human put them into a class of being from our future. So what did they want from us? Charlie spoke of the data for the creation of universe, he was not sure it was that simple. Can you trust an Irishman with the name of O'Hare being right? Even from beyond the grave? Fitch rocked his left hand to-and-fro in front of himself and muttered, *Ummm*.

The trolley was still outside the chapel where McCoy had walked off and left it. It was jammed between a chapel door that had refused to open the evening before – having swollen-from-the-rain, and a general lack of maintenance to the oak upright. As luck had it, with another night's rain, Tommy had had the foresight to leave the coffin in the ambulance.

Sin took one end of the coffin while Tommy took the other. For Sin there had not been time for any formal introductions, Gerty (he could hear her now), turning up at any time wanting to know what they thought they were doing putting a coffin into the chapel that was in this mess? And she'd be right.

'Where's it going?' Tommy asked, looking around at this wind swept, ramshackle of a place that was intended for a meeting of minds between God and Man, but looked more reminiscent of a barn now.

Sin would like to have said, Here! Where else? instead he nodded in the general direction of the ground.

'What, on the floor? Will it hold?' Tommy Scripps said stamping his feet on timbers rocking over warped beams.

Sin made the point, that if it were good enough to hold two rows of six pews it could easily support a coffin.

'Well, I've seen more comfortable chapels of rest, but, I suppose it'll have to do. As to those pews, considering the riddling of woodworm they'd be less heavy than they once were. Not ideal is it?'

Sin nodded at Scripps' structural assessments realizing he hadn't got a catafalque in place for the coffin yet. Gerty would not be amused. He was supposed to have organized the chapel. Clean, make good the window, fix the door, renovate the altar, all before the wake.

They dropped the coffin on the floor in front of the wooden table Gerty used as a devotional altar. The original dated back to the time of the oak door. Long since rotted away from the rain coming through the stained-glass window behind, it had been thrown out. Waiting to be renovated or replaced, crumbling plaster surrounded the window frame now. Another job waiting. Sin absentmindedly swept away the dead leaves blown under the door with his feet as if it was going to make any difference. Thinking better of the floor and Gerty's reaction to Charlie's coffin lying directly on it when she returned, Sin asked Tommy if they could use the trolley as a temporary catafalque.

Tommy Scripps felt he and Daniella had been ill used by first McCoy, and now this man. Everything was supposed to have been set in place for Charlie O'Hare by his relatives. He wasn't even related to the man, for this was a sad excuse for a chapel of repose.

'If you must, but it'll be extra,' he said more without thinking than actually meaning it. 'And I'm going to want it back . . . with all its wheels intact,' Tommy said far from pleased.

When they had finished Daniella and Tommy returned to the castle leaving Sin to lock up. Standing by the coffin with one hand on it he looked around. There were dead dry leaves that had blown under the doors. He moved across to one of the pews. Running a finger across the cap rail he looked at it, then rubbed it off on his trousers. There was dirt and dust everywhere. The pervasion of must he could do nothing, the result of age and damp. Scripps was right. It wasn't ideal, he thought. He resolved to give the place a good going over. The place was disturbing him, and not in a good way. He physically shuddered as he went to leave, and that hadn't happened to him before. He tried to dismiss the emotion as one of an overactive imagination; putting it down to Charlie's body lying in state. He saw himself lying there in a future that must come – perhaps. How old was he? One hundred and twenty-eight. Older than his nephew, that's for sure. Charlie had gone well before his time. Was he finally approaching the crossroad 'twixt life and death? One of a – not so rare breed as people would have us, striding the world. Passed their sell by date and some. Charlie was dead for sure, so were the twenty or so of his ancestors in the crypt below aged ranged between his father, two hundred; and his grandfather. He was born ten years after his grandfather passed away. The stone coffin in the crypt below testament to his longevity:

GERLOIS BÓRUMA O'HARE

A SON OF THE KINGDOM OF ORIEL

BORN 1372–DIED 1848.

Seventh son of any seventh son (for he was a third) had nothing to do with their long lives. *It was all in the jeans*, he said forcing a laugh.

Eighteen

WITH CHARLIE'S COFFIN NOW IN THE CHAPEL all that was left was the arrival of Sin's granddaughter, Gerty. At her pottery in Dublin she was expected to return to the castle today. A through and through Castle Rose woman, Gerty O'Sullivan had a husband, Clan. Sin smiled at the thought of her being married although he hadn't always thought well of the match between him and his granddaughter. The financial settlement from the man was useful though. He was thinking of the transfer of the property from the O'Sullivan's to the O'Hare's. Although the O'Hare's owned the property before the O'Sullivan's; and, but for a royal flush against his straight they may never have lost it in the first place. The luck of the Irish, eh! Not for all of them. At least, not all at the same time, Sin mused. Though to be fair, Clan O'Sullivan was an Irishman, and Castle Rose being the generous dowry it was, he looked on as poetic justice. He smiled to himself.

He swung his legs out of the bed and onto the floor pulling the bed covers off the woman lying with him. She whimpered pulling them back over herself. He downed what was left in the glass by his bedside table: the remnants of a whiskey from the night before, spilling it down the front of his legs. He looked at her, then pulling the sheet off of her he wiped his leg dry. Half asleep she complained. She turned over. Her night dress had risen up exposing her backside to the elements. He reached out and smacked it.

'Caffrey! Move your arse, I want me breakfast.'

She pulled the sheet over her exposed body and settled back down to sleep a little longer. The direction of the kitchen, with his demands for breakfast were not uppermost in her mind. Finding she couldn't settle she said, 'Do it yourself. Anyway, what's the rush?'

'Gerty!'

'Cleaned the chapel haven't you?'

He fiddled with his ear ring trying to play for time. 'Er, not exactly. Not yet.'

She sprung up. 'What's that supposed to mean?'

'Well . . . I've cleaned some of the leaves up. Nearly finished the catafalque.'

'He's not on the floor . . . SIN!'

'Of course he's not, what do you take me for. He's resting on a trolley, so he is. He'd be proud, so he would . . .'

'Yeh, I bet. Not as proud as Gerty's going to be though . . .'

'Erm . . . maybe . . . not as proud as Charlie . . .'

'Tell the truth now, you've made no attempt to clean the chapel have you?'

He smiled, 'Give us a hand there, Janice?'

She got out of bed.

'And you expect me to marry you. You must think me stupid. You're a bloody useless mess, Sin O'Hare. At least as housekeeper I'm paid. There's going to be nothing in it for my marrying you.'

'What about the sex?'

'I thought we were doing that already.'

'Well at least if we were married I couldn't be accused soliciting you.'

She turned and landed him a blow to the back of his head followed by another, and several more.

'Get off me woman, get off.'

'How dare you accuse me of being a prostitute. You damned, damn . . .'

'What?'

'Gypsy! An ill-mannered, hedgehog eating, horse dealing son-of-a . . .'

Her blows rained down on him while he, laughing, made playful attempts at protecting himself prodding at her with his finger.

'A horse dealing what?'

She ceased her assaults. She was breathing heavy. Considering his brown eyes she ran her hands down his rugged face and through his red hair before fingering his gold earring. He leaned towards her and kissed her forehead. Kneeling on the bed, he pulled his collarless shirt he had been sleeping in off over his head. She stared at him, grasped him around the neck and pulled him down onto her.

Below the upstairs bedroom, Ned McCoy, feeling plaster fall about his upturned to the ceiling face knew the frivolities were coming from the room over. The center of one of the ceiling joists, having long since seen better days, had over the years developed a spring in its step. This would have been unusual, if not impossible, had it have been replaced with oak, but there hadn't been any on the estate for years. Willow! In spades. Not wishing to take a chance on the ceiling coming down – it would only be a matter of time – he decided on a swift retreat. He dressed leaving the floor above to exercise itself in its own good time to the lover's usual cavorting tune – three times a week. Now there's a lucky boy.

McCoy was replacing the last of the screws into the oak door's hinges.

'There, give it a shove.'

Sin pulled the chapel door closed, shot the black bolt, released it, shot it again, releasing it once more he was satisfied the fifteenth century woodwork had been repaired.

'He was a bit of a celebrity, Charlie. In the States, you know?' Sin said. 'Gerty's been complaining about the wind whistling under this door for months now.'

'So I understand. I don't know how she prays here on her own, especially in the winter when its dark and all she has is a candle to light her way,' McCoy said.

'Faith, old friend. She has the faith. Nobody should be frightened inside of a church at night,' Sin said.

'Not the sinless, no.'

'No need to fear the inside of a house of the Lord when one's at one's devotions,' Sin went on. He was wrestling with thoughts from the night before when he was in here.

'So you don't even get a weird feeling with someone dead in here?' McCoy said.

Sin laughed, 'What's to fear? Thunnin' good keeper of Castle Rose I have in you, Ned McCoy. Frightened of the dark and the dead. We'll all be buried soon enough so you'll not have to worry about the dead then, only your Maker. Come on, let's get you out of here before your imagination runs across the courtyard leaving you for dead.'

McCoy hurried out. He had to admit to himself his imagination had got the better of him. That was Sin winding him up. He was half across the courtyard before Sin was leaving. The door still ajar Sin went to leave before turning around. The damned place was calling him back once again.

He looked around the walls. The old wooden pews in need of a rubdown and varnish were washed, the banners and battle insignia of past wars had been dusted down. Even the old battle flag of the Gaelic O'hEir, ancestors of the O'Hare's was, as always, still holding its color.

It had never needed cleaning. A chill ran up his spine. He shook his head saying to himself, *Bloody Ned. His imagination is bloody catching*. He closed the door allowing his eyes one last look.

But for all the reassurances he had given McCoy, there were ghosts here.

Ethereal ones! Not those below.

Nineteen

IT WAS AFTER MIDNIGHT. Sin wasn't sleeping. He thoughts were drawn to the chapel once again. He got up, he had to put his mind at ease. The castle was asleep. He wouldn't get a better opportunity. What he hoped to find: what he hoped not to find, with Charlie laying in state inside an old dark chapel, with ancestors in their progressed states of decomposition in its crypt below, in the middle of the night, he was not sure. God is our hope for the hopeless, he thought to himself.

He trod the gravel leading up to the tree line on to the chapel. The chapel door was open. Not by much. A crack did it. It had either blown open or someone had not closed it when they went out. He thought being the last out he would have remembered. He decided the wind had blown it open. A tingler of fear went down his spine. It would be too easy to shut the door and go back to the house. If he was going to get to the bottom of his anxiety, drive away the demons, so to speak, he was going to have to push on. He eased the oak door further open then startled. A spider walking toward the black iron door handle on its way home had gone across the back of his hand. He drew in a deep breath for relief and shook it off. *What's the matter with you, man?* He spoke the words out loud, more to give him confidence than for an answer for an actual assessment of his state of mind. He had to admit it wasn't in the best of condition at this moment. For reassurance over reason he called out the name of the only intruder that came to mind.

'Ned, you there?' He prayed for a reply.

The tingler returned. Involuntarily vibrating from the surface of his skin on his arms and legs before coming to rest along his bones. All of this, the emotions, the tremors, and . . . the frights, were unnatural responses to him; not part of his makeup. This was a first and he was far from enamored by it. There had to be a reason. Were they premonitions for sinister happenings to occur? He was known to be possessed of them.

'Ned! You there?' he called once more. A muffled echo of his own voice came back to him but no other. He was going to have to go in.

Charlie's coffin was undisturbed on its trolley. The ladder propped against the wall was where it has always been. At least to Gerty it was, who wondered if he was to ever get around to using it for what it was intended. Repairing the wood rot surrounding the cracked window was a possible suggestion for her to make to him. Already the ingress of wet had dampened the wall surrounding it threatening to put the whole frame out at any time. He looked along the wall when he noticed something out of place. One of the shields, the one having a deep crease across its center; the result of being struck by some spikey metal conker-wielding assailant in times past was missing its sword. One of a pair.

He took the torch from his pocket and flicked it on. Its artificial light danced from coffin to wall and back again. There was always the chance the sword had fallen from its mount onto the floor. Fallen from the shield from the vibrations of bringing the coffin in. He had to admit it had been a tight squeeze getting it in here. Perhaps it had bounced off the back of a pew and fallen between them. He ran the torch beam across the wooden floor. No sword there. Which left the gap between the skirting board and the floor running up to it. Another repair he hadn't quite got around to finishing, he thought. If it had fallen down there it would mean him having to go outside to the other side of the chapel and go in through the lower door into the crypt itself. Not a prospect he relished. Not this time of the night. He wasn't afraid of the dead, even so, who would go ferreting among them given the choice. If he turned his head to one side between the wall and the floor board and shone his torch down, there was always the chance to pick up the glint out from the rust of the sword's blade; come back when it was daylight and retrieve it.

He got down on his hands and knees. Whether he expected to find the weapon down there, or was looking from an act of bravado he couldn't say. Whether he would spend time down there searching would be another matter entirely. The point was, if anyone asked him if he had looked there, he had.

With the torch in his outstretched hand, he squeezed his head into the abyss. After brushing the musty dust from his eyes caused by his head being locked against the wall skirting and the floorboard he stared down. There was not so much as a glint from a coin. Gerty would pass round a collection plate on one of her special religious day ceremonies for the needy in the town. Had one fallen on the floor and rolled down through a crack. There was. A single washer. Well that's one tight bastard among the congregation, he thought. Only dust ridden cobwebs along with rotting coffins was all that was to see now. As he had already dealt with those, he would put them to the back of his mind once more.

He got braver.

For no rational reason he put his whole arm into the darkness and ran his hand underneath one of the flooring joists, fingering the knots and splinters as he went. Enough! Pulling his head back out, followed by his arm, he stood up to relieve the pain from arching his back. He stared back at the shield once more in the forlorn hope it was a figment of his imagination and the sword had returned to where it once hung.

There was the tingler again. There was the sword.

As if a magician, passing his hand over an empty space, causing a rabbit to appear from an empty top-hat, so had the sword, pinioned back into its holder over the shield. *By the Lord Puck, I was dreaming!* he said in a voice loud enough to wake those sleeping down below. It wasn't them he would need to worry about though, for he was in the full throes of fear now. He either needed a drink, or was suffering from its years of excesses. Either way he was going to have to get out of here. Here! he thought. The family chapel he had known all his life, no way! He would look through the glass portal into Charlie's coffin first. He would have to overcome the fear of seeing his face to check that he was alright. Overcoming his terror for such an outcome, he leaned across the coffin and stared through, his torch angled to one side.

God's sake! What now? he said in a voice loud enough for any wandering souls about once more to let any know he was not afraid, whatever state they were, and that he had a job to do. The lid of the coffin had been tampered with. Dead or alive – dead in the main, his demons would have to be faced down once and for all. For it would not have been anyone from the other side of death's veil that had carried out such an act. Nevertheless, Charlie was turned over onto his side, and that had not been done by any of his ancestors below ground. The hanging straps screwed to the top of the coffin to support the body while in a vertical position for transit, were unfastened. Had Scripps done this? Daniella? Surely not.

What have they done to you, Charlie? he asked attempting to remove the lid to put things right. A rhetorical question, for he was not expecting an answer.

It was the breeze of the sword blade took his concentration now.

Returned to its shield. The same weapon coming from the battle of Derry when the English raped and pillaged their way across Ireland in 1450. A hand-and-a-half, old and rusting, as he had seen it, was now a glinting weapon designed for slaying, which, from the half-light of a clouded moon shining in through a window in the chapel, was heading the height – assuming it continued the way of its wont – to slice his head from his shoulders in one fell swoop.

He ducked. He ducked quicker than he'd ever ducked in his life. And he'd done some ducking. From the law in the main. It was his head at stake here now – no question. And the lowering of which was his involuntary answer for its staying put on his shoulders.

Not giving any thought to his assailant he made an assault at the wall and the shield holding its twin. He pulled it away from its clip. Gripping it tight, he felt the pommel stop in his fist, spun the sword through 360 degrees, turned and held it in the parrying position ready for his assailant's next swing to take him through the skull. He was right. His opponent's sword was a thunderbolt, gliding down his own blade in a stream of sparks not stopping until it hit the cross guard.

He twisted and leapt a forward pew, ran down the seat and jumped out into the aisle. Now at least he had room to maneuver. Any thoughts of stopping the assailant were not uppermost in his mind right now, getting out of here in one piece and making a run for it was. For this was a match swordsman familiar with the weapon, while he, more handier with a shotgun; not unimpressed with his own abilities and chances to fight the good fight and win, now had his doubts as to any good outcome. Not sporting, he knew, but dying for no reason he could imagine became his reasonable thought. All academic now, for he didn't have a shot gun to hand.

He screamed out for McCoy in the forlorn hope he, or anyone nearby, could help him. Not that anyone would hear his cries at this time of night. The worst of it was, he would go down fighting his corner knowing not the reason why. For whoever this was had already drawn blood this morning. It was wet on the floorboard close to the coffin. Drawing on his adrenalin, he tightened his teeth, let out a scream, took the sword over his head and crashed it down into the enemy coming out of the darkness at him. He missed his target by a mile and stumbling out between the pews, his assailant was now opposite him in the aisle. Out of the darkness he went rolling under a pew, and came up the other side. Here he saw his assailant. A woman! Not any woman.

Who in the name of Puck are you? he screamed at her. She was to all intent naked. This woman possessed all the body curves of her femininity, none of a woman's . . .

Who are you? he shouted once more.

She wasn't going to answer him. She was not of his world and he knew it. Nor was she from the world of the dead. Somewhere higher.

She held the sword over him now, height ready to strike him down. He had no chance against this. She was going to kill him for sure. Coming out from between the pews he held his sword firm, the rusting excuse for a weapon up against what she had in her hands. A gleaming representation of a weapon handcrafted by Vulcan himself, and one he imagined, some would be proud of dying by. If they were of that mind-set. He wasn't. There was a tunnel under the crypt leading back to the castle, if he rolled himself across the floor, drop down the old steps, he could make an escape. The chance came and went. An idle thought, was now too late, unless. Not unless . . .

He lunged at her. A last desperate attack stance with a rigid straight arm and driving the rusty relic forward at her. She parried causing him to lose his grip. The sword clanged onto the stone floor. He was done. She had the weapon point at his throat. In the vain hope of slowing the inevitable he stepped backwards falling over an old hassock as he did so. His fight done he lay on the floor between the pews. If it wasn't before, the game was up now. He closed his eyes and waited for the hot metal point to sear into his thorax giving him pain of death. He lay there, his eyes closed, his chest heaving, as the seconds counted down until they had numbered too many for what would have been a reasonable time for a conquering adversary to run him through. He opened his eyes. Fearful of seeing his point of death playing out in real time he had no need to worry. She was changed. Standing over him was how he imagined a ministering angel looking. The whole of his body and thoughts went into an ecstasy he had never ever experienced before. Far beyond even a sexually climatic orgasm. He closed his eyes. If this was an application for his death presenting itself, then pass me a pen and ink. Where do I sign?

It was over.

He opened his eyes. She was gone.

Shaking he went to Charlie's coffin. His mouth dropped in horror. The lid had been replaced. He looked through the viewing window. Charlie was looking as normal as any other man dead in his coffin, except the fastening straps that had been interfered with were now back in place. Although bravado had overcome fear it hadn't prevented his heart beat racing. His feelings were that this episode was far from fully written.

After the excitement he fancied one of them needed to get out of here and get a drink. As the only living soul here, it had to be himself. He made his way down the aisle of the chapel. The moonlight showing through the broken stain of the window across Charlie's coffin although giving of an eerie feel, was now no longer something he should be frightened of. He bent down and picked up the sword replacing it into the retaining clip over the shield. What about the other damned sword that's missing, he thought. What plans has she for that one?

He made his way out of the chapel, closing the door as he went. He locked and moved the door back and forth making sure if there was anyone here they would be locked up until morning. What was he thinking. There would be no interment until whatever had gone on here had been put to bed. How he was going to achieve that without exorcising the ghost he had little idea.

The morning sun came up reflecting off the dust from the inside of the chapel, its rays of light in bars picked across the trolley. On top of the coffin, indiscernible from the sunlight she sat. *H*er eyes towards the chapel door. Cross legged, head bowed, she was clenching the sword. Its point dug deep into the coffin lid. The weapon she had come close to killing the mortal, while safeguarding her Creator's data must now be used for defending herself from the one appearing before her now.

Predator Guardian by passed −EVT crossing the Time−Verse directly into Sentinel Mother. Using part based mathematical and plausible universal scientific concepts then converting to a p-code binary language she downloaded her ultimatum:

You are not of this Verse. ALPHA OMEGA does not recognize your use of technology for advancement of life. Neither will He. The technology used to drive your world has been manipulated. You have misguided your race into believing that technology emanates from you. It does not. That manipulation is now your world's downfall. ALPHA OMEGA is still your First and Last Lord. Cloning human biology into robots is not sustainable beyond a

hundred millennium. The capacity to upload the program data
for creation will not mend your Time–Verse. We have isolated –
EVT. Without capacity for human emotion your Time–Verse is
at the point of closure.

–EVT read Predator Guardian. –EVT arrived in this verse as a powerful being. Downloading these observations, passing them through the matrix of Time–Verse reprogramming them back to – EVT's Time–Verse updating for the destruction of this Predator Guardian failed. –EVT was confronting her and it had no way to respond. –EVT sought guidance from Sentinel Mother to take this guardian down. Sentinel Mother had disengaged. –EVT was isolated from Sentinel Master and Sentinel Mother.

    –EVT would not be able to engage Predator Guardian.

    Sentinel Mother would think again.

Twenty

DUMPING HER CLODAGH wrap kilt unceremoniously into the garden sink, Gerty filled it with cold water. Sensing someone behind her she turned.

'You're back,' Caffrey said.

'I am.'

'When?'

'About four this morning. Everything all right?'

Janice hugged and kissed her on the cheek. 'And did you get the pot order finished?'

'I did. All packed and on its way to America. It was touch and go though. And Sin?'

'In the chapel finishing off cleaning.'

'Left it late as usual. I take it the remains of his uncle has arrived.'

'Last evening.'

'Good. I've heard a lot of him, although I never did get to meet him. He was a little removed from us, family-wise, so I'm not so emotionally involved as Sin,' Gerty said. 'Still, we're obliged as a family, however distant, to do our duty as we see it. Did Sin fix the chapel door?'

'As I said, along with the cleaning.'

Gerty laughed. 'I suppose he and McCoy have been out poaching and generally loafing around while I've been away?'

Janice thought what an absentminded, layabout Sin was at

times before sinking into deeper thoughts about him and what he really thought of her?

Gerty studied her. Janice often went into herself when it came to talking about Sin. Their relationship was not normal, and she wondered how long it would last. Some not knowing the couple would take it bizarre. To put it crude – grave-snatching. Plenty of women fall for men older than themselves, but a hundred years, that was bordering on the absurd. Gerty had reservations about Janice and Sin's relationship, resolved into a state of rationale open to all possibilities. The family harbored a different species of human being here. A throwback to Genesis and the Old Testament. Sons of Abraham. Some living a normal span of life while others, 2, 3, 400 years of age was her explanation, she had told herself. He is what he is, and discussion on the topic with him often led to tales of witchcraft – the devil himself. For the seventh son of a seventh son, carries burdens we couldn't even begin to imagine. Sometimes he wishes he were normal.

'No, not poaching. The other.'

Janice watched Gerty plunge her hands up to their elbows into the sink. The cold water had dissolved most of the clay up her arms. Her mind dismissing her relationship with Sin, she returned to the real world of household chores.

'What you doing there, Gerty? I'll wash those, I'm sure you've more important work needing your attention.'

'Clay from the wheel. It sprays everywhere, gets into the tartan. Bit of a nuisance. But, it's part of the act the public seem to approve. Makes them think I'm a throwback from a bog village.'

'It's as well you've not got your grandfather in the shop with you, one look at him will convince anyone you are.'

She laughed happy to change her thoughts.

'Did our Mary get herself to school all right?'

'Yes, packed off. When I prised her from Sin's arms.'

'He dotes on her. If he had his way she wouldn't go to school at all. He believes Gypsy ways are all that's needed, but as I often tell him the world's no longer a place for traveling folk.'

'Well, with the troubles over, your husband will have the time to become a better influence on her now.'

'Do you think so, Janice? I'm not so sure. Those troubles have been with us a long time now. What with being away from us, now spending time in Europe, he'll have even less now. He never did hand in his weapons when the IRA called a ceasefire you know. For someone working in the European parliament I find a worrying irony there,' Gerty said.

'As you said, those troubles have been with us a long time now. You can't expect 600 years of conflict with the English to go away. It takes time. You know it. You're of this country,' Janice replied.

Gerty loved Clan with a passion which hadn't diminished since they had first met at the Cahirmee horse fair. An annual event she, her mother, father and grandfather went – until her mother and father, mistaken for terrorists, were shot down and killed by the British army at a border crossing. Sin, her nearest blood relative left to look after her, had been super protective to her from what he called, predatory Irishmen. He put energy into keeping the interested Clan O'Sullivan interested in Gerty for her sake rather than his own. He did not altogether trust the man at first. Clan was from landowning stock, a gambler who won everything – including Castle Rose. A dowry to be later exchanged with the marriage. Convinced he was honorable and good enough for her hand, he conceded. And now a child. Sin, happy in the knowledge Gerty and Clan's daughter, the redhaired, double plaited, with a smile as broad as Loch Garman,

Mary, would continue in spirit pedaling around the great hall of the castle on her little blue tricycle until the end of time.

Sin was in the dining room. He had finished his meal when Janice came in and took his plate. She looked at Gerty.

'Are you ready for yours?'

'I am. Grandad!'

Sin looked up at Gerty. He had the face like a chitted potato.

'You okay, you've hardly said a word since I got back. What's the crack?'

He nodded and made an attempt at a smile. Who in hell would know he'd had a sword fight in the chapel the night before? Thankfully, it was not him she was attempting to slay. Taking up a glass of water he took a sip. 'A little under the weather, that's all. You know me. By the way, I took a call earlier. A guy calling himself Coxly Hess. Said he's with the CIA or was it the FBI, anyway, one of those. He asked if we'd come across a computer hard drive which may have come over with some of Charlie's belongings. Apparently it belongs to the United States government,' Sin said.

'A hard drive? Have you asked Mr. Scripps?'

'He handed over Charlie's old clothes and books. His bank cards and some personal items – letters, pictures. Nothing of significance. While I think of it I'd better call the bank and get them canceled,' Sin replied.

'Did he say what was on it?'

'Some details about old police operations Charlie had been involved. He said we weren't to worry if it wasn't here, it's probably in his office in New York,' Sin replied. 'By the by, did you say you'd be going across to the chapel to pay your respects later?'

'I'd better have. He needs welcoming with a prayer. Don't suppose you said one for him?' She looked at him. 'No, didn't think you had. Fr. Donavan has agreed to conduct later this evening.'

Sin nodded approval.

'Well, you'll be glad to know we've fixed the door. If you want me to come too, don't want the pair of you falling over in the dark.'

'Won't be necessary.'

'No, I want to come,' he said.'

She shrugged. 'When does Clan get back from Brussels?'

'Tomorrow.'

'I expect you've missed him. He's been gone a month.'

She nodded as Janice put her meal in front of her.

'Get some fishing done, after the wake.'

'And no doubt some horse trading. By the way, he's bringing a new suit for you with him. All the way back from Belgium. Can't have you looking like an out of work leprechaun much longer. Not in front of family and friends.'

He stood up with a hurt look on his face.

'What's the matter with the way I'm dressed, I am known as the King of the Leprechaun's in these parts?'

'Do you really need an answer?' She looked at Janice and shook her head. 'How many times has Janice asked you to get some new clothes?'

'Wasted my time, so I did,' Janice interrupted, 'I don't know about the King of the Leprechaun's. A Rolling Stone with a bad hair day.'

He feigned hurt. 'I'll speak with you girls later.'

He walked out to the tune of their sniggering.

Fr. Patrick Donovan from Graiguenamanagh, was standing by the lych gate leading to the chapel when Gerty and Janice arrived. Janice unlocked the door and pushed it open to let them through.

'Thank you for coming at such short notice, Father.' Gerty said.

'Not at all,' Fr. Donovan replied.

Gerty had never been one to use an electric torch when she came to pray in here, preferring instead the simplicity of flame on candle. Side by side they each walked passed the coffin of Charlie and knelt at the altar. Fr. Donovan lit two candles placed earlier on the altar by Sin and begun his liturgy:

'Lord, the death of our loved one . . .'

The words were no sooner out of Fr. Donovan's mouth when a lightning strike hit, followed half a second later by a clap of thunder which struck over the chapel threatening to take the medieval roof tiles from its beams.

'What the fuck was that?' Sin said forgetting where he was.

Fr. Donovan looked up into the roof beams.

'Is everyone happy for me to continue?' he said to the small gathering.

'Yes, you'd better had,' Sin said. 'I'll get Ned to check the roof later. Sorry for the language,' he said turning to Gerty.

'. . . has hit us hard. Ours was a relationship stretching across other lands. A friendship and its death is beyond value, and we find memories of him in many places. His passing has made us aware of our own mortality and challenges our faith. Yet, we hope in you, Lord. Your power over death with the rewards of your promised Kingdom to come the only consolations we can find at these difficult times. Maintain our love to all of those who cared for our friend and help us to be a source of support and comfort to each and all. Amen.'

'Amen.'

'Amen.'

They all crossed themselves and stood up.

Gerty opened her eyes and turned to the Father. 'Will you take a nightcap before you leave? Sin, lock up will you?'

Fr. Donovan nodded that he would. He was also relieved nothing more than a freak thunderstorm had hit, as opposed to the hand of God striking him down and missing for previous sins.

'Leave the candles to burn down, granddad. It's a bad omen to extinguish them only to use them once more,' Gerty said. 'And this place could still do with another sweep.'

Sin nodded. Still mindful of his out of place profanity, he smiled at the Father. He then hurriedly ushered them out in readiness to lock up. He watched them going through the front door of the castle. Now with the key in his hand, he looked back inside the chapel. He was still wary. His eyes were drawn to the temporary catafalque. They didn't linger. His mindset was on the leaves that had blown back in under the door now. *Yes, another broom in here I think*, he said out loud in the vain hope that any mythical slayers fancying their chances with him would think twice. He could not get out of his mind the beautiful woman with the long hair sitting on Charlie's coffin, her arms around her knees as if holding vigil. Of course, she was not Aoife, the warrior princess from Irish legend he was familiar from his days of studying Irish history. This one was from another place he was scarce able to say. An angel, if such existed. Charlie's guardian angel. A companion for ones final journey into the unknown. *Fairyland? Heaven?* What was it to be? Despite his Catholic upbringing he had a leanness of soul when it came to Christianity's heaven, preferring the Celtic Tír na hÓige or Land of Youth for any eternal rest he may be entitled, his life curse, in death likely more conducive to the young rather than the old.

She was a faded and imaginative apparition now. He spoke the words he had used more times than enough to justify and comfort his own condition when needed, *There are more things in heaven and earth, Horatio, than are dreamt of in your philosophy, and all that.*

With the illumination from the two candles shining over the coffin he pulled the door closed, this time locking it.

A Moriarty taxi drew up outside the castle the following morning.

'Here we are, sir. Dracula's Haunt.'

Fitch got out and paid the driver off. He picked up his case and overnight bag, and walked up to the front door. A black painted affair with reinforced iron bandings, tipped with square studded bolts sent an unexpected chill through him. With the taxi driver's words in his mind regarding this Prince of Darkness's abode (frivolous advice he didn't need, for hadn't he seen Satan for real). He summoned up the courage and in true, Our car's broken down and we need to use your telephone fashion he lifted the unpolished brass moulded knocker of a fox with a chicken in its mouth and banged it down. He was taken aback. The door was answered so quickly it seemed the servant was hiding behind it waiting for a delivery, instead of which, he had two empty milk crates in his hands. He placed these on the doorstep and looked up at him.

The man was wearing – *Abishter!* he said under his breath – skin tight black trousers with thin white stripes, a too shortened black jacket looking as if it had been stolen from a waiter along with his trousers. Neither having been tailored at the same time as they had white stripes of a differing width down their length. He studied his shirt. A white cotton affair, having no regular collar, enhanced (for want of a better description) with a pearl stud piercing it. The bottom of the shirt, part in and part out of his trouser waistband, which kind of matched a pair of pointed soft black low leather boots, having one inside his trouser bottom and the other outside the leg of the other. A shock of red hair and a rugged face showed to him the look of an Irish Gypsy.

Fitch said, 'I'm . . .'

He paused while he tried to decide whether this man was a servant or a stable hand.

'Can I help you, Mr. I Am?' Sin said.

'Hamilton Fitch.' The man showed bewilderment toward him. 'Charlie O'Hare's funeral. I was expected. Although it was short notice.'

'Ahhhhg! You'd be his colleague from the police, so you will. Please come. GERT!' He opened the door wider for him to enter, 'GERTY! A GUEST!'

'Not the police, no. I'm a newspaper man.'

Sin put his hand on his shoulder ushering him inside.

'Come in, come in, you're very welcome. GERTY! Charlie said you'd be here, and we were to make you welcome.' He hesitated. 'Of course we would. I mean. Before he passed away. Come with the coffin, didn't you? Newspaper man you say, you didn't work with Charlie?' Still thinking about the reference to Charlie telling him he was expected, he acknowledged he did come over with the coffin. 'Good . . . GERTY! Sorry about this only it's a big place, full of echoes if you call for anyone. Know what I mean?' He repeated his cry.

Fitch stepped into the hallway. Distracted by the sound of footsteps above him he looked up to see a woman at the top of the stairs. She was, best description, amply proportioned. Smiling at him through a rounded and ruddy face she gave an immediate welcome ease to him. She was wearing a chunky knit pullover, a kilt held up with a canvas belt, a bum bag in front, with what appeared to him to be a small dagger hanging from it. As women went, he thought, she was an all-round formidable person, with a pleasant demeanour, matching the servant opening the door for him.

'Did you call earlier? About a hard drive. Coxly Hess!'

Fitch's thought processes went into over-drive. CIA. Hard drive.

'No, sorry to disappoint, I'm Hamilton Fitch.'

The woman came down the last of the stairs and walked across the hall to greet him. 'I'm Sin's granddaughter, second cousin to Charlie. No, no disappointment, I'm pleased to meet you, Mr. Fitch.'

'Please, call me Hamilton. Charlie's second cousin you say. Do you know what, all the time we knew Charlie. All the time we worked with him. Well, he never let on he had a family. Tommy Scripps' mentioned there was a Sin O'Hare living here. His uncle?'

'He does. He's my grandfather,' she smiled. 'That's him. The scruff-bag standing next to you.'

Fitch stared at Sin O'Hare. The man he took for a servant was, Charlie's uncle. His father's brother. How could that be? The man didn't look a day over forty. He reckoned the math. If this Gerty lady was right, that would make him 130 if he was a day. *Oy vey!* They must have been drinking from the same bottle.

Gerty watched him doing the figures in his head. Sin had been so long getting to his years he never considered his great age as anything other than ordinary any longer. She took control of the family enigma.

'God! Sin. You losing your marbles? You're not Charlie's uncle,' she lied, 'you're his nephew. You trying to frighten Mr. Fitch, he'll be thinking you're on your way to two hundred instead of sixty.' She changed the subject, 'Was there to be a lady with you? Scripps mentioned two of you were coming over. Your colleague, wife?'

'There was, yes. Sister Marie was called away on important business in Rome.'

'To Rome! Now did you hear that, Sin? Rome, is it? Our Charlie mixed with people in Vatican circles.'

'Well, I don't believe Sister Marie ever considered herself part of the Vatican's hierarchy. She was a Carmelite nun until she became employed in their library. She's left the order now. She would have liked to have been here, but contented herself with being at his funeral, so it's not too much of a disappointment for her.'

'Ah! Right. A pity, so it is.'

He put to the back of his mind events at Kennedy. Carter had been called away for an important meeting, not Rome on this occasion though. She had been asked to attend the President at the White House for a report of what they had witnessed at the time O'Hare's coffin was being loaded onto a plane. Stories of an Alien wreaking havoc in New York were now abroad. Now it was rumored to have made an appearance at JFK the public were no longer swallowing news reports of any Iron Man or a Disney Fantasia movies being made. Quelling the potential for panic in the streets was now to be a challenge for Homeland Security.

Sin lay on his bed. He was convinced there was danger in the chapel. He should never have allowed Gerty and Janice to pray in there. But how could he have done that without going on to explain his being attacked by a woman with no clothes, no feminine identifiers, wielding a sword about willy-nilly. Sexual fantasies will get you into a lot of trouble in the real world. Still, they can't as yet do you for what you're thinking.

Four the following morning and he'd given up trying to sleep. He was going to have to face those demons once more. He eased the bolt of the oak door across. Waking Gerty or Janice, given his non-track record for starting work early in the day, would take some explaining. Still, with a broom and dust pan to hand. . . . He shone the torch inside and directed the beam around the walls and the floor, in fact, anywhere the guardian had chased his arse to put him to the sword. With nowhere else to go he shone it on the coffin. Holding the beam directly into the glass view port he drew in a deep breath. *As it should be*, he sighed relieved. Feeling reassured he went inside to his first port of call. Broom in hand he looked through the glass window set in the coffin lid. He shuddered. Charlie's face, ashen white stared up at him without movement. He whispered, *It's all right, Charlie, the cleaner's here*. He tapped the coffin more for his own peace of mind than the corpse and began sweeping.

The candles used the evening before by all of them were long since burned down. He made his way along the chapel's aisle sweeping as he went until he had a heap big enough to shovel into a sack. Pinpointing the walls with their memorial plaques and old paintings of the Sullivan's and the O'Hare's their families went back a time, fighting with each other for most of them. Bloody battles over bloody nothing other than bloody pride for bloody power and glory. Oh yes, the evidence was there that this was an armory containing implements for killing over show. Battle shields hanging with matching axes and long past rusting armour . . . and double-handed . . . *Sword! Fuck me, where's it got to now?*

He sensed he was not alone and that somebody was behind him. He spun around expecting a final fight. One to the death, for him at least, for he wasn't armed. He made to run to the wall to pull the other rusting implement from its mount stopped and turned. She wasn't after him. In point of fact she was ignoring him, the object of her attentions elsewhere in this universe, for she was sitting across the coffin cross-legged with the point of the sword dug into its woodwork once more. And for sure she was not expecting any challenge from him. The proverbial mere mortal was either too old to contest her, or she was waiting for an opponent that would put up a proper fight.

Twenty-one

'STAND THERE, AND DON'T GO OUTSIDE THE GATE. Your father will be along shortly.'

She scraped her unlaced shoe against the edge of the step.

The school house matron smiled, 'Don't do that dear, you'll scuff them. I'm sure he'll be along any moment.' She waited for affirmation but received none, the girl was too preoccupied roughing the nap off her shoe leather.

As the person, responsible for the pastoral well-being of her charges – the world came too fast for young ladies – this one had been granted special leave. Mother, father, brother or sister was more in keeping for a funeral, not for a great grandniece she thought. What possible benefit would a funeral be to a nine-year-old's frame of mind of someone so old and distant she had no way of judging, having never had a biological child to care for? While this girl's family was one of the oldest in the country, a virtual fiefdom by all account, she was in no position to express her view.

Mary O'Sullivan had gathered around a following of friends. She was popular. And although, not the only redhaired girl at St. Boniface's Preparatory (for boarders – *Ut Prosim*), she was the only one: double plaited. A smiling, happy-go-lucky girl; perhaps the death of a great grand uncle was closer to her than the matron imagined.

Clan O'Sullivan arrived by way of a sweeping entrance through the double ornate gates. Driving over the sleeping policemen humped up out of the gravel to slow vehicles down, along with its accompanying hand painted red lettering proclaiming, Five Mile An Hour Limit. Children Playing, he ignored it continuing to speed at 20 miles an hour.

The house matron saw him arrive first. She called the headmaster by telephone. He was awaiting this important parent in the lodge office. Arnold Barningham MA, was giving a final polish to his shoes, each at a time, down the lower half of his suit trouser legs.

Not one for overlooking a visit from a dignitary even if it was for no more than the formality of collecting a daughter, Barningham was out of the lodge and down the steps and at the girl's side. He placed his hand on the head of Mary with a satisfied grin and a look on his face of, Look how I've cared for your precious daughter, sir.

'Daddy!' Mary ducked herself from under her charge's hand running to her father to the dismay of headmaster Barningham, who, wishing for a more dignified hand over felt himself slighted.

'She's ready for you, Mr. O'Sullivan,' he called after her. 'Sorry it's under sad circumstances.'

Clan met his hand.

'Hello, Barningham. I trust she's been little trouble—'

He opened his arms in an act of ingratiating submission, 'Not at all. One of our brightest . . .'

'Thank you, Barningham.' He turned to Mary. 'Have you everything? Case.' He looked at the headmaster, 'Homework!'

She shook her head.

'Let's go. Barningham. Thanks.'

Clan opened the car door and let her inside. Closing it he got into the driver's side, waved his hand, and drove out of the school grounds into the main thoroughfare of traffic.

Barningham, turned to the house matron now at his side.

'I would have expected a member of the European parliament to have wheels more prestigious than a mere Renault Megane ... wouldn't you?'

Gerty finished reading the bedtime story for Mary. She had not waited for the ending having already fallen asleep. Gerty kissed her forehead and pulling the duvet up under her chin turned her bedside light down. She walked off down the corridor towards the stairs leading into the great hall below.

Twenty-two

THE EVENTS OF THE NIGHT came home to Sin in a way he had not expected. A series of fears from what had occurred had sapped the life out of him. Morning now, nine thirty. He was going to have to make a show of getting up and presenting himself for breakfast before people started getting suspicious. Despite his wealth, it was not unknown for him to have gone poaching in the middle of the night for rabbit, or pheasant on neighbours' land. You take the man from the Gypsy, you cannot take the Gypsy out of the man.

Tomorrow was supposed to be Charlie's wake, and he feared more acts of spiritual intervention were to follow. Against what though? He had fought with an angel of death for no understandable reason. As for the coffin lid, well, it didn't unscrew itself; the body of Charlie hadn't been unfastened from its restraining strap by itself; and there was blood on the floor. For sure, it wasn't hers. Not unless they carried it with them to whatever form of afterlife they came. And that's always assuming she came from a life we would recognize. As for the blood under the coffin, it could have belonged to Charlie. Which posed another question.

Which brought him back to her. Was she here to defend Charlie? Against what? Ah . . . hang on there, Sin boy . . . you'll have to reconsider that thought. Run it through a glass of whiskey or three!

He had not mentioned the incident to Gerty as he kissed her on the cheek. He would take a chance on her likely response if a naked spectre were to run amok slaying mourners with a sword from the chapel for his denying any knowledge of her. If he was to mention it now, she would not believe him, saying he had been too heavy on the whiskey. What would there be to say other that it was all a dream. *A dream! Some hope there*. He was of a great age, but he wasn't suffering delusions. What he experienced was what he had always known. The spirit world was closer than most realized, and this would not have been their first calling card as far as he was concerned. Delusion was never going to be an issue where the dead and their masters inhabited. Whatever this was, Charlie O'Hare would have known of it. Fortunately my saving grace is being an O'Hare. Not everyone this day would be of my stock, he thought. Some would be O'Sullivan's. He smiled to himself before the funny side left him.

Janice shouted for him bringing him back into the land of reality.

'Clan's arrived. Can you tell Gerty, Sin? I've things to do.' She passed through the breakfast room grabbing a piece of toast from the table spooning a dollop of scrambled egg onto it as she went, then, briefly stopping to consider his blank face added, 'Did you hear what I said, O'Hare?' Taking a hurried bite at the toast she dropped egg down the front of her. She shook her head at her clumsiness then brushed it off with her apron all the while looking at Sin's blank expression. Unable to get any response from him she shook her head and called him a lost cause. She went out the door as Ned McCoy was coming in. A co-conspirator in Sin's expression if ever there was one, she thought. She smiled at him as they brushed past each other. 'Sort the sad sack out will you, Ned!'

McCoy asked, 'Did you want me, boss? Problem?'

Sin's expression showed more concern than worry. He looked at McCoy. Did he? 'No you're all right, Ned.'

McCoy went to go out the door. He had a look of hesitancy about him. 'Sure? . . . I'll carry on then.' Sin's smile wasn't convincing. 'While I think of it, boss.' Sin looked up. 'There's blood on the stone floor by the coffin, did you cut yourself?'

Clan came into the breakfast room with Mary at his side.

'Clan. Coffee? Back in one piece – and Mary. How are you my little precious?' Sin asked. 'Come and give me a kiss.'

She went to him and put the side of her cheek out to him. 'Hello, great granddad.'

'Hey! What are they feeding you on at that school of yours, Scottish oats?' He looked at O'Sullivan. 'She's grown.'

'She certainly has. More and more into her mother, so she has,' O'Sullivan replied adoringly. He put Mary's case on a chair. 'Run along and find you mother, Mary. Daddy wants a word with Sin.' Sin sat down and poured two coffees. 'What is it, Sin? Gerty seems to think this funeral's getting to you.'

'Can you break me out a weapon, Clan. Something with a bit more beef than a shotgun?'

There had been little point in keeping it to himself. Whatever she was, despite what was missing, she had every appearance of being mortal. He mentally tossed a coin as to who he would tell. Ned or Clan? Gerty had not come into the equation. She had enough on her plate. And Clan, being an ex-IRA activist, was more than capable if trouble reared its ugly head. He hadn't handed all his weapons in, so he figured, a woman with a double handed sword would be little match for someone prepared to use a small automatic light rifle on them. Of course, that would have to be weapon of last resort were it needed, before any mourners arrived. Otherwise thoughts they'd been brought here not so much for a wake more as retribution for some misdemeanor or other of which there were plenty to be had. There was bound be a traitor in their midst. One with thoughts of revenge against them, trigger happy enough to jump the gun; laying waste to guests and family alike, ensuring wakes for the next twenty years. No, that wouldn't do at all, Sin thought.

He finished telling Clan over a pot of coffee. He laughed. More so after the description he gave of the woman. Clan's consideration of a woman bared of female genetalia sitting cross-legged on Charlie's coffin was a difficult picture to conjure. He was winding him up, surely.

'You come out with a fairy tale and expect people to swallow it. You say you hadn't been drinking, well tell someone who knows you, they'll think you're having a laugh.'

'I'm telling you I hadn't – had a drink I mean. God alone knows what would have happened if it had shown itself the evening Gerty and Janice had their mini service with Fr. Donovan.'

Clan could see Sin was not himself. His option, given all these circumstances, cancel the wake? And what excuse for not giving a reason would he use without telling Sin's version of events. In the normal run of life's trials and tribulations Sin was up there with the optimists. Now, he was questioning his sanity.

'Forget I mentioned it. We'll carry on and hope for the best.'

'It's not a question of you mentioning it, or hoping for the best. It's putting your delusions to the rest of the family. What do you expect them to do? Gerty! What do you think she's going to make of it?' Clan said. 'And what do you want a weapon for? If it's a ghost, apparition, call it what you like, shooting up a creature that's not flesh and blood is not going to get you anywhere.'

'It was flesh and blood when we clashed swords! There's blood on the carpet, so to speak.'

Twenty-three

FATHER PATRICK DONOVAN officiated in the manner of a novice fresh out of Donegal Roman Catholic Church of Teaching. To him a wake was a ceremony of closure to life no matter the spin of joviality some put on it. It was no different from any other funeral. Whether disposal into the ground or firing up the gas at a crematorium to him they were all the same. The delay in proceedings between closure and burial academic. As far as he was concerned, man or woman, they were off this mortal coil at heart's last beat. The ritual was no more than a tidying up. A throwing away of a shell no longer needed.

As for the saving of souls to a place of celestial beauty, to him, all the pontificating, all the philosophy the books and manuscripts from some of the sharpest minds humans were capable of producing was no more than wishful thinking. For all the visions of saints and sinners, the crying statues of Madonna in stone and flesh, all this and more and not one shred of evidence an afterlife was any more a reality than a life before. A death we have all gone through since time before birth. Before being or after being. What difference was there? Waiting for arrival or departure, both lounges were filled to capacity.

Fr. Donovan could not remember when he had first doubted his faith. Although. He had feelings. Those drawn to children. He deluded himself into believing he had not interfered with any of them, only touch them in a loving way commiserate with God's understanding. At the start it was photographs. Exercising a carnal lust with himself became less and less satisfying, it would only be a matter of time before the face of Satan turned towards him, as the face of God looked away.

Religious formalities done and dusted the guests moved out of the chapel in a procession carrying the coffin of Charlie ahead and back to the castle and its great hall where all had been set for the wake.

A hostess in a starched white blouse was giving out clay pipes stuffed with tobacco for the mourners. Fitch tried to pass without taking one. She was having none of it. She reached between two guests ensuring he would not miss out. He smiled and thanked her. While looking at it, wondering what he was to do with it someone clapped him on the shoulder offering a taper to light the pipe and a glass of whiskey to light his soul. Thanking him, and not wishing to offend, Fitch sucked on the pipe drawing in a lungful of smoke. He had a burning cough. Tipping the whiskey down his throat for relief made it worse.

He watched as a small gathering of men manhandled Charlie's coffin into an upright position in the corner of the room. They took off the lid then replaced it with another that had a half hinged door. He shuddered. Before him was his friend, not looking as he once did in life for he seemed to be older now. Although he knew this was going to happen the reality was far more than he imagined. The sight of him dressed in a suit, wearing a bowler-hat took his breath away. In this position his arm was casually set on the lower part of the coffin lid. Tradition demanded a glass of whiskey was to be placed in his hand and a clay pipe put between his lips. The contrast between his blue lips and the white of the stem of the pipe was apparent. With that done, Sin O'Hare, with the clay pipe lady on his arm, called the congregation to order:

'Ladies, gentlemen, will you please charge your glasses with your appropriate tipple. Ah, that'll be whiskey, then.'

There was a general swigging of what had remained before their glasses were re-charged by several hostesses moving among them. When he was satisfied everyone had a full glass Sin called in a loud voice, 'I give you our kinsman from across The Pond, Mr. Charlie O'Hare, FBI.' He turned to the coffin and with all their glasses raised he called out in a loud voice, 'CHARLIE!'

A murmur of his name went around followed by a cheer. Fitch self-consciously did the same, putting away his whiskey in one swallow to ease the cough still hanging in his throat. Up until this point he had allowed the clay pipe to settle in his mouth and hand. With the conviviality of the company he felt able to smoke it. He was beginning to understand the meaning of a wake and was fast coming around to the tradition.

An applause went up as small band struck up with, If Your Irish . . . to great applause. As the evening moved on guests sang. An accordionist and violinist played. Nodding in time with the music and the infusion of whiskey and pipe smoke, Sin, began dancing with Janice. A dance Fitch took to be Irish judging by the flashing footsteps. He smiled remembering the occasion he first saw Charlie doing the same when he was alive. He had been rather good at it as a boy. Sin – now too out of breath – waved for an excuse me. Gerty took him up. Not a slim woman, nevertheless, she came to the dance with gusto, giving Janice a run for her money. Her footwork below her Clodagh kilt, now lifted from her lower legs to allow better movement, was electrifying. The pair danced as if in one mind, looking at each other for the next jam. Only when the glass of whiskey Charlie was holding jumped from his hand and smashed on the floor did it end.

The band in a cacophony of disorganized musical notation left the flautist to finish the piece in a bad ending.

—EVT dispensed a seeking probe into the body of the human being. It took a trillionth of a billionth of a second before hitting a wall of physics the Alien was not programmed to counter. The probe vaporized. An unexpected fire wall had been put in place. Reacting in half the time, White Bear Angel returned the probe to its source with an attached virus. The Alien's program was paralyzed. Having no capacity for a counter assault. —EVT disengaged.

Janice and Gerty ceased their dancing.

Sin felt a spirit passing through the world using him as a conduit. Up until Charlie's arrival his sensitivity to ghostly phenomenon was negligible, not anymore. He looked at Clan. The look on his face was showing he was feeling it.

Clan seized the moment.

'And that wouldn't have been the first time Charlie O'Hare has tried to catch the eye of a bartender to get a drink,' he said trying to lighten the mood others in the room felt. For something had gone through here and it wasn't alcohol. He gestured for a hostess to pour him another glass of whiskey. Taking it he put it in Charlie's hand. There was an eerie silence from the shocked guests before they picked up the thread once more continuing with the wake.

Mary had been allowed to stay up for the evening. She was standing close by Charlie, sipping lemonade through a straw while at the same time trying to emulate her mother and Janice's dancing. Everyone was now getting back into the routine when she tugged at Fitch's jacket. He flashed a smile at her – when an adult smiles at a child they generally reciprocate, unusually for this child she did not.

'What is it, Mary. Do you want some more lemonade?' Fitch asked.

'No thank you. Over there. Great granduncle opened his eyes.'

Fitch, preoccupied with events did not at first comprehend what Mary had said. He asked her to repeat what she had said. Having been brought up by consummate parents and surrounded by people of a clan always looking out for her welfare, she repeated herself in a matter-of-fact fashion as an adult would.

'His eyes opened and he looked at me. Was he asleep?'

His eyes opened, repeating to himself what Mary had said. He looked at Charlie. He saw nothing untoward. She must have been mistaken. He regretted the notion. She had far too much common sense for mistakes. He looked at Charlie once more and a sense of horror came over him.

Gerty – from the other end of the hall – was seeing what Mary and Fitch were seeing. Charlie had his eyes open and was smiling. She screamed out the cry of a banshee, *NOOOOOOOOOOOOO!*

And that was the end of Charlie O'Hare's wake.

The officiating priest, the white robed Fr. Patrick Donovan from Graiguenamanagh, now a little worse for the drink, had left. He made his apologies and thanks. Passing the chapel, he went out along the lych way to its gate when he became aware of a young girl standing in its porch. She looked fifteen. He was immediately taken by her youth and beauty. The drink he had consumed had left him morally vulnerable. He needed to have her.

Twenty-four

. . . Take thou this vial, being then in bed,
And this distilléd liquor drink thou off;
When presently through all thy veins shall run
A cold and drowsy humour, for no pulse
Shall keep his native progress, but surcease:
No warmth, no breath, shall testify thou livest;
The roses in thy lips and cheeks shall fade
To paly ashes, thy eyes' windows fall,
Like death, when he shuts up the day of life;
Each part, deprived of supple government,
Shall, stiff and stark and cold, appear like death:
And in this borrow'd likeness of shrunk death
Thou shalt continue two and forty hours,
And then awake as from a pleasant sleep . . .

Friar Laurence from: William Shakespeare
ROMEO AND JULIET Act IV, scene 1

O'HARE HAD TAKEN A BULLET in his side. A weep of blood the doctor was able to stem was barely visible now. O'Hare had been threatened more times in his life than enough by people wanting rid of him.

Scripps and Daniella had got him away from the Wells Fargo offices as quickly as they could. He was in a bad way despite the bullet proof vest he wore when on active service. Even when he wasn't. The decision made at the time was that he be moved to another country for his safety. In this case, his ancestral home in Ireland. Apart from Dr. Hermenbergur Aloyious, Tommy Scripps, President Howe and Nathaniel Johnson nobody else was in the loop. A much advertised State of New York funeral was organized with the sole intention of informing as many people as was practicable he was dead. He would be interred in Green-Wood Cemetery, Brooklyn under his promotional age of sixty:

CHARLES SEAMUS O'HARE

AN IRISH NEW YORKER

BORN 1938–DIED 1997.

He had agreed to the methods to be employed. As he said at the time, his age put him into the general category of those who no longer cared whether they recover from death, planned or otherwise.

As to the success for a favourable outcome of the experiment being performed, it was put at less than fifty-fifty; his chance of a normal life from those out to kill him – about the same. His chance of going on to damage Star Birth beyond repair, again, about the same (assuming it remained in Europe and no western world democracies fell to defeat in war). Implanted in his brain from the hard drive by White Bear Angel was the data for the creation of the universe. He knew if he submitted himself to the greatest brain specialists on the planet to delve, psychoanalyze, defer to trepanation, nothing would show. While Birth Star were after the string of data (even though incomplete), that once opened would bring a catastrophe of neither man or nature's making. But one of divine. A change for once. For the balance of life being as finely tuned as it was, was destined to end in an instant with its opening. The fateful encounter hypothesis whereby two random single cells come together to produce a hybrid, the wiping out of the dinosaur, the creation of oxygen from bacteria; all leading to mankind inhabiting a planet the right distance from a life giving star were, in a word, a miracle.

Had all these events and more, not occurred in the way they had, who was to say the chance affect of data, creating another life form coming from another place, would not have occurred. Had the mystery of all we have, not brought everything together from a sloppy soup of complex chemicals, it would have been only a matter of time before another had. The data for our current creation undone and replaced by another in a flash. If he died in the interim the data would go the way of all data lost to the operator: unable to be retrieved – out there still – to be downloaded by another when the technology to do so came.

Dr. Hermenbergur Aloyious was the leading authority in America on the study of hibernation of mammals. He was in great demand from people needing to disappear: as in permanently; no longer being a threat to tyrannical state leaders. For tyrannical, O'Hare thought, read criminal.

They were at the offices of Scripps and Daughter Inc, in their Madison Avenue branch. Here Charlie was interviewed by the doctor prior to his procedure. A simple procedure requiring the careful administration of drugs for putting him down before reviving him later would be dangerous. If he agreed he was to be placed into a haloperidol-induced catalepsy to be revived with rapamycin. He would have rigid body and limbs, loss of muscle control, a breathing rate close to zero, and no concept of what was going on around him. To anyone seeing him in this state he would be dead. This would get him to Ireland where Dr. Hermenbergur Aloyious would be waiting to bring him back. Hopefully! For there were no guarantees with any of this. Fortunately, he hadn't already left for Ireland when the Alien smashed up the coffin with Charlie in it. While Tommy was tidying up the coffin, Dr. Aloyious was seeing to the welfare of the man inside.

Mary O'Sullivan tugged at her mother's skirt. 'What trick did uncle Charlie use to open his eyes?'

'What!' Gerty interrupted her daughter after having seen the same event, while at the same time calming the tone of her voice, 'Just your imagination, dear. Janice, will you take Mary upstairs, please?'

Gerty took a firm hold of her daughter's shoulder and directed her away from this ghoulish tableaux.

'He did open his eyes, I saw him. So, did Mr. Fitch. He was standing in front of him when he did it, he saw. And, you know the glass of drink he had in his hand, well it kept going down and Mr. McCoy kept topping it up.'

Caffrey hurried Mary out the door. 'An old trick, Mary dear. We use a glass with a little tiny hole in it. The spirit runs out and evaporates down his arm. Looks as if he's toasting health along with everybody else.'

Sin snatched the tablecloth from one of the well-charged tables in a magician's fashion, without the flourish that would allow the glasses and plates to remain off the floor, brought crockery and miscellaneous items crashing down. Charlie was now laughing beneath this hasty covering reminiscent of a shroud. Sin wanted to know from Scripps what they were to do now?

'Help me get him out of that box. Have you got an empty downstairs room we can put him while he's recovering?'

'Recovering! Recovering from what? Yes. Somebody give us a hand here,' Sin called out.

Scripps called for his daughter and between everyone they

moved Charlie to a back room. Dr. Aloyious came in and closed the door. He began examining him.

'What's going on, father?'

'He's come out of an induced coma before he should have done.'

'Well he's back in it now,' the doctor said.

'He wasn't dead! All the time you knew he wasn't dead. What's going on here, father?'

'Not our decision!' Tommy said. 'None of it. Charlie's a wanted man—'

'Well he's going to be after this.'

'This is a conspiracy. I smelt a rat from day one. That time you didn't want me to call a doctor in to look at him after I found live blood on his shirt. It's immoral, unethical, illegal what you're doing here and I want nothing to do with it. You do know we could lose our licence,' Daniella said to her father. 'And what's he doing here. Is he part of all of this too? An elaborate insurance fraud,' she said pointing to the doctor. 'I know you, don't I? You're the one the papers call Dr. Fake Death, the Resurrectionist, the body snatcher, peddling your filthy drugs around.'

'It's those filthy drugs I'm trying to revive him with,' Dr. Aloyious said.

'Right! After you killed him in the first place.'

'Ella! Ella!' her father said trying to calm her down. 'Charlie was never dead.'

'Don't Ella me. I should call the police.'

Dr. Aloyious was listening to O'Hare's heart. He was unconscious, but his heart was steady. He was hesitant about using the drugs to bring him back while he was in this state. After all, it could have been the noise and general commotion that had brought him round prematurely. Rest and quiet may be the best order of the day. He looked up at Tommy Scripps.

'He's back in a coma. He's heart beat's back to hibernation levels. He's waking may have upset his metabolism, I'm not going to bring him out until later, the shock may be too much for him. For the moment we'll leave him where he is.

'Fair enough, you're the doctor. Ella, we need to speak.' She took a deep breath. She was disappointed with him and all of this, he could see that, he took it on board. 'I really need to speak with you about all of this, Ella. For what has occurred here is part of a larger picture; one that Charlie asked for, agreed to, and knew the risks he was to embark on.'

She reluctantly agreed saying, 'And this had better be good.'

McCoy had to leave to carry out his rounds. Dead people waking or not, Ireland was still at war with Northern Ireland, and with a member of the European Parliament in the castle extra security was needed. Not being a man to relax his responsibilities, he always kept himself several drinks shy of sober whatever the occasion.

His duty done, he excused himself. It was while crossing the courtyard he saw Fr. Donovan. He was about to acknowledge him when he stopped himself. For what he appeared to be doing took him back. Close to the lych gate, the man was lifting his cassock and pulling at his underpants. McCoy's first thought was the man was about to have a piss, and although it was not nature's calling one generally succumbed outside a church, he supposed when early day's seal has been broken – king or pauper – you've got to go again. There was more going on here than a man of the cloth relieving himself though. Not there a second before, a girl appeared from a mist.

Fr. Donovan looked about him. The light was fading and judging by the raucous ribald from within the castle the wake was well in progress. Nobody would be coming out here now. Even if they did, the lych gate was obscured from the castle porchway. With his erect penis in his hand he exposed himself to the girl standing before him. Not as young as he would have liked, but she would be his first and was to be welcomed. An excitement carried through him.

To his surprise she was not reacting to his advances. She did not move away, scream, or show any other sign to him of shock. He smiled at her, moved right up to her, and layered his penis between her legs. She was wearing some sort of kilt. Closing his eyes he ran his hands around her waist to pull her nickers down. Joy. She was not wearing any. He would enter her where she stood. Failing at first, he pulled back, before pushing his erect penis harder forward for the sudden entrance that would burst upon him. There was none. Instead his penis caused him to wince. He would feel around, reposition himself. He put his fingers between her legs feeling for her vagina. The shock was electric. Her womanhood was not in nature's place. Her vagina was smooth skin. She had no place for a man to enter. He stepped back in horror. Looking into her face a chill went through him. What was at first he saw as the face of a young girl full of innocence and beauty was morphing into something quite different. Her face hideous, the skin melting and running down the skull was as ink. He was staring into an abyss and was sinking into it. With his penis still rigid, he tried to pull his underpants and trousers up together. He needed to get away from this creature, but it was too late now. His penis deflated. He felt her hands, old and jagged each side of his face. Locked tight between those hands he tried to move his head. She had him trapped. Her face engulfing his as her hands entered his head. The sensation going through his body was unbearable. His whole body was burning. He was naked inside a metal container. The fire from outside licked at the metal burning the flesh from his body. Despite efforts to contort his body from the sides of the searing hot vessel the burning continued. Without the mercy of death, she carried his version of this world into another where his soul would continue forever in a state of torment until the Lord God returned to revaluate its worth.

Fr. Patrick Donovan from Graiguenamanagh had found the Pale horse ridden by Death, with hell as its stable.

You dirt-y bas-tard! McCoy shouted across the courtyard.

He ran to assist the woman then stopping when the full horror of the scene came upon him. The Father's assailant was finishing off his mortal remains. He strained his eyes to take in what he was witnessing. He watched as the archeries and veins, the stumps of flesh and blood hanging from the priest's head were thrown to the ground. She had torn his head from his shoulders with her bare hands.

The man, still conscious, was still standing.

With the decapitated surgery complete she pulled the sword fastened to the back of her naked shoulder and lanced it forward driving it through the man's chest. Not sure who the assailant was here, McCoy drew his revolver and fired over their heads. The woman took neither notice of the shot or him. She was gone, leaving the priest pinioned up against the lych gate's upright woodwork.

McCoy ran to the lych gate. Before he had time to turn his head away carrot soup was passing through his mouth on its way to hitting the ground splashing the Father's trousers and underpants down around his ankles. With the pool of blood at his feet becoming a lake, McCoy brought up another stomach full. The upcoming forensic examination, well compromised now, resembled the Massacre of the Innocents. Or would have done had anyone here been innocent.

Wiping his mouth with his shirt sleeve, McCoy gathered his wits. What wasn't fully into the priest's chest was gleaming steel. One of a pair of swords he recognized hanging over the shield in the chapel. Not used since medieval times, the priest's blood down its channel the only testament to it having been used in the here and now. He watched in amazement as it reverted back to the rusting weapon he was familiar.

Sin was trying to placate the guests into thinking everything was normal, not immediately aware McCoy was trying to attract his attention. When eventually he saw him he shouted, 'What is it, man? I've a crisis here.'

He whispered in his ear, 'Crisis! You'd better come outside, boss. You think you got a crisis here, that priest who conducted the service is nailed to the lych. Now that's a crisis!'

Sin went outside and looked across to the lych gate. He didn't need to guess who was responsible, he knew it had to be her. He came over in a cold sweat.

'Get rid of the guests. Take them out the back way. Charlie's wake is over.'

Twenty-five

BLEACHTAIRE CIGIRE PETER CUTTER with his Bleachtaire Sáirsint Jack Mander were at Enniscorthy District Headquarters for the Garda Síochána at County Wexford. Their secret mission was to collect a hard drive; but their story mission was to oversee security arrangements for the upcoming European meeting in Brussels with regard to the Good Friday Agreement and the protocol for the island of Ireland. That was to advise Clan O'Sullivan of those arrangements. As everything else in Peter Cutter's life none of this was going to be straightforward.

Cutter was Dublin Garda's National Cyber Crime Bureau's specialist. Jack Mander, his assistant was learning the tradecraft. Circumstances being what they were in Ireland he was hardly ever there.

Prior to the Good Friday Agreement they had to make frequent trips to London, slipping into MI5's backdoor to 'help out' when IRA activity in London demanded. This time MI5 had rubbed shoulders with a United States government department. A sensitive piece of technology had to be taken out of America, flown to Ireland, then returned. His job was the halfway point in all of this collect and bring. Collect was Castle Rose from some character by the name of The Undertaker; bring was the London Network working out of MI5 for the American Embassy.

Why all this shenanigans? he had asked his controller. He could see from the man's blank face he wasn't to get an answer; so back to

Ireland he and Mander went.

In the office of the Chief Superintendent for the local area, Bleachtaire Ard-Cheannfort Patrick Polkinhorne, they politely sat and listened to him telling them all they needed to know about Clan O'Sullivan and Castle Rose (like they'd never heard of the man before). How an ex-IRA soldier became political (and his weapons) . . . when Polkinhorne's phone rang.

Polkinhorne had taken a call earlier in the day from the landlady of The Jigging Leprechaun telling him that a member of the IRA had been dining in her establishment with a priest. With that in mind he put two and two together, made three, put his phone down, then informed Cutter that murder overriding what he was here for he was duty bound to inform Dublin, further, that as Cutter and his Sergeant were on the ground he was making them the investigative team until Dublin sent replacements.

'So who's been murdered? Did they say?' Mander asked.

'Didn't I say. Sorry. A priest!' Polkinhorne said. 'In the grounds of Castle Rose. That is where you're headed, isn't it?'

Great! Cutter thought. That's all we need.

Cutter studied the body before him. His mind was not on the task. This was not his remit. He was to recover a stolen hard drive belonging to the FBI; with murder having pushed it down the charts he was back to basics. He stood next to the body, while Mander, older than Cutter's 35 years by ten was on his knees alongside of him. He was trailing a finger through the dirt below the body of the Father. The deceased man, perfectly erect apart from rounded shoulders, was well lanced. His head some distance away on its side, to Cutter, seemed to have a look of horror on his face. Mander looked up at him saying.

'Judging by the depth of the blood soaked into the ground the man's been dead . . .' Mander rubbed the sensation he had felt through his fingers and sniffed them. 'God! Vomit! Smells like the floor of a sticky carpet club the morning after Saturday night closing. Three hours tops, sir.'

'Shall we leave it to forensics. Right, clear the area please,' Cutter shouted out to the few gathered guests that had ventured out to rubber neck. 'This is a crime scene, I want you people back inside. Jack! Go wash that stuff off your hands, it may be contagious.'

'Are you leaving him there?' McCoy asked Cutter.

Cutter studied the man, 'And you are?'

'Ned McCoy. I work for Mr. O'Hare. You can't leave him with a sword sticking out of him like that, it's not Christian.'

'Well . . . Mr. McCoy . . . until forensics have examined the scene, I'm afraid it stays where it is. While you're there, a question, was it you that called us in?' Cutter asked.

Sin was hurrying along past guests returning to the house. He was eager to keep McCoy from answering any questions to the detective inspector of what he knew of the sword.

'No, it was me,' Sin called breathlessly across trying to resist the Guard from moving him back.

'All right, officer. I'll speak to him. And you are, sir?' Cutter asked turning to the man while at the same time eyeing him with suspicion. For any man dressed the way he was had to be a suspect. An itinerant if he ever saw one.

'Sin O'Hare.'

'I take it you rent the caravan on the lawn over there,' he asked looking at the run-down bow top wagon parked up.

'No. I own the caravan over there,' Sin said pausing to add, 'As I do the Castle! . . . On the lawn! . . . Over there!'

'Oh, right. I see. And do you know what happened here?' Cutter asked.

'Here. No. Inside. We were enjoying a wake for my nephew before we were interrupted.'

'By the murder taking place?'

'Correct.'

'Do you know who it is?'

'Patrick Donovan. Father, as was by the look of things.'

'I take it he was here in an official capacity?'

'Yes and no. My nephew's funeral had already taken place back in the States. In fact, he was one of yours. FBI. He's to be interred here.'

'FBI, eh. Certainly not one of ours, sir. But I take your rough comparison as a compliment. So, an ex-officer of United States law is brought home to rest bringing his own priest with him.'

'No,' Sin answered. 'Father Donovan was a friend of the family. He had a few drinks with the rest of us before taking his leave. I went outside for a piss to find him here.'

Cutter studied the man closer. He was about to ask why he didn't use the bathroom in the castle. On second thoughts, judging from his appearance, he would not want the bother of going upstairs. 'And did you see anything suspicious, apart from the obvious, when you came out?'

'Not until I looked up from the hedge over there.'

'Where you were piss . . . relieving yourself. Well, we're going to have to speak to your guests. Let me have a list of names of all those here, and any that have already left. If you would go with my Sergeant and organize that I'd be obliged. Jack! Go with Mr. O'Hare will you. I shall stay here until forensics . . . ah, here they are now. They didn't waste any time.'

Cutter called after Sin as he was walking away.

'Mr. O'Hare,' Sin turned back to him. 'One more thing, sir. I shall need to speak to you about your nephew later if you wouldn't mind.'

'Not a problem. . . . All done?'

'For the moment, sir.'

Dr. Alice Mabin was forensic pathologist for the local Garda. She was a woman in her mid-fifties, which Cutter was happy about. The relationship between a police officer and a doctor was not always acrimonious, and someone knowing what they were about was always welcome. With one wanting instant answers for time of death, the how's and whys, with the other reluctant to commit, especially if they were younger and played it by the book. An experienced person would be more open. With one of the questions being apparent, time of death, evidence of damp blood on the ground being near enough to within an hour or so, it wouldn't be too long before Cutter had his man.

She made a preliminary examination. Her assistant took photographs.

'We'll have him down now. Can I have a couple of bods to give a hand please, Inspector?'

'We'll do it,' he replied. 'Mander, give a hand here.'

She gave them plastic aprons and gloves to put on.

'Okay,' she said.

She took the handle of the sword in a blue gloved hand and pulled. It was stuck fast, and she had to move it from side to side unpinning it from the wood it was fastened to. She began withdrawing it. Cutter thought he heard the sound of a suck as the sword came from the priest's body. But it could have been his imagination. Both policemen stepped forward to take the weight of the corpse as the sword came away. They then lowered the body to the ground onto a plastic sheet. Her assistant passed Mabin two bags. She put the sword into one and the head into the other. The body was then put into the back of the ambulance.

'That's it. Thank you all, I'll be in touch.' She acknowledged both men. 'Detective Inspector, Sergeant.'

'Peter.'

'Call the office in the morning, I'll have the prints from the sword by then. DNA, anytime in the next two to three.'

'Thanks, Doctor.'

She smiled and left.

'Peculiar that a priest happened to have been murdered with us coming here. Don't you think that's bizarre, sir?' Mander suggested.

'Coincidence, yes. Bizarre, no. Go and organize the fingerprinting and DNA swabbing will you.'

Both Cutter and Mander found themselves in the unusual position of being able to interview people not pushing to go anywhere. In fact, they were more than happy to carry on eating, drinking and smoking. Probably immune to violence, he thought.

Forensics discovered it was Ned McCoy's bile splashed about the priest's headless body when it came back. That had come as no surprise to Cutter seeing as he was first on the scene. They carried out a visual inspection of those in the castle, looking for traces blood on any. There was none. Fingerprinting and DNA swabs were carried out over that day. Where guests had returned home tests were carried out there. Family, servants, were all straightforward.

Everything had come back from forensics with negative match results for everyone that had been at the castle that evening. The sword, well, Sin O'Hare did confess to ownership of it. Passed down through the ages, a battle trophy from 1450 that hung on display with one other in the chapel. There were two causes of death here, both as mysterious as the other. First, running through with a sword was perfectly possible for someone of average height and strength. The second, was more difficult to comprehend. The removal of a someone's head. How do you do that? What could do that? Cutter thought. He put it to Mander.

'A brown bear, grizzly?'

He got Mander to check the nearest zoo for any escapees. A list came back ranging from exotic birds to small mammals along with one other. 'A beaver! Are you kidding me?'

'Have your leg off, sir.'

'After you've pulled it, Mander.'

Mander went on to make the suggestion that two people would have had to have been involved. One to run him through, while the other attached a rope around the victims neck and the back bumper of a jeep, or something similar, driving off at speed.

'Where's the tyre tracks?' Cutter said. 'Where's the rope mark round his neck. And most importantly, something Alice Mabin wrote in her report, the head was turned and turned until it just came away leaving the mess we saw on the ground. . . . Jack!'

'Sir.'

'Call National Bureau of Crime, see what they got on this Fr. Donovan fellow? While you're at it, ask if there has been anything similar anywhere else . . . and I mean anywhere . . . anywhere in the world like this.'

Dr. Hermenbergur Aloyious had returned to attend to Charlie. He would need to bring him out of his cataleptic state. His one overriding concern was his untimely awakening before lapsing back into a coma. He had been put down with drugs and it was drugs that were to revive him. He listened to his heart then checked his brain activity with an electroencephalogram. It showed he had undergone major brain activity to a level he should not have survived. His heart rhythm showed signs of arrhythmia, in his case tachycardia, which he would have expected in someone of his age. He listened to his heart once more. It was steadying. With no apparent external cause for this brain activity indications were it must have emanated internally. Internally may indicate the onset of death. He decided to inject rapamycin. Too late. He was convulsing for a second time.

Sentinel Master–EVT hit into the brain of the human. In a trillionth of a billionth of a second it had taken to go through eighty billion neurons of a human brain. Finding the nucleotides containing the stored analogue information for creation it attempted to download it back to its own time. It hit a fire wall.

Sentinel Mother disengaged Sentinel Master from –EVT cutting –EVT adrift. Sentinel Mother attempted to pull the $10\wedge124$ bits fragmenting for a lack of Space–Time of creation of the current universe into some semblance of order. Universe–Verse–Time threatened to crash not only their Verse but others. It was at the point of breaking up. For the Gateway holding this onslaught of data in check, all Space and Time threatening collapse with entropy ceasing, would all come to an end. $10,000^8$ trillion years of creation's existence span threatening to have been brought forward in a trillionth of a billionth of a second; were prevented by a Creator they knew – Nothing!

O'Hare moved forward into an upright position and clutched at his head. Dr. Aloyious steadied him and waited for his first thought, that a cerebral hemorrhage was going to occur. There was no swelling to the optic nerve, no seizures, no difficulty in his speech, he had no hand tremors, no dizziness. Aloyious got him to stand. O'Hare stood, shrugged, opened the palms of his hands and asked, *I don't know what all the fuss is about?*

There was fuss, for the man was showing all symptoms of having had a massive overload of energy to his brain, which if it happened again would kill him.

Cutter was standing in the doorway. A man previously occupying a coffin at his own wake, now sitting up in a chair, sent a mild chill through him. He demanded to know who this man was they were attending.

O'Hare turning around to face him answered with a smile, *Why, I'm Lazarus of the Four Days.*

Daniella Scripps prevented him from entering the room. As far as she was concerned this was a private part of the house and was not to be trespassed on from anyone other than family. Cutter saw things differently. Seeing the man that had supposedly died alive and talking warranted an investigation. Through the door there were people he did not recognise; those he had not interviewed. The one with a stethoscope listening at the heart and lungs of the man for starters. A doctor? There was equipment in use here that in the normal course of events he would only expect to see in a hospital. They would not have been brought in on the off chance that the dead man would suddenly spring into action. Which he had. They were brought here for purpose.

He called to the man that appeared to be the doctor, 'I shall need to question, Mr. O'Hare when he's fit to talk. Soon as you like.'

'Daniella!'

She looked O'Hare in the eyes. Kind and smiling. Happy to be alive eyes. She had been told everything; and although not completely happy that her own father had not involved her in the beginning, she would settle for Charlie O'Hare being back to normal (if he ever was in the first place).

'Could you ask my cousin Gerty to come and see me. I've caused a lot of trouble with the family. And family means the mistress of the house. I have a lot to explain and apologise for.'

'Of course.'

He looked at the doctor. 'And some breakfast and a whiskey, perhaps.'

Mander was taking a call when Cutter came into the room. He held his hand up to Cutter to hold his attention. Thanked the person at the other end of the line then turned to the Detective Inspector.

'That was Garda's National Bureau of Crime about Fr. Donovan . . .'

'And were there?'

'Accusations of child abuse while carrying out pastoral work for a childcare center at the Archdiocese of Dublin. The police were called in. The church said they would handle it and not to bother. A week later he was moved to another diocese.'

Sounds about right, Cutter thought to himself. Washing hands in the time honored fashion, for the Catholic church when it came to child abuses, never did stray far from mode.

'If someone's taken the law into their own hands, we need to secure a connection with his past. Make a start on questioning the family, but don't let on what we know though.'

'What are you going to be doing?' Mander asked.

'What we were sent here for.'

Since he first arrived not one of the American's have made any mention of any hard drive. He was beginning to wonder if it was all a fool's errand; and that he had been sent here to investigate the murder of a priest. Hardly likely, given his murder didn't take place until they arrived in Ireland.

Cutter, Charlie, and Sin, along with McCoy and Fitch stood by the lych gate. Cutter was hoping that all of them here together might kick some life into his inquiry.

'This is where it happened,' McCoy said to Charlie. 'I was no more than thirty yards away,' he said turning to Cutter, 'But then that's all in my statement.'

'No need not concern yourself, Mr. McCoy. You're not a suspect,' Cutter answered.

'A young woman, defending herself. You've never seen her before?' Charlie said.

'She was definitely not on the guest list if that's what you're driving at, Charlie,' McCoy said.

No, she definitely wasn't, Sin thought to himself, who had known exactly who this woman was without knowing where she came from. Clan had not believed him when he recounted events of his fight with a sword-wielding woman in the chapel. McCoy's statement has since altered that.

'Detective Inspector Peter Cutter is it?' Charlie said turning to him. 'You were not sent here to investigate a murder were you.' O'Hare said.

'Are you the Undertaker?'

'Would you like to sing a song, Inspector.'

'Sorry, don't know the words to Lola.'

Fitch looked at Charlie, 'Lola?'

'Leave it, Hamilton.'

Cutter followed Charlie into the chapel. He watched him turn the discarded coffin lying alongside a wall onto its side. He felt along the base until he came across a small wood knot. He pushed it. A small section of wood came away revealing a plastic case. Charlie took it out then unzipped it. He then removed a small hard drive from inside.

'That's to go to the American Embassy in London, but then you know that, don't you?'

'I do. But tell me, why bring it here only to send it back to America?'

'From now on it stays in London.'

He needed to get to the bottom of this murder before he went anywhere. A slaying such as this was not one of your routine murders, this was out and out sinister, intriguing, with all the hallmarks of it having been carried out by professionals whose intentions were to make it look as if pedophiles' had been killed by demons. Ridiculous as that thought came to him, for he knew it had nothing to do with the supernatural, it had an air of something bigger about it. Knowing he had once been a detective he asked Charlie for his opinion.

'Your duty is commendable, Detective Inspector, but you will spend the rest of your life looking for the culprit for this one. I'm told he lost his head; and not with it hanging over a block. You have no ideas of your own then, Inspector?'

He had to admit he hadn't. Everyone had been fingerprinted, DNA's taken, there was no evidence that anyone in the castle had committed the crime. There were no fingerprints on the weapon, no marks on the ground, apart from the victim's blood and McCoy's spew. Forensics had gone all over the castle grounds and had drawn a blank. Polkinhorne got one of his constables to go to the Jigging Leprechaun with a photo of the dead priest's face supplied by Dr. Mabin. The landlady had said it wasn't her priest.

'My Sergeant and I are still looking into the evidence.'

'He was a pedophile, wasn't he?' O'Hare asked matter-of-factly.

'How did you know that?'

'Concentrate on doing what you came for, Detective Inspector. Forget everything else, for its critical you return to London. The free world depends on your success, Detective Inspector.'

That supernatural thought Cutter had came home to roost when Mander called him to say he had back reports of similar incidents to the one here.

'Dave Carson, a deputy sheriff, from Cheyne Valley, close to Nebraska was found in a cave with his trousers around his ankles and his head torn from his shoulders,' Mander said.

'When was this?'

'Nineteen ninety-seven.'

A little over a year ago, Cutter thought to himself.

'Earlier another. In 1920, a man was found in bed with his head under it. Doctor put on the death certificate, hang on I'll read it, Died from head being twisted and torn from the neck due to flesh fatigue. He was commissioner of police in New York, name of Harry Rivers, arrested by the Bureau of Investigation on charges relating to corruption and child trafficking.'

'You've done well, Jack.'

'Want one more?'

'You're joking.'

'Again earlier, still in the 1920s though. A local hoodlum name of Runfeldt. Found dead by police from New York's 7th Precinct for the abduction of an infant. He was sitting in a chair when he lost his.'

'And no one found for any of them?'

'Guess who one of the officers was? Well, you won't, Inspector so I'll tell you, Detective Sergeant Charlie O'Hare from New York's Lower East Side precinct.'

Twenty-six

ROISIN KRIEMHILD looked up at the sky. Deciding it would not rain in the next twelve hours she laid the sack containing the Barrett M82 with its two 10-round detachable box magazines tight under the muddy overhang of a ditch. She covered it with bracken, then made a phone call before returning to Crossmaglen.

The landlady asked Hess in passing as he was leaving the public house, while at the same time knowing full well who Roisin Kriemhild was, 'And the lady you dined with, was she a birdwatcher too? She could have stayed here, I have vacancies.'

'A coincidental chance meeting with someone I met up with at the New York Theological Seminary last year. No, she wasn't. On her way to Dublin,' he had replied.

Hell! If you're not lying about your birdwatching activities, you are about everything else, she thought to herself. She was a member of South Armagh Sniper's. A section of the Provisional Irish Republican Army. An arms dealer and go-between with Libya. *Now who would this twitcher be?* she asked herself before phoning the Guards and speaking with Polkinhorne.

Hess had taken up a position as a twitcher in a field overlooking Castle Rose. A pair of binoculars, a British Isles guide to birds, a flask of coffee and sandwiches (provided by the good landlady of the Jigging Leprechaun), along with a semi-automatic pistol from Roisin.

He was to be a priest enjoying a week's holiday hoping to record sightings of raptors; waiting for the rest of his club to join him if anyone asked. He no longer needed the clothes of a priest now and discarded them. He had needed to get into the castle to get the hard drive. Kriemhild mooted that it would be in the coffin O'Hare had come across in. Coffins meant churches; in this case chapels. That had been a day ago . . .

. . . Close to midnight, when he had made the move.

He had pushed open the oak door enough to squeeze himself in, then pulled it closed. Flicking on his torch there was the coffin. He went straight to it. Thumb screws, he thought. Four of them. No need for any screwdriving. He undid them and lifted off the lid and looked a the man laid out. *Hello, old son, me again! Sorry for the intrusion.* He unfastened the strapping from his body and rolled him on his side. That's wide for a coffin, he thought. More room to roll the man over than he thought there would be. Handy.

He then went round the inside feeling over the lining for any concealed sections that might hold a hard drive. Nothing. He then went over O'Hare's body feeling trouser and jacket pockets. There was nothing here. He looked around for signs that it could be anywhere else. It appeared not. There were some steps in the corner. A door three steps down that looked as if it led somewhere. A crypt! That's going to be dark down there. Fortunately he did not suffer from the dark, midnight, or horrors the squeamish associated with graveyards. In this case, Crypts! Was the door unlocked the question he put to himself. Only one way to find out. He went down th steps and tried the handle. A brass knob end affair covered in cobwebs and verdigris. It was sticky. He turned it, the door clicked forward. Looking behind to make sure no one had followed him he went down the steps pulling the door closed as he went.

Shining the torch around there were coffins in various stages of rot, stone sarcophagus, and all manner of funerary laid out haphazardly. Not a place that lends itself to being cleaned up and organized, he thought. Surprisingly, apart from must and damp rotted wood, it didn't smell as bad he expected.

He had not gone a few steps when he came to the first of the coffins. This one was new. Its lid was to one side as if waiting for someone to take up residency. He looked inside. This one only had a crape lining. He shone his torch inside and began searching its interior. There was nothing. He then slid its lid over shining his torch on the top and startled. *What the fuck's going on*, he said out loud. Realizing the volume of his voice he looked about him and listened before going back to make sure he hadn't imagined what he had seen. He hadn't. Screwed to the its lid was a brass plaque with the inscription:

CHARLES SEAMUS O'HARE

AN IRISH NEW YORKER

BORN 1890–DIED 1997.

'Well, one of us is lying, Charles Seamus. And as sure as hell it 'ain't me.'

Roisin's plan for an assault on the castle to find what they were looking for was going to have to happen after all. He made his way back up the steps dragging his hand through as much cobweb as he could. Making sure he closed the door he then draped it over the door knob. Easing the chapel's oak door open he went out taking in the night's fresh air. Then he heard the castle's door open. He would need to get back to his hillside retreat. What an idiot, he thought. Covering his tracks with cobwebs on door handles he had forgotten to close the chapel door properly.

A helicopter appeared from the gray morning mist settling itself down on the ground close to where Hess lay waiting at the edge of the woodland. He picked up his binoculars and looked back towards the castle and its chapel.

Five people got out wearing white paramilitary Strurmbannfuhrer uniforms. Among them, was the woman he recognized as Roisin Kriemhild. She directed the men to unload the weapons and ammunition. Hess, shook his head in disbelief at how these people were dressed. To say they had delusions of adequacy would not be an over exaggeration.

'You took your time, Kriemhild,' Hess said. 'Wasn't there a second helicopter to get me out of here when all of this is over. There won't be room for me and your private army in that one.'

'Tied up in a shoot out. Now what's the situation on the castle? Did you get the hard drive?'

'Not yet.' She ignored him and began dialing her cell phone. 'What are you doing now?'

'Calling Ireland's member for the European Union. You obviously can't work on your own initiative. Hello, you know who I am.'

Clan O'Sullivan recognized her voice straightaway. He agreed, they had gone back a long way. 'A long way back, not now. Times have changed, you haven't.'

'The old days you refer were our allegiance to the IRA, mine to the second world war and our cooperation with Germany. And now it's Germany once again, my cousin, and Birth Star. If times have changed, they have only changed for you, Clan. You got a house guest. Supposedly dead. We want what he brought over in that coffin of his. Do that and you can get on with your life.'

'He is dead! What'd you think he brought with him, a change of clothes?' Clan said.

'Be bollocks, he's dead. He came here with a hard drive that has data not belonging to him. If it's not up his arse, then it's up Sister Carter's. Bring it out and our job's done here. When you're done, bury the Irish *bastard!* Alive if you have to. By the way there's a brand new coffin in your crypt complete with his name plate. Now get on with it before we reduce you, your kin, and your pile to bodies and bloodied flesh. If you don't know it already, you soon will. You're looking down the tube of an 81 mm high explosive mortar bomb. I assume you still know the damage that can cause?'

'I have no knowledge of any hard drive. So let's say you've been wasting your time, shall we?'

Clan was listening trying to gauge where she was calling from. His days as a paramilitary with the IRA hadn't been wasted. The chirping flight call of a hen harrier over the woodlands above the castle told him all he needed to know. He answered her in a soft voice, 'Go and fuck yourself, Roisin.'

Polkin was on the horne of his dilemma, were the thoughts now. The oft times phrase used by his staff when he wasn't supposed to be listening were coming to mind along with, 'Oh! Back villains!' used by himself. A section of his assault team – ordered out by Cutter to deal with troubles at the home of Clan O'Sullivan – who according to their Commander were coming under a sustained and overpowering force. Polkinhorne needed orders from on high if he was to go in.

He asked himself, *What the fuck's going on here?* The next nearest tactical unit was in Dublin. They would take hours to organize and get here. His own people's intelligence coming back to him were these people were neither IRA, Real IRA or Republicans. His own ears on the ground in the name of, *What did she call herself?* The landlady of the Jigging Leprechaun in Wexford when she called the Guards; saying a woman by the name of Roisin Kriemhild, one she knew to be an arms dealer from the South Armagh Sniper's was entertaining an American priest on a bird-watching holiday. *God! Roisin! I thought she'd been shot in the back years since. She should have been.*

This is what happens when the man- (himself) in-charge is kept in the dark by his superiors. Not Ireland's Garda, but London's MI5. He had called for clarification from the Crime and Security Intelligence Service. For all the good they had been he may as well have called the Chief of Staff for the Salvation Army. *Two officers in danger and still the murder of a priest to be investigated*, he said to himself.

'What was that, sir?' Donnelly asked.

Polkinhorne tried to decide his next best move. His options were scarce on the ground.

'We need to know . . .'

'Sir!' Detective Constable Donnelly asked once more.

'If they weren't IRA or Republicans, who in hell. . . ? Organize an armored Land Rover, we're going to Wicklow.' He removed his jacket and went to his cupboard. He then hung it on a coat hanger and took out a bullet proof vest. Putting it on, he went to his desk drawer and took a belt out. Doing it up around his waist he said, 'While you're doing that, I'm going to get us tooled-up.'

'Sir!'

'Sorry. I know it's your first week. In all this confusion, we're going to need somebody to record this incident and submit a report. You're going to have to come with me. In case one of us gets shot and killed. Roger that!'

Clan wasn't prepared to wait for any armed back-up from the Guards.

If they turned up at all was more the question (for although being a member of the European Union, with a track record with the Irish Republican Army, the Guards were not convinced of his commitment to peace), he would deal with the situation as it was.

'SIN!'

Sin was already ahead of Clan's game.

'Don't tell me, we need the weapons for a cross border ambush.'

McCoy was with him. A gun room holding muskets, swords, shields; in the ordinary course of events, totally useless for a modern-day assault were not its total. It held a secret. A cellar.

Accessed from below an oak table taking up most of the room was a hatchway flap under one of its matching chairs. McCoy and Sin were on their way down the stone steps leading to an ante room. From there, another door, hidden in the wall. This led on to a weapons store. Here boxes of automatic weapons and ammunition were stacked, along with grenades, smoke bombs and rocket launchers. More than enough to start a war, prolong, or end one.

They carried them out and into the main lobby of the castle and up the stairs. From there they would set themselves up from the castle's roof to defend themselves.

'All this for one man,' Cutter said. 'Why not wait for my people?'

'We will not have that luxury. They have a high explosive mortar bomb alongside those woods. One of them will easily take a building this old down. We have to move now, Inspector. If not for our own safety, there's yours to be considered.'

'Here! Take this,' Fitch said throwing him the hard drive.

Once again, he and Carter, had been enlisted as stage management assistants for Charlie's illusions. Not all of them, not all of the time, for appearances suggested he was responsible for carrying a Members' List of names toxic for anyone outside of their organization to know . . . although he wasn't involved, not until Carter had relieved him of it, did the penny drop that this was planned. Right up to his 'death', Charlie had organized one enormous conjuring trick involving misdirection time after time, one on another. He had to hand it to him, he was smart. Except now, this could well be the end of the line for him and all here, for Kriemhild's Star Birth were about to go to town on them.

Fumbling it with one hand, Cutter juggled it, coming close to dropping it in the process before getting a second hand on it.

'Thanks, I think,' Cutter said.

Having got nowhere to discovering the person responsible for the death of the priest, at least he had what he'd been sent for. Question was, how did O'Hare know MI5 in London were the acting go-between with the United States Government for its return if he had not organized it himself?

The recovery of a hard drive had been his orders. The murder of the priest, an investigation he had failed to solve. Informing Polkinhorne of his true reason for being here was not going to happen. For any information on the device Polkinhorne would insist on opening and look at before London spelled out to him that DI Peter Cutter and DS Jack Mander were not there to solve the murder of a priest, but had other work. His refusal in not allowing CS Polkinhorne to handle the hard drive would amount to disobedience of authority. What of that?

'There's a professional assassin out there, Inspector. You're going to have to try and get the hard drive out of here and away,' Fitch said.

'Not before I call for armed back up, I won't. Jack! Get onto Tacaiochta Faoi Arm. They'll soon sort this lot out.'

Twenty-seven

WHEN CAFFREY WENT to fetch Mary one of her worst fears for the care of a child was realized. While everyone was preoccupied, Mary O'Sullivan had wandered out of the castle and headed towards the chapel. She had left her hair ribbon on one of the pews and had gone to fetch it. She was already in the chapel when a rattle of bullets from an automatic raked across the oak front door taking out chippings of wood as it went.

Hess shot-up the door of the castle, more as a warning than an actual attempt to gain entry for the taking of prisoners. Kriemhild had told him, Clan O'Sullivan was among them. Alongside him, Ned McCoy. Hess shrugged. *Is that supposed to frighten me?* he asked.

'They were both serious fighters for the IRA back in the day, and I don't suppose for one second either of them have lost any of their talents for killing. No, there's going to have to be a better way.' She looked down onto the castle's courtyard through her binoculars, adjusted the focus, saw the girl coming out of the chapel and said to Hess, 'And there it is.'

Mary had heard the gun fire and was showing signs of caution. The nine-year-old, happy, smiling, double-plaited red-haired girl knew Ireland's history as she did her father's, her great grandfather's as well as McCoy's involvement involvements.

Her mother, not wanting any nasty surprises by way of innuendo and taunts by her school friends that her father was a murderer, had made sure she knew the facts. Her family had been fighting a war with England. She knew for instance, Ireland was one country with two histories all dating back to the English king, Henry the Eighth, when he broke the ties holding the Catholic Church to the Pope and Rome. To her, and most people in Ireland, her parents were fighting a just cause, and there would always be disagreement in the two countries over what was right or wrong. Her mother went on to say despite all of this fighting, there was no future for any of them if they continue. Her father had turned his back on violence becoming a member of the European Union pushing for peace through the 'Good Friday Agreement' through both countries.

She didn't say he was supposed to have handed in his weapons.

Cached under the castle.

She crept around the magnolia bush outside the chapel and looked toward the castle door. It was all broken up on the outside. The brass knocker with the fox with a chicken in its mouth was hanging off. The milk crate with the empty pint bottles great grandfather put out in the mornings was smashed. The glass scattered over the doorstep. She took a tentative step forward enough to expose herself. She gave a little scream.

Hess had her.

Caffrey clutched Gerty around the waist and tried to stop Gerty from both screaming and trying to open the oak door.

The strafing from the machine gun fire onto the outside of the door had ceased. To Caffrey the question was for how long. The sound of the gunfire echoed around the high-ceilinged lobby, although having ceased, left a resonance of sound ringing in both their ears.

Caffrey needed assistance to get Clan down from the roof, which would mean leaving Gerty to go up there alone. And going up there would leave Gerty vulnerable. Her instincts to go outside and find Mary would far outweigh any thoughts for her own safety. Whoever was out there hadn't given any thoughts to anyone coming out of the door while they tore it apart with gun fire, why would they have any conscience when it came to killing someone trying to rescue a child, getting themselves killed the result?

Clan, Sin, and McCoy had heard the screaming. Gerty could scream for the world, heaven and all the angels, when it came to the protection of Mary. McCoy and Fitch would stay put while Clan and Sin would go and find out what was happening. Grabbing his AK-47 assault rifle, Clan ran down to find out what was going on Gerty would scream the dead awake for.

'Mary's gone, Clan,' Janice said to him when he appeared.

'You sure?'

'Of course, she's sure. You bloody idiot, Clan. As for you, Sin, a damned good great grandfather you've turned out. That's your great granddaughter out there, and Charlie has been a liability to this family. All this nonsense about him being dead, wanting to be brought home to rest. And now he's not. And now there's an army out there, and if they haven't got her yet, it's only matter of waiting,' Gerty said. 'What was all this for, eh? The protection of a man who should have retired from crime fighting years since.'

'Get Gerty upstairs, out of it, Janice. Sin, go back and man the fort. Get Ned down here. Tell him to bring the other RPG with him. You cover me while Ned and I will make a search for Mary. I'm guessing . . . I'm hoping, she's gone to the chapel. The magnolias will provide some degree of cover.'

'I'm sorry, Gerty. Clan'll get her back, I'm sure,' Sin said.

She'd turned and faced him from the bottom of the stairs.

'You'd better had, granddad,' Gerty said with tears in her eyes.'

'Come on, Gerty. Leave it to the men. We've been down this road before, we're used to it,' Caffrey said taking her by the arm.

'What're you going to do?' Sin asked still smarting from the tongue lashing his granddaughter had given him.

'Give them what they want,' Clan replied.

'You're going to take the hard drive back from Cutter? What all this was about in the first place,' Sin said. 'What would have been the point?'

'No! A fight! Soon as Kriemhild woman got herself involved with me and mine, she was doomed without knowing it.'

Ned stood in the lobby. A rocket propelled grenade launcher strapped across his back and an AK-47 cradled in his arms.

'Ready?'

McCoy nodded. He took the latch off the door.

'Let's do it, boss,' McCoy said as they went out the blasted door, pulling it behind them.

They ran for the magnolia bush.

'Cover me,' Clan said. He went to the chapel door and pushed it open. '*Mary!* It's your father, are you in there?'

Gerty picked up the house telephone to answer it. A woman's voice, blunt and to the point, said her daughter was being held hostage by a psychopathic killer and if she wished to see her alive again – not necessarily after any compliance – her husband was to hand over a hard drive being held by O'Hare.

Caffrey came out when the phone rang. Gerty had collapsed taking the phone onto the floor with her.

McCoy's mobile rang as Clan was informing him Mary wasn't in there. It was Caffrey to tell them they had better return to the castle.

Twenty-eight

SENTINEL MASTER–EVT needed program instruction from Sentinel Mother. The gateway to the Transparent Portal Field was still closed to it.

When it howled, the team of scientists and soldiers guarding the Donut (now its adopted and affectionate name given it by Jean Ronstandt) in its newly constructed hangar in Area 51 all they could do was stand and stare at each other. Some had heard the sound of a dog howling before. A Belgian Malinois, from where the sounds and images had been picked up from the United States Base of Fort Sam Houston by the Army Signal Officer, Sgt. Tamsin Tass. It had all ended badly. With the slaying of twenty marines by an Alien coming through to visit Earth; having taken out its hosts, everyone here now feared for their lives.

A streak flash of light emitting from the center of the Time–Portal: some said they could imagine, if the universe was to give up its vacuum, the sound it would make would be the same.

Sentinel Master once separated returned through the Time–Portal alone to the Sentinel Mother leaving –EVT stranded with the downloaded program compressed to an infinite size within its system. With its Fatal Exception System having been declined, it would have to dump down the program manually. With contact with the Sentinel Mother having been denied it would have no other option than to return the program to the Sender Source if it was to return to its own Verse.

An action terminal to the conduit.

Polkinhorne and Donnelly arrived in the Land Rover to find the small unit of his Emergency Response Unit being held down by, *What the hell's that uniform they're wearing?*

'Nazi Stormtroopers,' Donnelly replied.

'Stay here,' Polkinhorne said. 'No sense in both of us getting killed.'

He ducked down under the temporary border fencing and went in closer until he reached the commanding officer.

'Oh, it's you, sir. Have a look through these.'

Polkinhorne took the glasses.

'They have you pinned down,' Polkinhorne said.

'Do you know what their intentions are, sir?' the Commander asked.

'To keep you from Castle Rose, where the rest of these Nazi looking bastards are holed up. Detective Inspector Cutter and his Sergeant are in trouble, and I don't think even they know by how much.'

'Do you recognize them? Because if you don't, and they are plain criminals, no matter how they're dressed, if they are preventing officers of the law from carrying out their duty, me and my men will be ready as soon as you give us the go-ahead,' the Commander said.

Polkinhorne felt proud and honored that he had such a team of men behind him. He looked through the glasses once more. His unit was being held down by snipers that was for sure. Mindful of recent legal cases being brought by relatives of differing paramilitary groups common to both sides of the border being taken against the police and the army for killing innocent people, he would need to be careful.

'How many did you say?' Polkinhorne asked.

'No more than half a dozen, sir.'

'All wearing German army uniforms?' Polkinhorne asked. 'Any of your officers injured or killed?'

'One injured. Though by more luck than judgment on their part. The second bullet got jammed in the sniper's rifle.'

'Very well, I'm satisfied, take 'em out. Call for paramedics when the job is done. No sense in any more people being put at risk by these terrorists.'

'Terrorists!'

'Terrorists, Commander. For we cannot say that about the IRA or the Provos, now can we? For they were never dressed in uniforms of the Third Reich.'

'Very good, sir. Terrorists it is. TAKE THE BASTARDS OUT MEN!'

When all arrests had been made, the dead and injured taken away, Polkinhorne set to rescuing the two officers on his patch. Intelligence coming to him was that they were not here to talk about security arrangements for Clan O'Sullivan and his trip to Brussels. Which begged the question, what were they doing here?

Roisin Kriemhild received word some of her people had been shot and killed. The rest arrested for acts of terrorism by an assault task force of the Garda. She put the responsibility squarely on Clan O'Sullivan's shoulders. Her cousin, Direktorin Elke Kriemhild switched the blame to her.

'If they were dressed to impress, stomping around as if they were Obersturmbannführers, they don't me, Roisin. How many have you lost?'

'Enough. We have the child though.'

'An example by way of retribution I think. It will open the eyes to our member of the European Parliament, if no one else, we are not here for the short term . . . we will cut an ear from Clan O'Sullivan's daughter. If that doesn't spur anyone to hand over the hard drive . . . tell him our next option will be to kill her!'

When the call came through to the house, Gerty stormed over to answer it. Fearing who it might be, for they were being threatened by an army of violent people, Caffrey tried to stop her. It was too late. Caffrey called Clan. It was someone giving his name as Coxly Hess.

'HESS IS IT?' Gerty screamed down the line. If you're the same CIA man came a knocking on my door asking if we had a computer device belonging to your government. Well, tell your American government, they can go fuck themselves. It stays put.'

Hess laughed at her intransigence before changing his tone of attitude. 'Listen lady, if you want your daughter to keep both ears you'd better tell old man O'Hare to bring out that hard drive. Your daughter will be returned and we can all go home. Dig!'

'Well, listen to me, you piece of shit. The only digging we'll be doing is when the time comes for burying you. So start counting the seconds you have left to live. Harm one hair on my daughter's head, and I'll personally go at your throat with one of my steel pot cutters leaving your head to come off quicker than clay from its wheel. Dig!'

For the first time in his life Hess was taken aback. Frightened even. For this woman was no push-over. Of course she couldn't cut his throat, nevertheless . . . he swallowed hard. 'Look out your door, lady. A second thought, perhaps.' He rang off.

She did look. On the ground outside by the chapel was her daughter, bagged up as a sack of vegetables. There was no movement. Standing over her smiling was a woman in German uniform. She was cutting the top of the sack open with a knife. She screamed and went to run out. McCoy and Cutter pulled her down as a bullet whistled over their heads.

She was hysterical. He had put the family in danger as he had in their previous life and told him so. He placed the AK 74 against the wall, we're going to rescue my daughter, *My daughter!* he repeated for her benefit.

'My daughter,' she replied. 'Is trussed up in an old sack with a gun to her head. With all your weapons, you won't get five yards before that bitch holding her takes you and McCoy down. Look on her, Mr. Clan O'Sullivan, go get the fucking hard drive and throw it out.'

'We don't have it any longer.'

Gerty O'Sullivan an O'Hare by birth, a normally mild mannered woman had many ways of responding to trivial argument. Now close to being out of her mind with grief when it came to the safe keeping of her daughter she had just the one. She turned away from him after his inappropriate remark concerning, *My daughter!* as if she was not part of the equation. She then turned back to face him, only this time she struck him full in the face putting him on his back with a fist from the hand of a woman who could throw a fifty pound lump of clay onto a potter's wheel and work it.

'NOW GO GET IT! or I'll kick your balls so far up your arse you'll have to open your mouth to piss.'

Twenty-nine

–EVT ATTEMPTED TO CROSS the threshold of Time–Verse in its efforts to return home through the Transparent Portal Field. An automated program response, allowed an –EVT separated from its Sentinel Master to return had defaulted to a non-return program through its installed fault tolerant system.

–EVT responded. A Belgian Malinois. With its self-destruct capability timed to bring what remained of an advanced transmutation of species, robotics; with all the combined program technology at its disposal, it was destined – Created Universe program and all – for Another's oblivion. For this servant of Sentinel Mother GOD sent to Earth to duplicate and download the defaulted and applied Created Universe program from Another was at the point of being abandoned by Sentinel Master. Sentinel Mother could not allow that to happen that would give away their being in this Verse. For they had moved too far away from their human roots.

The ululation from –EVT was likened to an afterburner being fired up from a fighter jet. With the program for the Creation of Universe and Man firmly locked into its own system –EVT had one option. –EVT would have to liaise with Predator Guardian as well as Hartley Hare if it was to save itself. For Sentinel Master the conduit between them and where the link up would have to be made for –EVT to return. Already the journey across the Time–Verse by Alien craft to prevent that happening had been launched by the Sentinel Mother, its weaponry locked-on to take Sentinel Master down.

Thirty

IT WAS AN INSTANTANEOUS reaction from the Alien. And a devastating reaction for the human. –EVT downloaded the program back into the mammalian brain of Hartley Hare; while the Predator Guardian uploaded it to herself in an identical frame of time. With all 100 trillion synapses in O'Hare's brain firing at once (twice) he went into a coma.

Dr. Aloyious examined him where he lay. There was no pulse, and his breathing had stopped. The doctor began cardiopulmonary resuscitation. An anxious twenty minutes passed before ceasing the exercise. He looked up at everyone and shook his head.

'I'm sorry. Looks as if we've lost him for the last time. Someone take over while I fetch my bag of tricks?'

'I'll do it,' Fitch said.

Fitch began the rhythm of compressions to O'Hare's chest. The doctor came back with an electroencephalogram and attached it to O'Hare's head. There was a few anxious moments before someone dared to speak.

'Well?' Sin asked.

Fitch looked up while still pumping at Charlie's chest.

'There's only bloody life in the old dog. Keep going, Hamilton,' Aloyious said. 'Long as it takes.'

'I'll take over if you need a break,' Sin said to him.

Despite Gerty turning her back on Clan and not giving him the phone,

Clan had heard the demand from Hess. He was going to take it back from Cutter.

'Sorry, Mr. O'Sullivan. Our orders come from London. The hard drive stays with us,' Mander said.

Clan pointed to his nose and asked him if he wanted one of these?

'Or let me put it another way. None of us is going to get out of here if anything happens to our daughter.'

'Well, we've had a call from our Chief Superintendent to say they've secured the task force and will be here in half an hour,' Mander looked at Clan. 'Inspector Cutter's orders were to recover the device from the Undertaker and and taken it to London. As far as we're concerned those are still our orders, Mr. O'Sullivan.'

'We'll see about, Sergeant.'

Clan went out and took up the AK 47 propped up against the wall and returned to Mander. Cutter was with him, the hard drive under his arm.

'Sorry, Inspector, you're going to have to take my orders now. They want the hard drive in exchange for my daughter's life. Hand it over,' Clan said levelling the automatic at them both. 'I haven't time for the Seventh Cavalry to ride in.'

Thirty-one

FOR THE TIME IT TOOK −EVT to download the data inside O'Hare's brain, then for the Angel to upload it to herself was the same trillionth of a billionth of a second −EVT took to remove it on the first occasion. Natural Earth time of $10,000^8$ trillion years from beginning to end was negligible due to the irrelevance of known physics for any meaningless of time. For physics to handle such a mind-blowing amount of data in such a manner was a miracle forever hidden from all − except Alpha Omega. The clicking sound (familiar to O'Hare in another time) being evidence a third party was involving itself.

The White Bear Angel, unseen and weakened as a bird with clipped wings, was doomed on Earth. The second shift of data had done it for her. She was cross legged on the upside down empty coffin waiting to find in which divine direction she was to fall. For this was confront and challenge a second time against Him. While O'Hare would recover, having been the conduit rather than the transfer port, she would perish.

Thirty-two

IT WAS A SIMPLE MATTER for Polkinhorne's task force to overwhelm Roisin's Nazis from the hilltop. And although he hadn't personally led the assault, he rather enjoyed the day out. The Commander came to tell him the helicopter had moved off and they were keen to know where it had come from and who owned it before they followed it. Despite calls without success to local airfields Polkinhorne came to the conclusion it was a private plane belonging to the IRA, hangered up in any number of deserted barns and farms in the area. He would track it down later from its radar co-ordinates – always assuming it hadn't turned off its transponder, a dangerous practice if they did he thought to himself.

The Commander gave him the bad news. Seen by one of his men. Events had taken a dangerous turn in the courtyard of the castle.

'They have a hostage, sir. A child.' He passed him his binoculars.

'Oh! Back villains!' Polkinhorne said trying to make sense of the scene below. 'Have we got the castle's telephone?'

'Yes, sir.'

'Let me have it. There's civilians involved here.'

Bleachtaire Cigire Peter Cutter was passed the phone by Clan O'Sullivan. Where he was to go with all of this now he had little idea, and while he was no particular fan of chief superintendent's from rural communities, he was glad of having this one's ear now.

'What does he want, Cutter?' Polkinhorne asked.

'A hard drive belonging to the Americans.'

'And is he American, Cutter?'

'Yes, sir.'

'There's your answer then, give it to them.'

No matter the circumstances was the directive. Those circumstances had paled with Polkinhorne's simple statement. London wouldn't get it, for it was to be delivered into the hands of an American assassin instead. He laughed, then said out loud, *Then get himself out of Ireland with it.*

'I have her in my crosshairs now, sir,' a marksman said.

'And I have Hess,' said another.

'Oh! Back villains! Not through those trees you don't,' Polkinhorne said. 'With them moving about in this wind, you'll hit the girl for sure. Keep your position though.'

Clan pulled open the splintered remains of the castle door and walked out into the castle's court yard, the hard drive in his hand.

'Thank you, Mr. O'Sullivan. You have better sense than your wife.'

Hess took it and walked away. Roisin had hold of the sack, her knife over her head threatening the child inside. She saw the hillside above was held by Garda. She knew as soon as Hess got away she would be captured – or killed. For the moment though her leverage over Clan O'Sullivan and his wife, with their daughter tied up in a hessian sack stenciled, PICK OF THE CROP would be short lived. Hess had got what her cousin had sent him for. For him his job was done. Hers however was not.

Thirty-three

RONSTANDT DESPATCHED A COMMUNICATION via wire to their US London Network in Thames House on Millbank.

```
TOP SECRET & CONFIDENTIAL (GREY ZONE): Jy/56/49021
Dame Margaret Wise,
Dir. Gen. of the Security Service.
Madam. The request from the United States
Government for the London Network with yourselves
to act as intermediary for the recovery of a
computer hard drive belonging to the US Government
has now been rescinded. No liability for the
failure of its recovery has been/will be put at
any one person's door. No intelligence is
available as to how the enemy will leave Ireland
and return to America.
```

Ronstandt was now clear in his mind the Alien seeking the same hard drive one time held in Charlie O'Hare's possession, would now switch its search to its new owner, Coxly Hess. He was now if it managed to get hold of it, it would return back from where it came using the Time–Portal in Area 51.

Any of his people not happy about waiting for this to happen, with dangers to come, were given the option to quit the battlefield. To a woman, they all opted to stay and monitor their equipment in what is being seen as the biggest single breakthrough of life existing in another Time–Verse they were ever likely to see again in their lifetimes.

The Alien had already made one attempt to pass through the portal. Each exercise being as futile as the last. To the scientists watching the Alien seemed as if it was running into a brick wall, going back, before coming forward once more searching for a breach. Somewhere its efforts were being thwarted. These humorous attempts to return from where it came invoked a degree of wanting it to accomplish the task. After the roar of a dog, Ronstandt was not so sure. He had responsibilities. To add more deaths to those twenty marines at Becland and two plane loaders from Kennedy would be construed not so much as incompetence, more inaptitude to the American people, shouted to them to get out.

Konig was having none of it telling Ronstandt so. As for the rest of his team, Simpson, Prishna, and Mitchell, they were going nowhere. For where else would they ever come as close to an Alien time portal in their lives. Now they had seen the Alien attempting to return through the Donut the rest of his team were of the same mind. What amazed those here was not the fact it couldn't get through, it was the reason preventing it given it had mastery over time. For it had no trouble going out through the hangar walls.

Finally breaking through it gave a roar of a Belgian Malinois leaving everyone to wonder where it would, and when it would return. Some clapped as it left. It didn't return. What came next was more spectacular than any Alien with the appearance of a glass-fronted grandfather clock from the waist down: part human upper. If they thought the roar of a dog coming from it was ear splitting enough, what came next blew eardrums and downloaded second degree burns over a wide area. One of the engineers responsible for first building

AG-MX-960 was cremated beyond recognition.

The portal expanded to ten times original diameter taking out and bringing down part of the roof structure of the hangar. What came next, came slowly. As if it was testing the amount of room it had. And to Ronstandt, later relaying his impressions to Howe, *If it had side view mirrors, Mr. President, it would have clipped them off.*

Konig and his team, when asked for their impressions sang from the same hymn sheet, *It resembled a long slither of rock chipped from the side of a mountain.* [KURTZ KONIG, Post-doctoral fellow, FAIR Accelerator Project Helmholtz Centre for Heavy Ion]

It wasn't that. *It could have been from an asteroid.* [WILFRED SIMPSON PhD (Conseil européen pour la recherche nucléaire) CERN]

It was an Alien craft. For sure, you'd never find it if it settled on the ocean floor. [MARLYN GIBBS, National Geographic]

The heat trail was awesome. *Of iron and rock to withstand the friction of entry.* [STEFANKA PRISHA PhD CERN]

The alien craft picked up speed. The cameras around the site recorded an increase in velocity from five mile an hour to an estimated light speed in less than three seconds of breaking away from the hangar. The multitude of flashes of lightening and thunderclaps from it breaking the atmosphere of Earth was likened to the sound of Krakatoa with attitude. There was collateral damage around Area 51: not one pane of glass was intact in any of its surrounding buildings or vehicles. Sentry, the Earth Impact Monitoring system used for cataloging close encounters of asteroids had picked up nothing coming in. Conclusion. They now had evidence the Alien had not come from the known universe. It had come from a multiverse. One of an infinite number according to Konig.

Of concern. *Was this an invasion of the planet for its own sake or for what O'Hare had secured?* [JEAN RONSTANDT, Assistant Head to the President for Homeland Security]

Thirty-four

O'HARE MADE HIS WAY to the chapel by way of the tunnel coming out in the castle's crypt. One he didn't know existed until Sin happened to mention it. He needed to pray for the return of White Bear Angel. If anyone would take pity on their situation – more so with regard to Mary, a child, being held hostage with death hanging over her – it would be her. He came out of the crypt covered in dust, cobwebs and generations of husks of dead insects over his head and clothes. When it came to arachnids he had never been popular with them. One or two, disgruntled at being disturbed, were trying to crawl off him in their efforts to return. He brushed himself down before going to the task in hand. *Brhhr! Size of dinnerplates!* He saw his previous resting place. The coffin that had carried him here was back in position resting on its plinth. She was gone. He went to the oak door and drew back the bolt. Opening it no wider than a light crack of sunshine he looked out. The scene was gruesome shock. He had been told it was Mary. If it was she had been tied and bound up into a sack good and proper. Standing over her, the former IRA woman, embedded back into her family roots from the second world war's German Abwehr, Roisin Kriemhild. He thought about rushing out and taking her down himself. He might have done had he been in his teens, for now there was no way of covering ten yards of gravel and taking her by surprise. Not at his age.

He closed the door and locked it. Turning around, he gasped. She was there once more. Sitting on the coffin cross legged as a living statue, the sword from the Battle of Derry once again gleaming silver, its point dug into the coffin lid capable of taking the head from the shoulders of any foe, was sheathed waiting for another day, for there was to be no blood running its channel this day. Arming herself with the sword now had been a meaningless gesture, for she was finished.

He stood beside her and looked up. She never gave him so much as a backward glance even though she had known him: protected him for more years than he cared to remember. She never had. Never a word. All communication from her, from him to her, coming through thought. Why had she the need of words? She was not of this world, even though, there had been times he thought she was Irinushka, daughter of Fariq and Oonna Mihalyvich, traumatized by a child trafficker. Marco Giuseppi, who had sold out to Satan, before he himself had been used by others. The crimes inflicted by this demon, transcended her to the state she was now. An assassin for the innocent.

He could never be sure she had gifted him mortality. Or whether it was the one universally known as the divine spirit. He had not needed his Catholic faith to know he had been in the company of such a creature, whatever spin others put on it. He knew he had.

What of her now?

Helpless herself. Helpless to give assistance to his own great grandniece.

He leaned forward across the coffin and tried to take the sword. With such a weapon he would be invincible.

Excalibur!

A thought no sooner came to him than he felt ashamed. For wasn't that the mentality he was fighting. Domination of one human over another was so easy a trap to fall into. Any thoughts she was about to spring into life as a cavalry coming over the hill, well, she was going nowhere. He startled.

A single shot rang had rang out across the castle's courtyard.

He dropped to his knees and cried out the power phrase he knew was ineffective, *My God, My God, why have You forsaken us?*

Roisin Kriemhild stood over Mary. A gun to the head of the girl she was about to murder. The screaming from inside the castle from the women for somebody to help them fell on deaf ears. Roisin was committed to a cause that saw genocide as a way to removing half the world's population, enslaving the remainder under a dictatorship of a people's autocracy. She would take one with her, then die for the cause.

The family would come running from the castle. O'Hare imagined Clan, Sin and McCoy automatic weapons primed to burst into life to shoot down this bitch of a woman that had murdered an innocent child. There was a lot of it about and this organization was following a well-trod path of violence. Priming itself up for more to follow. All races carrying the wrong blood (according to their twisted doctrines) around the world, in their quest to wipe out what they saw as inferior races. Though what he thought she would be thinking inferior about the Irish he couldn't imagine. She was a daughter of Ireland after all. He tried to prevent the hatred from rising in his throat, for Mary would be dead, his anger only turning in on itself. The occurring thought was far from inspirational when it came to him. He was too simplistic for much else given the present situation. He would run to his own death into a shoal machine gun fire to kill the woman that had taken her evil decision. Dying once more, this time for the last. A proper death.

*   *   *

A single shot. A 9mm round from the Luger P08 pistol hung freeze-framed in the air. Time virtually prevented further forward velocity of movement from its explosive discharge. From mycoplasma genitalium to Antarctic blue whale, for one trillionth of a billionth of a second all living creatures, flowers and fauna slowed relative to this time. All except −EVT. A race with technology to conquer Time−Verse. Without Sentinel Master or Sentinel Mother to guide her. She blew the round into another place then went for the executioner. She needed a mucus feed.

Roisin Kriemhild didn't know what hit her. As Alexander Wulfhere, the trailer bum who had stayed in Area 51 too long, her chest was ripped apart ribs and all, with the liquid overspill sucked dry from her.

Unable to hold back time any longer real time caught up with − EVT. She was caught up in a shower of machine gun fire Earth had inflicted on her from the day she first came through. She was morphing. Fitch, Tommy and Daniella had seen this change before. They knew what this creature was capable.

Gerty screamed out to Clan to bring Mary in. He couldn't be sure how many of Roisin's people were still out there now she was dead. He would consider no other choice.

The Alien had twice attempted to get the data from O'Hare's coffin with him in it. Tearing into Roisin's chest cavity, was for other purposes. Was it to save Mary, or purely for sustenance?

The Alien was changing. Not of this Time−Verse it would need to return. The morphing of the man in the bowler hat into a large dog before taking on the form of a human being (of some description), wrapped in technology, some might imagine we ourselves would be in a future. Was this a creature from another Time, hundreds of thousands of years ahead of us? Or behind. Who could say? The bombardment of Earth pollutants to −EVT's systems was beginning to cause malfunction. It no longer needed the program to reboot their own. Predator Guardian had passed through Time as a courier, where it had been conditionally given. . . .

At the bottom of the North Atlantic Ocean, an Alien ship waited.

O'Hare had a dilemma. Star Birth has his original hard drive; and although the data for creation is no longer there the other file folder is. The mystery file, as he would have it, containing data equally valuable to creation. And now Hess has the key. How he will get himself out of Ireland with it is another question. With two possible options, sea or land; both will require Kriemhild's people to pull it off. He was still thinking about a boat when Gerty called. Far from a happy woman, she blamed him for bringing all this trauma to their home, not least, Mary. She was by his side when he took the call.

'And don't want anymore trouble, O'Hare. Whoever it is, whatever they want, you're not doing it under my roof. I want you and your people gone. And to make certain there's no more skullduggery, I'm listening.'

'Annie Carter,' Charlie said.

'Oh, the nun, Sister Benedicta Ma-ma-ma. Forgotten her second name. Her of Rome and Vatican fame. Marie,' Gerty said.

He nodded.

'Well please send her my blessings. I was about to say, it was a pity she couldn't be here, given the circumstances, it's as well.'

'Oh bless. Gerty! Your second cousin, isn't it?' Carter asked.

'Well remembered. Would you like to speak to her?' Charlie replied.

'Look, I'd love to. Later. Charlie, listen, I've had a call from

Tubman. Your Wharfmaster .'

'Y-e-s. Not always trustworthy. Go on,' Charlie replied.

'Seems the assassin is to be picked up by boat . . .'

Just as I thought, he muttered to himself.

'Say again.' Carter asked.

'The meanderings of an old man. Does Wharfmaster offer a date and time when this is to take place?' Charlie asked. Communication must be being passed from Germany to Hess. 'Times and dates, Annie.'

'Right. Madeleine didn't ask the question, I guess she's thinking there's a good reason for him not to volunteer them at this time – given the importance it could be what you might call a, goes without saying moment. Yes?' Carter added.

'Well, let's hope so. If it is, he'd better get on with it, for time is not on my side, if it's on his,' Charlie said.

'Assuming you have the means to thwart Hess's plans.'

'Well, yes.'

'And can you?'

'Speak with you later, Annie.'

There was only one way out of Ireland for Hess, and it wouldn't involve walking. Information received confirmed it was to be by boat. A submarine. For what he needed to do now would be sensitive and not without a degree of danger. He had connections, but they were going to require an inline fuse to fire them up. For that to happen he would need Clan O'Sullivan and his European friends with Eastern alliances. A sensitive international call to foreign lands was required. A regular landline call from a house occupied by a member of the European Parliament was bound to lead to awkward questions being asked by Great Britain's parliament. Questions of espionage being sounded around the House of Commons had sway. For sure United Kingdom's security services had the castle's phone tapped. He needed his pin to block them.

O'Sullivan wasn't particularly happy with what Charlie had asked of him. Reminded that his own daughter had been put at risk by these people brought him, not round to the idea, but more amenable. Further argument by Charlie that this man was responsible for putting Mary at risk, and that he would now get away with it, finally persuaded him.

'Ring this number, tap out the row of digits underneath. It's long. Make a mistake and it will cut you off. Rather it will cut my access off until I obtain authorization from the Irish government, leaving me with a whole load of explaining to do.' He handed him the card. The look on his face did not reveal an expression of confidence to carry out such a simple procedure. 'Shall I do it for you?'

Charlie took the card from him and studied it. Were it not for the logo of the European Union in the top corner, with the addition of the member of parliament's name in the center, it could have been credit card.

'No. You're all right. Leave me in peace?'

Thirty-five

THIRTY FEET BELOW THE WAVES of the Atlantic Ocean, off the coast of Ireland, the boat stationed itself waiting to break waves to engage with the man. The submarine commander had already been seen. He knew he would. There would be nothing anyone would do about it other than shout international waters and what was it doing here? Or they could ignore all of that and just drop a lightweight honing torpedo on him from a helicopter and be done.

Hess watched the scene on the ground. For a man of violence, even he had to admit to himself the horror of seeing Roisin being torn apart was uncomfortable. He had heard about an Alien attacking one of the staff at the German consulate back in New York. He'd also heard it was a film in the making. This though, well, this was for real. That was no film in the making in New York, and for sure there wasn't one being made here in Ireland. This was a full-blown Alien, and he was not going to hang around to be its next meal. He would pass his condolences to Elke, say she didn't suffer, and call it a day. Although, anyone hearing her screams would have soon put that down as fake news. He could hear the blade slap of a helicopter in the distance now. Fully armed, there would be nothing the Garda task force could do to stop it. It would strafe across the hilltop on its way down into the valley to a place of shelter until the time came for him to be picked up.

* * *

Polkinhorne stood aghast. The woman, Roisin Kriemhild, a one-time commander for the IRA was, Being eaten!

'Are my eyes deceiving me, or what?' he called to the Commander.

Clan O'Sullivan had released his daughter, and now his wife was running to her aid. It was over.

'Oh! Back villains! We got to get down there,' Polkinhorne said to the Commander of his Task Force team.

'Wait! Chief, wait!'

Both men heard the sound. The Commander was turning his head to gauge the direction it was coming.

Polkinhorne listened. A helicopter was headed in their direction. Garda's Task Force Commander was right. He was looking straight at it now.

'Have a look,' the Commander said passing Polkinhorne his binoculars. What he saw gave him cause for concern. It was armed. He passed back the glasses.

'We can't match that weaponry with what we have here, sir. If he comes in close and lets rip with those machine guns,' the Commander said to Polkinhorne. 'We're sitting ducks.'

Polkinhorne tried to reason why it was returning. Vengeance, or to rescue Roisin Kriemhild. If it was she was dead. They were about to go down there to clean up the mess and arrest the CIA officer. Unless. It was on a rescue mission to collect Hess.

It wasn't with him now.

'It's going in for Hess,' Polkinhorne reasoned. 'There, its veered away from us. He's over there, can you get a clean shot at him?'

'When it clears the ridge. Give it a moment.'

The helicopter came down in a cloud of dust leaving no clear line of sight to take it out. Polkinhorne called for air support on his radio asking them to track it or bring it down if they have to. Too late it lifted off above the ridge and headed north west. Polkinhorne radioed the Garda pilot approaching Wexford from the north to head north west as his quarry appeared to be headed across Ireland in the direction of the North Atlantic.

The Commander took the radio.

'With your permission, sir. Task force Commander to Garda Air Support, who's flying today? Quick man, quick.'

A voice came back, Alpha Sierra Two, Flight Lieutenant Randolph at the rudder, Commander.

'Continue north west.'

'Roger that, Commander. I fear . . . radar's showing his faster than we are. I've no chance of catching him.'

'He's heading out to sea, keep north west, in the meantime the Chief Super will call the Coast Guard in. If he decides to do a run along the coast, oh, I don't know. Do what you can.' He handed the radio back to Polkinhorne, 'Sir.'

'Nice work, Commander. CONSTABLE DONNELLY! Where are you? Oh, there you are. You're going to be my go-between with the Commander, I'm taking a couple of men, Commander, armed to the teeth please . . .'

'Aren't we always?'

'Garda Air Support. Alpha Sierra Two, Flt. Lt. Randolph to Commander of Garda Task Force, we've tracked Rebel One. He's transducers operating. And he's running toward the Dingle. ETA thirty minutes. OVER.'

Donnelly struggled with the radio. He wasn't expecting it to spark into life. He pulled the phones over his head hooking one ear out of align before disentangling it. He picked up the microphone, then looked at it trying to work out what button to press. He pushed one, anyone, found another and spoke into the mic.

'Commander's not here, I'm Detective Constable Dermot Donnelly, and I'm to pass any information over to Chief Superintendent Polkinhorne.'

There was a pause.

'ROGER THAT! Very good, Detective Constable Donnelly. Now make sure when you radio talk with an aircraft in future you, ROGER THAT if you understood the message, OVER when you've finished speaking as in, ROGER THAT. Now pass this message to the Chief Superintendent please: Lost them over the coast. ROGER THAT? OVER AND OUT!'

Four days later Hess was headed out to sea. He had finished dressing in a survival suit and was standing by the open door of the helicopter, the hard drive in its sealed container strapped to the front of him. The co-pilot had a pair of binoculars and was looking ahead of him. The transponder pinged into life. The submarine was four nautical miles ahead of them.

'No green light on this plane, Mr. Hess. Listen for my shout,' the pilot said.

Hess waited nervously. He hadn't done any jumping out of planes for a few years now. Nearer twenty. The pilot was bringing the helicopter down until it was about fifty feet from the surface. There was a swell in the sea which would make it difficult for the spotter crew to see him from the conning tower of the submarine. He hoped his orange survival suit would show up to his rescuers.

The submarine broke surface in an explosion of heavy waves, sea fume and swell. The pilot of the helicopter, seeing the change in sea pattern, strained his eyes to double check he was in position. He looked at his co-pilot for confirmation.

'You're on it, Captain.'

'GO! Coxly. GO!'

'See you in New York,' Hess shouted as he stepped wide from the helicopter into the air. He hit the surface in an explosion. A roar of sound from waves breaking over crest tops was deafening. Cold sea water was forced up into his nasal passages down into his throat. His eyes burnt from the pressure. He instinctively brought both hands up to his mouth and nose exhaling with as much effort as was possible. Coughing out all trace of sea water from his throat and eustachian tube. Hitting the water at twenty-five odd miles an hour he was sixteen feet under the waves now. Here he could risk a second cough, but not follow it up with any breath. He kicked for the surface. Pulled in all directions by the swell from the waves he pulled goggles and a snorkel on. He could at least breathe easy while he looked for the sub.

The gray hull of the boat was 300 yards from him. Even though he was a powerful swimmer the current was taking him away. Pulling hard he began to shorten the distance. At least, he thought, he would drift in the same current the boat was drifting. Whether they could see him in this mess of waves was another question.

An officer and a crew member were on the conning tower with binoculars searching. They had watched their man drop out of the helicopter and gauged his approximate position in the sea.

'ОН БУДЕТ ТАМ!' a crewman shouted.

A crewman came down from the conning tower with his commanding officer close behind him. 'THERE, OVER THERE!' Gathering up a recovery float and a coil of rope he threw it out to into the sea. Missing the man first time, he pulled the rope back in and threw it once more. With the second attempt the man caught it. They began hauling him towards them.

The welcome relief of being pulled along reassured him that he was now safe. Salt water crept in around his goggles that had been pushed from his face burning his eyes, even so he could just about make out the gray of the submarine and the lettering on its side in the dark green swell of Ireland's share of the Atlantic Ocean. When they finally cleared enough for him to see; pulling his head back alarm bells began ringing in his head.

The Type 212 German sub, was a Soviet-class K-278 Komsomolet.

Thirty-six

HE STARED INTO HER EYES, THANK YOU! Then turned away.

As the past he had been gifted thirty biological years younger. He swallowed and gave a deep sigh of breath, for this act alone told him none of this was settled. There was to be a repeat performance. Which of course he guessed as much. One of several one-act plays each in turn ready to play out; each in turn brought to finality before moving on. Ladies and gentlemen, time to ring down the curtain until the next show. You've had your laughs, you've clapped, you've gorged on popcorn, the fat lady has finished her song with an applause. The bad have been banished to hell while the good have gone to heaven (were that a truth). All have left the stage, the lights have come up, and now ladies and gentlemen, time to vacate our seats, go home and forget about what occurred here.

Not too deeply. For this world, this life, is no show for some. For others, hell a relief; heaven a drudge. He lit a cigar; swallowed a whiskey. For now he will leave this place and return to America. Only those with a true understanding will know what's in his soul. He laughed.

All were preoccupied with Mary (and why not?). There are few creatures on God's Earth having had their lives saved by an Alien, that to all intents and purposes had shown little regard for this version of the human race. Although, he suspected, it wasn't personal.

Fitch had already left for America. All missed his leaving, Gerty especially expressed a desire he return for a holiday and to bring

Annie Carter with him. He promised he would. Detective Peter Cutter had not got to the bottom of who murdered the pedophile priest, Father Donovan as I told him. With no weapon, and no forensic evidence to reveal the blood being any more than his own, he would return to London with his deputy, Jack Mander where more would be explained about other matters concerning the hard drive.

Cutter came into the library with Mander interrupting his cigar and whiskey moment. Charlie smiled. They had a serious disposition about them and didn't return the greeting. Sin was with them. It was clear to him his face showed a recent argument bordering on threats with the two police officers. This was not looking good, he thought. The spy catchers have tapped in.

'Mr. Charlie O'Hare,' Cutter said to him. 'I'm arresting you for the murder of Father Patrick Donovan, you are not obliged to say anything unless you wish to do so, but it may harm your defence if you do not mention when questioned, something that you later rely on in Court. Anything you say will be taken down in writing and may be given in evidence.'

'Right! Thank you, DI Cutter. You do know I'm an agent of the United States government and as such you cannot arrest me.'

'Only if you're living here, Mr. O'Hare. If my memory serves, although you technically came over in a coffin, presumably to take up residence in the crypt below, you are now alive and a visitor. I can arrest you.'

'When we last spoke, you said you had no forensic evidence, and no fingerprints on the weapon. Why would you think I was responsible for the man's death now?'

'He was a bloody pedophile anyway,' Sin cut in.'

'All right, Sin, leave this to me,' Charlie said.

Cutter looked towards Mander.

'The evidence we have is that over the years there have been numerous similar events of people being murdered in America, everyone of them involves you either being present or in the vicinity. In 1920 two people were found dead in similar circumstances . . .'

'Ninety twenty! How old do you think I am? Anyway 1920, that would have been my father,' Charlie interrupted smiling.

'Not the one in 1997 it wouldn't have been. A deputy sheriff from Nebraska found with his head torn from his shoulders looking very like the one we had here. You were the investigating officer looking into crimes of abuses to children then,' Mander said.

'Were you perhaps taking the law into your own hands, Detective Sergeant O'Hare from New York's Lower East Side precinct? I'm sorry. You'll need to come with us,' Cutter said.

'This is all bollocks,' Sin said. He turned to Charlie, 'I'll get Clan, he'll soon sort this out.'

'Not unless he's confessing to it himself, he won't,' Mander said.

With nowhere else to hand for any immediate rescue Hess allowed himself to be hauled aboard the Russian submarine. He watched as his $50k pay check disappeared over the horizon. He had been stitched up by Herr Direktorin Elke Kriemhild and he hadn't seen it coming. Perhaps if he had thought about the amount on offer it would have come to him sooner. Free lunches and all that, he thought to himself. If he gets out of this in one piece, perhaps it wouldn't be such a bad idea to throw his lot in with the honorable member for the FBI after all.

The submarine commander climbed down from the conning tower. He had a machine gun under his arm pointed at Hess. The officer and the crewman stepped to one side.

'Coxly Hess?' He smiled. 'Any relation to Rudolf?

'A long way removed.'

'Is that the hard drive you have there?'

'Not for you it isn't, sir. No.'

'I think it is. Pass it to me . . . carefully now, for we know you are a dangerous man.'

Hess unfastened the sealed container and went to pass it to the man.

'No. Put it on deck, and stand away. In fact, all the way back. Closer to the edge. Back into the sea even. A short swim, Mr. Hess. Seven nautical miles. No problem for the man that attempted to shoot dead Liberty Valance. Da svidaniya, Mr. Hess. The man from CIA's inner sanctum; and almost as corrupt as its outer.'

O'Hare! Hess exclaimed.

'With the compliments of ex-President Sergei Bezukladnikov,' he replied.

Hess went to step off the submarine; instead thought about his situation, then turned. He took a dive towards the commanders legs pulling him over. Holding his arm up behind his back he hauled him to his feet and attempted to take the hard drive back. The crewman had his machine gun pointed at them. There was nothing he could do, they were swinging around so much he might hit the wrong man. The commander held onto Hess attempting to push him off the boat. Hess was at the point of losing balance, then, holding firm the commander's sea sweater took him as a brother-in-arms over the side. Both men were fighting and struggling in the heavy sea before washing along the submarine's hull length then disappearing under.

Other crew members hearing the commotion from the crewman for help came clanging up the ladder attached to the inside of the conning tower out onto the deck. It was too late. Both men had vanished into the blue. All that remained was the water proof bag floating away.

Polkinhorne asked questions that no one could answer. For instance, how did the burnt out wreckage of a helicopter turn up on the beach at Brandon Bay on the Dingle peninsula without anyone knowing where it came from, who owned it, who the pilot was, and where did that submarine come from before it dived?

A Note at the End

Hello there Reader,

This is the story of the story. The result of all those creative juices putting a book to bed. I say creative juices, what I really mean, are the influences bringing everything together to make the book an enjoyable experience for the reader. For creative juices, read the brain.

If you have finished this book, like any other book you have read, you have got into the author's brain. For that is where I get my creative juices. I have bared all. Exposed myself to all my thought provoking vagaries and laid them before you.

The Sentinel Mother is the second book in the series of, 'An FBI Agent Charlie O'Hare Novel'. If you read The Seventh Gift you've met NYPD Sgt. Charlie O'Hare for the first time. An Irish beat-cop immigrant who becomes an FBI agent. You've bumped into Lt. Frank Weinberg, the cursed third generation of the same family following the same crimes. He is Charlie's boss and between the two of them they uncover a conspiratorial plot to bring (best description here) to Earth the Holy Spirit and download the creation of the universe it contains. Here it goes into the paranormal/fantasy and there is more.

And it is not about religion.

A difficult subject some would define as biblical paraphrasing. Which, to an extent it could be described. When writing stories of adventure and crime, of greed and people wanting to take over the world, you cannot not delve into religion.

Although the title of the first book happens to be the name for God's gift of education and science to man, is where it ends. It could as easily be entitled, Downloading the Physics of God. And that's pretty much the crux for the basis of the story. A three-generational race to prevent data from being opened, and the consequence to man if they are.

I mention the influences brought all this together in the first place. Now I know you're going to say it's a cliché; an overworn one and one I had to come up with, as if I had been selected by some divinity to pass onto the world great revelations, no, not a bit of it. I'm the same as everyone else when thoughts and ideas come into my head, and if a pencil and paper are at hand written down for future reference, if they are not, they are gone for all time.

In this case the inspiration for the series came from . . . wait for it . . . Indiana Jones', Raiders of the Lost Ark, Dan Brown's, Da Vinci Code. And there the similarity ends. Well, I say that. The scene at the end of Raiders of the Lost Ark where Strurmbannfuhrer Arnold Ernst Toht, the Nazi Gestapo agent (played by the late, great actor, Ronald Lacey), has a face melt-down by an angel did it for me. I was asleep dreaming about it when I snapped awake from the fright. Voila, the series was born. Not all at once mind. Creative juices dripped, bit by bit.

Of course, Raiders of the Lost Ark had religious connotations.

Angels and Demons despite religions' subject matter, a raucous adventure film made close to $400m, and is still earning. Dream on Gil Jackson.

Having met Charlie O'Hare you'll know he has a bit of an age problem (haven't we all, or at least, God willing we will have). Now most authors when they are presented with a character going on for years and years, the result of the success of the first book in their series going from strength to strength, it's a problem.

Take Mickey Spillane's Mike Hammer, the private investigator. Spillane's first book, I, the Jury was published in 1947, his last, Black Alley, in 1996. Hammer was a World War II veteran fighting the Japanese, which made him, I don't know, about twenty in 1945, and in his nineties in 1996 when Spillane's last book was published. Heroes, if they are required to be recycled, cannot die, certainly not get older.

Or so it goes.

And as the fictional Mike Hammer, Charlie O'Hare is the hero as well as the main protagonist and sometime narrator for the series. So bear with me on the age of the person, and try not to let too many figures get in the way of my attempts to write a good story.

The other problem an author has is trying to keep away from typical characterization. Well, you can do nowadays, not so easy a hundred years back, when everyone looked more or less the same, and carried the same typicality. And Charlie O'Hare is an epitome of an Irishman. That is not to say, out of any laziness on my part, in finding a more original character description, he is the epitome of how an Irishman would have looked if he had been born in 1890. He would not have looked any different.

How else can the son of an Irish immigrant farmer from Wexford County; after their family escaped the potato famine of 1850 to start a new life in America's poverty struck New York look? He's going to look Irish. As such Charlie has the typical features of an Irishman: the ruddy cheeks, a casual attitude to life, a sense of the humour – which no-one other than a student of Irish philosophy would understand – and what a bookmaker wished on other people's of the world: the luck of the Irish. And of course, the Emerald Isle water, straight. And when he can't get it, as all non teetotal Americans, settle for good old Kentucky Bourbon.

As a young man he attracted the attentions of an Irish girl by his footwork (another Irish trait), drawing the attention of Paddy O'Flaherty. O'Flaherty was an exponent of the Irish dance and an entrepreneur who teamed him up with a young girl by the name of Mary O'Grady – she being adept in the art of 'proper dance' – where they performed together at Irish evenings. O'Flaherty had a variety show popular among the new immigrant Irish masses becoming eager to enjoy an otherwise dull and difficult life for them in New York.

So, when characterization is next to impossible, you have to fall back on epitome.

There are two consistent protagonists that run with Charlie's life into the third book of An FBI Agent Charlie O'Hare Novel series. The Carmelite sister, Benedicta Marie (pre-nun, Annie Carter), and crime and political editor for the New York Post, Hamilton Fitch (real name pre-Jewish death threats, Arnold Z.

Weinberg).

Both are involved big-time in crimes perpetuated by the organization known as the Order of the Most Divine Third Circle. That organization, although coming close to being shut-down in the first book, continues to operate under the new name, Star Birth. Based in Bavaria, the home of the Illuminati, the similarity ends, for unlike them in that they were a secret society on the lines of freemasonry, the Order of the Most Divine Third Circle seeks to destabilize democracies across all countries where they currently exist leaving one super authoritarian body accountable to none to rule the roost.

As a footnote figures for democratic and autocratic countries is complex, in that they fall between full, flawed, hybrid, and authoritarian regimes; a weighted average is democratic countries, 110; authoritarian, 57.

Those statistics show democracy is not a spectator sport.

Of course there is a whole host of other characters in this series. Some will come, some will go, and some will keep returning back as bad pennies, antagonists and protagonists alike. And as the rest of us, they will endure in equal measure life, suffering, and death, falling between the cracks of the good, the bad and the ugly in equal measure. Doesn't mean to say I don't sense grief when I lose one of them, for the story, when it flows takes its own course; and the author is merely the instrument for mystery and suspense; often with little control.

The last book in the series (I think) will go to the year 2000 – possibly beyond. With the first book moving apace through the generations, putting Charlie in the mind of the reader into an obvious increasing age bracket, I decided that he would become, and stay the years as they went.

He is not the only one with an age problem. The result of confrontation with the Holy Spirit, four characters, protagonists and otherwise, are also of similar age. All four are next to immortal. Although, they can be killed.

At the ending of The Sentinel Mother Charlie will be 108 (he looks sixty with the added bonus of the angel knocking another thirty years off him). Charlie's only protagonist/antagonist left standing (not yet known which side of the fence he is on to you) is Nathaniel Johnson. There is one other that will throw a spanner in the works age-wise though. His father's brother, Sin O'Hare (didn't I love that name when it came to me). He never did come across any Holy Spirit, for he is the seventh son of a seventh son of a seventh son. A natural immortal. Honest. Would I tell you a lie?

All my books are destined for the indie publishing world. And of course (in answer to your anticipated question) I tried going down the traditional route for publishing; and of course, as all other indie author with a story to tell, having been rejected over the years, went the indie route.

For some reason, I don't know why, I ignored self-publishing for so long it surprises me and the people that know me that I didn't do it sooner. After all, I have a background in books and printing: it being my trade and all. It was as if, the plumber that has the worst kitchen in the neighborhood, I never got around to having one fitted out properly. The thought was, that self-publishing would be a five-minute wonder, and that there would never be a way around traditional publishing. Well, there is nothing new in self-publishing, some of the best known writers indulged in it at one time or another. The likes of Alfred Lord Tennyson, William Blake, Beatrix Potter to mention a few. And that was before pc's and publishing tools were available to writers. In my case it was a mental block that needed overcoming, for I could have had it all done by myself through the trade that I knew.

Traditional publishers had the know how to originate a book (so did I), the way a book is be laid out (so did I), they had access to proof readers and editing services (so did I), they knew printing processes (so did I), they knew how to design and layout a book jacket (so did I), they had the ability to promote titles to an international market (ah, no, I never had that). That takes money and resources. There are ways and means.

The traditional route did open for me on a few occasions. One publisher, keen to take me on, went out of business even before the lick on the acceptance letter had dried. Another, shall we say, a vanity publisher wanted my book along with a few thousand dollars. Oh, I renounce the devil and all his works, the pomp and vanity of this wicked world, and all the sinful lusts of the flesh. Amen. Needless to say, I kept my money.

Not that vanity publishing is wrong, no, no, no. For not everyone wants to publish their work to any more than a wider audience than themselves and perhaps close family and friends. The problem comes with the charging and publishing, and although they are not all in the same boat, the claims made of how successful they will become is stretching the fib a bit too far.

The other coming close to being traditionally published was when I wrote a three-part tv drama about a tiny blackhole that had landed on Earth, getting itself lodged in the ground.

So I set to investigating this self-publishing game starting with that famous on-line retailer that has the same name as the longest river in the world running through South America.

For some reason, there comes a 'cocking a snook' in certain quarters when it comes to the mere mention of the, that river's same name. To my mind, having them on board, got me off the ground. I could download a Word document onto their site and it would produce a reasonable rendition of an e-book. Not brilliant. Half tidy. Of course when they first came on the self-publishing scene the word for self-publishing was e-books. Not until it became possible to self-publish a paperback from a pc did it begin to take off. Once that happened, the whole world opened up for self-publishers becoming what it is today. A multi-million dollar industry that probably eclipses today's traditional publishing market.

When I said (so did I) I meant it. I was apprenticed in London's Old Covent Garden (no, not selling bananas to monkeys), as a compositor (letter assembler) to the advertising industry producing ads for national magazines and newspapers. After I came out of my time six years later I went on to book production and graphic origination with other companies finishing up as manager and origination manager. So there it was, when I said (so did I) I did and had.

To widen my writing appeal onto other publishing platforms I bought the ISBN's for my books. That is, I own and manage the rights of where those books are published. As a result they are available for sale in most of the major book outlets as well as online around the world. Now that's pretty smart. Innit?

The aforementioned three-part tv drama series in question is, The Tinners Hut. A Barrister Phileas Cluff Novel, with the byline: '24 seconds to save the English crown from 300 years in its past - time is not Cluff's greatest asset!', will ask you to consider the theory that quantum physics expounds, that parallel universes are possible and are not to be interfered with. It has great characters, more police and security forces than you can shake a stick at. And with Phileas Cluff alongside the founders of his 2008 law firm based in Lincoln's Inn Fields, Zac Ellick and Hilary Waite alongside Edmund Skull the charismatic judge with his son, Ventonwyn, from 1716, it all becomes very weird and compelling.

Set on Dartmoor national park in Devon, England. A place steeped in history, myths, mysteries, ghosts and ghoulies (who has not heard of the Hound of the Baskervilles, a Sherlock Holmes and Dr. Watson crime story by Sir Arthur Conan Doyle?) and is an alternative history story. It sends a young lawyer back through to the time of King George the First and the Jacobite Uprising in 1716. Here, the young Phileas, sporting his Nike trainers, has to defend a man in a court of law already hanged (truthfully), without modern day forensics to aid him, while his fiancée, remains mainly in 2008 to collect the evidence. The bringing back of the hanged man will allow his descendant to save the lives of 300 children being held hostage at a school in Bristol. With all that, how could it fail?

Problem. Television drama departments asked for my agent (haven't got one); agents interested in the manuscript wanted the name of the tv company interested (I haven't got one). So I began ringing around. Of course, they all understood the dilemma. *How does anybody get into television drama and films?* I asked pleading. There was a pause, before one said, *Let me have a look at it then.*

So off it went to the dear lady, and funnily enough, she loved it and said so. We're going to put this forward to our publishing department for approval. Bless her! I bought a new car, put a deposit on a house, had a holiday, then: *We need the accountants to give it glance over. A formality!*

Ah! Accountants, eh. Don't you love 'em. Their foresight and daring, their willingness to take chances. Um! Along comes the inevitable response: Historical tv dramas are not popular at the moment. We've used our budget for this year, come back next. A year goes by and I remind them once more . . . Sorry, not quite our style. If you could only turn it into a book!

Well, that last suggestion, I did. Sent it off to them before it got rejected; before being sent on its world tour of literary agencies.

As before, they all loved it, Not quite our style, though. Writing is subjective, other agents will take a differing viewpoint. Keep trying.

Of course, writing is subjective. As are all art forms. As the late American painter (another great), Bob Ross often said on his tv programs, When it comes to putting paint onto the canvas, it's your world, you can do what you want. We don't make mistakes, we have happy accidents.

I take that same reasoning when it comes to my writing. My books, my rules; happy accidents and all! Respect, Bob Ross. Respect!

For the painting of a story will always be subjective. Hope you enjoy my versions of its subjectivity.

Good luck team, and take care of yourselves,

Gil Jackson

Plymouth UK. 2022

Also by Gil Jackson

FICTION

The Seventh Gift
An FBI Charlie O'Hare Novel
Paperback: ISBN 978-1-8382326-3-4
Ebook: ISBN 978-1-8382326-2-7

The Sentinel Mother
An FBI Charlie O'Hare Novel
Ebook: ISBN 978-1-8382326-9-6

The Tinners Hut
A Barrister Phileas Cluff Novel
Paperback: ISBN 978-1-8382326-8-9
Ebook: ISBN 978-1-8382326-0-3

NON-FICTION

The London Apprentice
An Autobiography: Makes tea, smokes cigars, sets type
Paperback: ISBN 978-1-8382326-5-8
Ebook: ISBN 978-1-8382326-4-1

Hiram B. Good's The Multi-Drop Drivers' Manual 2021 Edition
The Definitive Drivers' Manual

Paperback: ISBN 978-1-8382326-7-2
Ebook: ISBN 978-1-8382326-6-5

Hiram B. Good's From Stone to Amazon!
The Pica Thumpers' Text Book Bible (available on Amazon only)
Paperback: ISBN-13: 978-17178531-4-1
Ebook: ASIN: B01MPVSP4L

<u>*ALL BOOKS AVAILABLE WORLD WIDE*</u>

Throw me *a-Buoy!*

If you like my style of novel writing, you can help me reach out to others with a few acts of kindness by reviewing my book.

Go to your favorite book platform where you bought the book, search for the title, and leave a review. It will help me, and I would appreciate it.

Perhaps you'd like to go further and subscribe as others to my email list. Here I regularly keep in touch updating you with all my latest releases as they are published. There will also be FREE DEALS on my ebooks downloaded directly to your device. **The Mane Verse** is one such book, *A Spine Tingler of a Horror.*

https://giljacksonbooks.com

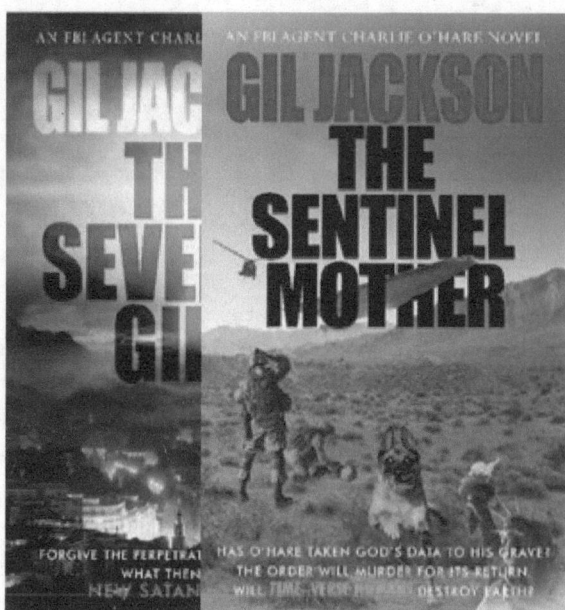

AN FBI AGENT CHARLIE O'HARE NOVEL

GIL JACKSON

THE
SENTINEL
MOTHER

HAS O'HARE TAKEN GOD'S DATA TO HIS GRAVE?
THE ORDER WILL MURDER FOR ITS RETURN.
WILL TIME-VERSE HUMANS DESTROY EARTH?